Catching Lameds:

Reflections on an Unconventional Life

Catching Lameds

REFLECTIONS ON
AN UNCONVENTIONAL LIFE

TED RICKLES

StoryTerrace

Text Ted Rickles with Eric Wyatt, on behalf of StoryTerrace
Design StoryTerrace
Copyright © Ted Rickles
Front Cover Concept art & design, Ted Rickles
and Lincoln Creative Writers
Back Cover Photo of author on HaAri Street, Tzfat,
Israel, June 2022

First print December 2022

StoryTerrace

www.StoryTerrace.com

A Publication of the *Genesis II Frontier Project*
www.GenesisIIFrontierProject.com

www.catchinglameds.com

CONTENTS

"I believe the future is only the past again, entered through another gate."

Arthur Wing Pinero,
English Playright (1855-1934)

DEDICATION

For all our parents, grandparents and teachers
who have guided our paths this far. . .

And for their childrens' children who, in their
contributions, will light the path onward.

ACKNOWLEDGEMENTS

My inspiration to write this autobiography came about as a desire to leave a little something behind for family and loved ones- when I can no longer be sought out to discuss the events of a good life. What makes any life good?- I think it begins with gratitude to G-d. Beyond that truth, I was specifically motivated by Michael Crichton's narrative in his own autobiography, *Travels* (1988), and Scott Rosenberg's scripting for the 1995 film, *Things to Do In Denver When You're Dead*. In that film, the main character, Jimmy "the Saint" Tosnia operates an agency called "Afterlife Advice". The book you have before you, *Catching Lameds*, is a kind of repository for my own experiences and changing views on life. But unlike the fictional "Afterlife Advice", instead of the responses being put to video-tape (or DVD), the topics and my experience are here in your hands in book format. However, just like a video production, this book couldn't have been produced without the hard work of a talented "behind-the-scenes" production crew, knowledgeable experts- and a cast of good associates, great friends- and family who were never "extras", but always integral to every moment of life.

First and foremost, I wish to thank my parents and

grandparents, and aunts and uncles for the amazing family I was born into! I'm also motivated by my siblings who started their own families and have likewise brought inspiring nieces and nephews into my life. So, in large part, this book is for all of them. It's also for all those I'm no longer able to thank, because they are unfortunately no longer corporeally with us. Here is grateful acknowledgement for the friendship and inspiration I benefited from in association with: Rabbi Dov Aaron Brisman; Dr. Peter Goldstone; Frances Gordon; Klebs Junior; Dr. Robert Kleiner; Bertram "Buddy" Korn; Dr. Leo Rigsby (former Chair Of Temple's Sociology Department); Andrea Sakim; Arthur Tobias; Chuck Tooley and Kristl Lynn Wiernicki.

The "production team" that helped put this book together, and enabled me to speak of these friends and experiences, deserves all the credit for publishing the accounts you'll read in these pages. The folks at *Story Terrace* (www.storyterrace. com) deserve much thanks, including my co-writer, Eric Sheridan Wyatt (www.wordsmatter.com) and my project editor, Brian Burnsed. Brian is an amazing coordinator and he handled every aspect of our communication and tasking with aplomb and professionalism. I could not have gotten more fortunate than to have his input and handling throughout this project! Over at *I-Universe* (www.IUniverse. com) I would like to thank project coordinator Ellie Go and editorial Consultant Nolan Estes for pushing the project along toward what I hope to be the second edition of this book, to be released sometime before the end of February, 2023. Finally, the publishing agency, Lincoln Creative Writers (www.lincolncreativewriters.com), whom I engaged to help market this book is a home to some incredible, and incredibly diligent talent- Including Senior Project Director, Marvin Mahoney; Project Coordinator, Zane Cole and copy-writer Michael Anthony. They did an amazing job creating the artwork for the cover (along with some artistic insight from my nephew, Axel Beckett). I wish to acknowledge the research assistance I received from Margery N. Sly, through Temple University's SCRC, for archival material on Temple's Ambler Campus and Kristl Wiernicki's academic degrees. Thanks to Thomas Wieckowski, chair of the Cheltenham Township Historical Commission for recalling the January 12, 1994 *Philadelphia Inquirer* article on the fire that destroyed the old high school building. Thanks to Laura Kessler for information, photos and background on the Kessler family.

Thanks also to good friends: Michelle Greenberg-Fleischer, Bashira Charles, Joe West, Ray Bistline, Sharon S. and Denette A.

Throughout the years I've kept the memories fresh of all those I was privelidged to know in high school. They've all been amazing people! In this effort I have not been alone, and have had the privelidge of working with like-minded alumni from Cheltenham High School's Class of 1981. At one time or another, the following individuals have comprised a hard-working reunion committee, that has included our Class President, Patty Smith-Hinchey; Brenda Hecklin; Leslie Fine; Julia Turner-Mozka; John Donnelly; Adam Yaller; Joe Desch; Hope Grossman-Canonico; Judi Fox; Robert Cohen; Nancy Stuart-Portnoy; Rose Mealy-Pfender; Steve Gross; David Dienstman; Adam Kazan and Marc Frumer (If I've left anyone out across four decades of wonderful reunions, please forgive my aging memory-you're all very wonderful people!)

I am grateful to the community of Elkins Park, Pennsylvania to which I've established a deep connection across four of the six decades of my life. To that point, a special thanks to Israel Roling and his family for their wonderful baking of skunk cookies during several holiday seasons and allowing me to share those cookies with our community. Through my assembly of worship in Elkins Park-(their spiritual as well as administrative leadership)-I have been strengthened as a person, and without all of whom, I would be much impoverished as a human being.

Across those forty some years, the membership of my religious community has varied. People raised their families, and moved away. It's impossible to name everyone, but I wish to acknowledge a few former members of the Young Israel of Elkins Park who have moved, some even to Israel. Thanks to Howard and Cathy; Liz and Yoni; Jeff and Shelly; Danny and Vivie; Sharon and Shooki; Omid and Rachel; Lee and Alyssa; David and Renee; Ron Tabas; Ira B. and Jerry S. - Great friends, one and all!

For almost as many years, I've derived inspiration and motivation to write through the annual PHILCON science fiction conventions. Thanks here to fellow attendee Wallace Kemp for many thoughtful and provocative late night discussions over the years. However, age and disability are creeping up on me, making my annual pilgrimage to that assembly of imaginative people more and more difficult. (Even before PHILCON, Felicia you worked your magic on me as a great physical therapist- so know that I haven't forgotten you, either!) Anyway, back to PHILCON, which has more recently been held at the Doubletree Hotel, Cherry Hill, NJ. Their staff has been most helpful and accommodating toward all of PHILCON, but has been a godsend to me in-particular, in consideration of my disability. Thanks to Double tree staff: Camara, Mohammed and Diane Delazano- you and the people whom you work with are all truly wonderful!

Finally, It's with mixed joy and sadness that I acknowledge the contributions of those who gave of their time and support of the never-published graphic novel, *Genesis II: Alone Against Tomorrow*. I recall with appreciation a brief but meaningful conversation that I had with the late (Great) Dorothy D.C. Fontana in 2002 in the Pasadena Convention Center during a Creation Convention. I told her of my efforts to contact the Roddenberry's to promote the project. In just a few words, she gave me the impetus to keep moving and work toward that connection. Thanks also to

Jeff Marriotte, who during his time at IDW Publishing was supportive of our creative effort. In the pages of this book, I acknowledge David Campitti of Glass House Graphics for introducing me to artist Klebs Moura Junior- with whom I shared a wonderful creative partnership and friendship. There were those such as editor, Chuck Tooley and artist, Luke Ross, who have visible credit on the project, but there were others who worked behind the scenes and until now, were never officially acknowledged for their contributions on the project. To that end, I'd like to acknowledge early sketches and proto-art created by artists, Eugene Forehand and Tom Pollock. Also, a shout-out to Michael Lovitz, Esq. a friend and intellectual property lawyer who provided some answers to questions of copyright use. Finally, I'm grateful to Majel Barrett Roddenberry, Eugene "Rod" Roddenberry and everyone on their team who, however briefly, entertained the possibility of a true sequel (graphic novel or otherwise) to the films of *Genesis II* (1973) *and Planet Earth (1974)*.

The rest, as they say.. is history...

Thanksgiving Weekend
November 27, 2022

AUTHOR'S NOTE

Portions of this autobiographical work recount my experiences (when young) with explosives, witnessing their destructive use from within a deviant group in which I was then a member. I brought some of that experience with me to college. College experiences aren't always ideal. And no matter how supportive an environment a college campus tries to provide, the students as well as teachers are what make the experience a positive one. My freshman year at college remains one of the most difficult years of my life. Under the stress of that experience, I considered briefly, the use of an explosive device- not to harm, or cause destruction- but simply to "wake people" into wondering and to consider that perhaps change was needed. Thankfully, I never committed that act. Though I was expelled by the university on account of planning it. I was barely nineteen years old. It was 1982, and that place was the Ambler Campus of Temple University, in Bucks County, Pennsylvania. I'm glad that I chose, in advance, not to do that dangerous and destructive thing. Further, whatever negative feelings I had, either toward the campus, or the town of Ambler— vanished years ago.. In fact, I join with the many students, faculty and administrators who courageously and effectively restored the Ambler Campus in the wake of devastating destruction caused by Hurricane Ida, over a year ago (September 1, 2021). Life unfolds - and I have not returned to the Temple Ambler campus in some 39 years- I am strengthened by the fortitude of those who came after me and who have been positive stewards of the Temple Ambler institution. I have an appreciation for all the students, faculty and staff whose lives continue to be improved and advanced through Temple Ambler's wonderful education, meaningful friendships and most valued community commitment.

I also gratefully acknowledge the support and collaboration shared with my co-author, Eric Sheridan Wyatt (www.wordsmatter.com). I could not have successfully written this book without his patient, understanding and thoughtful partnership in penning these events to paper. I have done the best I can to recall events as they happened. However, as they are my memories, I take full accountability for any and all errors that may exist in this book, either grammatically, or in any unintended errors in recalling the events themselves. There are Numerous relationships that I've had over the years contained in these pages. In instances where an individual is no longer alive, I have freely referred to them here under their actual names. In the case of living individuals — it's more of a mixed situation. Some individuals have specifically requested that I use a pseudonym. Other individuals have given me carte-blanche to use their real names. Alternatively, some individuals, because of sensitive Issues, have given notarized legal permission for use of their real names. Still others are mentioned by their real names because the references are briefly circumstantial, based on a limited presence in University or religious affiliation. Finally, in some sensitive instances, I chose myself to provide pseudonyms to protect aspects of persons' private lives (marriages, families, etc.)-or because of those health issues in which individuals might not have the "where-with-all" to provide permission. All References to Rickles family members who are my parents or siblings are reported using their real names. The members of the Kessler family (while not related by blood to my father's mother's family) and referred to in this book, are also reported using their real names. This is a work of non-fiction. All accounts of situations and circumstances are true and accurate to the best knowledge of the author.

FORWARD TO THE YEAR 2133

(As of Now, Possibly 110 Years Early)

From the 1940s through the 1960s, it seemed the future being forecasted called for science, technology and colonization of new frontiers! Magazine illustrations and film animations from that time braced us to expect that by the year 2000, there would be lunar colonies, high-speed inner-city elevated rail systems, fully automated homes run by AI and – ubiquitous flying cars. The 1980s witnessed scenic artists like Robert McCall and Syd Mead still actively generating visuals for such a world of tomorrow.

What we ended up with instead were some books like, "Where's My Jetpack: A Guide to the Amazing Science Fiction Future That Never Arrived" (2007) by Daniel H. Wilson. Technology promised "linkages". Some things did come true in areas of medicine and communication— and electric cars. (We even have flying cars, but so far they've been deemed impractical on a large scale.

Many prescient science fiction writers, like Arthur C. Clarke, or yes, Gene Roddenberry, took a more tentative approach to the diffusion of technology. Clarke theorized and designed the early concept for geo-synchronous satellites in 1945 (though it wasn't until 1963 that the first such satellite was actually launched into orbit. Flying cars have been with us for a while now too, in one form or another. (Among the latest is the Samson company's "Switchblade" (2022)). But whereas some concepts, like the jet-pack and flying car have come much more slowly into actuality, others in the area of regional high speed rail transport are here. They have a constant presence, and have quickly transformed our world.

Futurists and many science fiction writers succeed with audiences by consulting existing R&D companies to find out, in the present, what is in their current "pipelines" for development. Gene Roddenberry did this in 1964 when he was conceiving his 23rd century world of *Star Trek*. Gene consulted physicists at the Rand Corporation as well as Isaac Asimov, the Air Force and NASA before depicting such a future world. At that time, mobile phones had been in development. Bell Labs had worked up an early version. Those were bigger, clunkier and were linked then only by base stations. They were more like walkie talkies. But, once the fictional *Star Trek* "communicator" debuted on TV in 1966, it seemed to "seal-the-deal". It inspired those engineers and designers,"in-the-know"and "on the job" to hasten their development for the eager reception of a world just waiting to have mobile communication in their pockets and handbags. In a similar vein, the fictional concept of "transparent aluminum" presented in the film, *Star Trek IV:*

The Voyage Home (1984) led to the real-world engineering of actual transparent aluminum (aluminum oxinitride)..

Gene Roddenberry followed that path with *Genesis II* (1973). In that made-for-television film, he portrayed Earth in the year 2133 as a post-apocalyptic world. But he he needed some "gimmick"or "macguffin", as it's called in the writing world, to provide hope to the communities that survived- something that could link decimated societies across vast distances. The idea he developed stemmed from a question of sorts... What if something remained from our time... some "old technology" from before the "great cataclysm" that survived into dark times? If such a tool could be used by noble men and women, perhaps it could link the disparate and far-flung communities that were in need of aid and re-civilization? In many ways, *Genesis II* was to be like *Star Trek*. The key difference was that instead of starships spanning galaxies in exploration, bringing aid to colonies, and discovering new societies— such adventures would occur here - for an Earth trying to heal itself after a Great War. Instead of starships bridging galactic distances, the stewards of civilization would rely on the remnants of a trans-oceanic underground high-speed sub-shuttle system, which remained functional, even while aging into dystopic times.

How exactly did Gene Roddenberry anticipate the construction of a world-wide underground subshutle system ? I've often wondered that. I don't think Gene himself knew until the early summer of 1972. At that time, nearly six months had passed since he'd returned from filming a movie in England. He'd thought *Star Trek* was over, and likewise, that he and television had parted ways. But then, two enthusiastic network reps had shown up to greet him at the very first *Star Trek* convention in January, 1972. Their message was a simple *mea culpa*. They admitted that the untimely cancellation of *Star Trek* in 1969, had been a mistake, not accurately based on its true success with fans. They prevailed upon him to return to television writing. They gave him an office in the Warner Bros. Studio, which he moved into in May, 1972. A month went by- and suddenly, Gene began writing *Genesis II* into existence.

Gene tapped Matt Jeffries, familiar to *Star Trek* fans as the set designer who created interiors and props for the original series. Jeffries is credited with coming up with the film's "gimmick"- the high speed world-wide underground subshuttle system. Gilbert Clayton, an uncredited contributing art director, designed the sub-shuttle car itself for the film. It was a timely idea. A scant three weeks after Roddenberry had submitted his initial prospectus for *Genesis II* (May 16th), the L.A. Times featured an article on June 11, 1972, titled, "L.A. to N.Y. In half an hour? 10,000 M.P.H. Tunnel Train Plan Developed". The article was a brief summary of the work that physicist R.M. Salter was developing at the Rand Corporation, based on principles of electromagnetic suspension first proposed in 1905 and then patented in 1912.

The science behind the fiction was based on the development of magnetic-levitation technology, which has in fact become much more developed and integrated into urban and regional transportation across the fifty years since *Genesis II* first aired. Prior to the March 23, 1973 airing of *Genesis II*, the more common view of inner city and regional transport was the monorail system. Monorails don't levitate, but rather follow a fixed-guide in the ground, and thus friction from the guide-path becomes a limiting factor on how fast a monorail train can travel. The monorail had publicly debuted as part of Disneyland in 1959 and was subsequently integrated into the 1964 New York World's Fair. But other than theme-park transport, and concept art for visions of the future, the growth of monorails, at least within the United States was at a very slow pace. It was different in popular film. A few James Bond films, including *You Only Live Twice (1967)*, *The Spy Who Loved Me (1977)* and *Moonraker (1979)* all featured monorail transport within their vastly large evil lairs or corporate spaces. However, one reason why monorail trains have been in more limited use is because at a typical top speed of around fifty miles per hour (80 kpm), the alternative "two-guide"system utilized by most metro rail is much faster.

However, *Genesis II*'s plot was based in a faster, or more "frictionless", high-speed transport system, that was relegated mostly to concept until 1984. That year, the first commercial MAGLEV, or magnetic levitation train debuted in Britain to link the Birmingham International Airport with the Birmingham International Railway Station. It marked the beginning of a greater range of speed and coverage in inner city as well as rail transport. Maglev trains, which can attain speeds from around 50 mph up to 250 mph or more, utilize two sets of electromagnets so that the train doesn't actually run on the guides at all. One set of magnets pushes the train up, while another set of electromagnets pushes the train forward upon a cushion of air. As of this writing, the fastest maglev train in the world may be in Qingdao, China achieving a top-speed of 600 km (373 miles) per hour.

So, March 23, 2023 celebrates the 50th anniversary since *Genesis II* was first aired. Sadly, It retains the reputation of being a relatively obscure "made-for-television" pilot for a never produced television series. Despite, Gene Roddenberry's additional outlining of eight never-filmed episodes, *Genesis II* is remembered as the failed product of the CBS network's interest in filling a Fall, 1973 program block carved out for a science-fiction TV series. In fact, though, the networks turned down the *Genesis II* TV series concept- twice! Subsequent to the CBS network's decision to opt-out for another series in that time slot (the short lived, *Planet of the Apes* TV series), Roddenberry tried again with a second pilot, *Planet Earth* (1974). But, ABC also rejected the concept. So, fifty years later, why care about it now?

In the film, *Genesis II,* it is 1979 when NASA scientist Dylan Hunt travels aboard a high speed underground shuttle of the very type we're theorizing. In fact, his subshuttle travels from Vandenberg Air Force Base, CA to an underground "NORAD -like" research facility in Carlsbad Caverns, NM. In the film, the trip takes only a little over six minutes, traveling at a velocity of 1135 km/hr and only utilizing 40.55% of the available power and speed of that fictional system. The theory of how a train could achieve even close to 1135 km/hr was advanced over a century ago by famed father of American rocketry, Robert H. Goddard back in 1904. The concept involves a super-fast maglev train traveling through a vacuum-tube - a special tubular tunnel in which all air has been mechanically removed. It's often referred to as "hyper loop technology. In the absence of all air-friction, a maglev train could attain mach-speeds of 4,000 to 5,000 mph (4,600 to 8,000 kph)- literally 4-5 times the speed of sound!

If that all still sounds like science fiction, it may be

Lines depict a "world-wide" subshuttle network linking continents, as presented in "Genesis II" (1973). Art courtesy, Klebs Junior. (2005).

because it was only much more recently, starting in 2003-2004, that engineers began to conceive the means to create such underground tunnels, even laying them across the ocean, to link continents! Even the idea of boring such tunnels through the earth was itself science-fiction until a short while ago. Tunnel Boring Machines (TBMs) have been with us since the 19th century, but they have advanced technologically so that in June, 2015, the world saw the largest TBM, the "Tuen Mun- Chek Lap Kok" built by the German Herrenknecht company. It is a mixed shield boring machine, 120 meters in length, and having a cutting-edge-shield with a diameter of 17.6 meters and a torque of 27,000 kilonewton meters. In 2015, the Tuen Mun tunneled at a rate of more than 30 meters per day, excavating two undersea tunnels of five km each under the region of Hong Kong. These tunnels are located 60 meters below sea level and were opened to vehicle traffic in 2020.

With this kind of advancement, the question arises- can we advance safely to creating undersea tunnels at deeper than 60 meters or so, too...say, laying them beneath the Atlantic Ocean, more than 4 kilometers down, subterranean to the ocean floor?? The engineering feat alone would be daunting, and it's integrity would be challenged by enormous atmospheric pressure at such depths (400 atmospheres). In addition, it would continually be at risk, as a result of crossing the geologically unstable Atlantic Ridge.

Those issues certainly suggest the whole concept of a

transatlantic subshuttle system, as presented in *Genesis II* would be untenable in the real world. Yet, even in the last twenty years, scientists have begun to conceive alternative ways of moving beyond these concerns. For example, instead of burying the tunnel so far down, and beneath the floor of the Atlantic Ocean, we could instead, prefabricate the sections of the tunnel above ground and tether the completed tunnel to the ocean floor (with steel cables) so that it floated, submerged only 200 meters below the ocean surface. That would be a depth high enough to avoid occasional turbulence from the Atlantic ridge, but deep enough to avoid occasional icebergs moving across the North Atlantic sea. The construction would be a massive undertaking! Such a 3,000 kilometer long submerged Atlantic tunnel would require 33,000 pre-fabricated sections, each one being 92 meters long and 17 meters wide! Submersible robotic vehicles would need to work at depths of 4-5 kilometers down in order to attach the 400,000 km of flexible steel cabling to the ocean floor which would anchor the transatlantic tunnel. Then, in order to transform it into a vacuum tube, once assembled, it would take the work of 100 jet engines, running 24 hours a day for two weeks straight, to suction all the air out of the 3,000 kilometer underwater tunnel. Subsequent to completion of that tunnel, it would be joined to additional connecting overland segments between New York and Canada on the western end, and Ireland and Britain on the Eastern side of the Atlantic so that, as Dylan

∞

Hunt's character in the film could proclaim, "the subshuttle would bridge its first continent!".

What would be the benefits and costs of a transcontinental subshuttle network? On a purely dramatic level, it would be a major time savings over current transatlantic air travel. A typical flight from. New York to London takes 7 hours (plus advance time allotted for security checks and terminal-to-gate walking time). However, a subshuttle that could make the trip from New York to London in 5 hours would mean being able to have lunch in New York and dinner and dessert later the same day in Paris! But, it would be a massively expensive and time laden project. The estimated financial cost could be $12 trillion or more! It would require huge supplies of steel and material and would likely be beyond the capability of any one nation or government. So, the project would necessarily involve many countries, both in resources, financing and political and economic consideration. But the greater benefits, economically and ecologically (cutting down on a significant portion of atmospheric pollution from the current jet travel). It's also estimated that it would take over a century from now to complete (which is ironically when the narrative of *Genesis II* takes place. In 2003, I created the *Genesis II Frontier Project* as a platform for the discussion, advocacy and advancement of major ideas presented in the film for real-world adoption. Right now, for various complex reasons, including the growth of social media, that platform remains a tiny voice amidst a plethora of liberal and extreme views. Tribalism of all kinds and sorts is fracturing our world despite the current shrinkage in distances. But the ideas of *PAX* (with some tweaking of their unisex ideals) represent a call for unity and repair of our world—and this is *very* "Gene Roddenberry" in its hopefulness. It's a hard haul, admittedly. This is true in all areas of change and growth, but perhaps markedly so, in the area of constructing a world-wide high speed transcontinental maglev system with hyperloop technology. However, to paraphrase President John F. Kennedy, in his 1961 speech to Congress, calling for national support of the goal to land a man on the moon… And as regards a world-wide subshuttle system: "If we make this judgement affirmatively", marshaling the necessary political, economic and social resources to construct a reliable and safe subshuttle system to link continents . . . it would not be any single nation's advantage, but rather it would be the triumph of World Humanity, for truly all of us would be joined together in getting there.

Information in this Forward, concerning Gene Roddenberry; *Genesis II (1973)* and Maglev Hyperloop technology was incorporated from the following sources:

Alexander, David. *Star Trek Creator*: *The Authorized Biography of Gene Roddenberry*. ROC. 1994.

Cushman, Marc. *These Are The Voyages: Gene Roddenberry*

and Star Trek in the 1970s-Volume 1 1970–'75. Jacobs/Brown Press. Frazier Park, CA. 2019.

YouTube: "The $12TRN TranAtlantic Tunnel Proposal". Futurology. 2021. (https://youtu.be/Q82Z0netZqk)

INTRODUCTION

Wednesday, May 25, 2022
(Possibly 127 Years too Late!)

"Please, give us some room, "the paramedic urged the crowd to back away..

Gentle hands, four pairs of them, swept around me and cradled my resting body. Slowly they lifted me up from the ottoman and onto the nearby paramedics' gurney. I was in a light daze, — conscious and able to hear everything around me. But the "will to move", even to flex or twitch a muscle was diminished within me. I let them do their work.

"Sir?," the paramedic was inquiring of me, "Are you diabetic"?

"Yes," I mumbled in response, and added, "but that's probably not the problem."I suspected that my diabetes was under control, and had nothing to do with this predicament.

I opened my eyes briefly as the room tilted and a momentary "clatter" sounded while they adjusted the gurney and moved me out into the hall, and down toward the building's exit. My body rebalanced with the guerney, as we proceeded over a bump.This problem with sound was new to me. The harshness and disorientation that sounds and some visual experiences were now causing me was only about 6 months old. How much worse would it get?- I wondered. What is the endgame of my disorder?

"OK- we are taking you outside now to the ambulance." The paramedic spoke English, but with a European accent, specifically the Austrian accent appropriate to Vienna- which is where we were.

They had transported me from the second floor of Bergasse #19, the prior office and living quarters of the famous Psychiatrist- the very father of psychoanalysis- himself- Dr. Sigmund Freud. Some eighty-four years earlier, Freud and his family had left this location for London, fleeing from the German Reich, which in 1938 had annexed Austria and which would soon fully occupy it. So, in fact, I was a century and twenty-seven years late, if I'd dreamt of any possibility that Freud's personal experience and understanding of hysteria could help me.

Freud's old office and family residence at Bergasse #19 were now curated as a museum, a celebration of his work and influence on psychoanalytic theory and practice. Admittedly, in my condition it was perhaps a mistake to attempt the tour.

I'd arrived close to 10am when the museum opened that day. At that hour, few patrons or tourists had arrived. I presented to the clerk the pre-purchased admissions ticket I'd bought online prior to leaving the U.S. I ascended the stairs from the ground floor to the mezzanine level. On either side of the mezzanine landing, there was a door. The door to the right led to Freud's medical office where he practiced his psychoanalysis on visiting patients. The door to the left was his private residential apartment, separate from the upper level apartments for other family.

I chose first to venture into his medical office. I spent some twenty-five minutes wandering amongst the glass-enclosed cases of his various papers and hand-writings, all with English and foreign translated descriptions. There were articles and notes. I looked with interest to see if there were any standout references to his work on my particular neurological condition. In 1892, Freud had studied the case of "Anna O.". She suffered from a number of physical anomalies that Freud and his fellow physician, Dr. Josef Breuer had associated with trauma and repressed anxieties. Freud had already gained some understanding of hysteria through his tenure as a student under Jean-Martin Charcot at the Salpetriere Hospital in Paris between October 20, 1885 and February 28, 1886. I was curious as to what other papers that might be referenced here, or what other patient profiles might specifically relate to my condition.

After the first twenty minutes or so, other patrons began to filter into the spaces of the medical office. Most looked like tourists. There was the young redhaired woman, perhaps in her twenties, who wore a stylish fedora. A similarly college-aged couple were viewing a glass-enclosed document nearby. There were also a few solitary older men and women who carefully and methodically viewed each display. I wondered if any of these had specific ties to psychoanalysis and some fervent connection to Freud and his work.

Beyond that, I wondered if somehow Freud himself, or rather his spirit was somehow looking down from whatever sphere of heaven to which healers might be dispositioned. Could his spirit in any way discern that I was here in Vienna, venturing into his old clinic and seeking understanding for my condition as well as ascribing kinship with some of his other patients? It seemed impossible to obtain any answer to those questions for now.

Feeling that I had seen enough of his office and clinic, I exited back onto the landing and went through the other door I'd seen earlier. I thought to take a brief opportunity to explore Freud's personal apartment and salon. Some of his renowned personal items, glasses, a cigar, and some furniture were there, but there was also a sense that much was still present in London, where the Freud's had moved to safety ahead of the German occupation of Austria. By that point in my visit, I'd been walking and taking in the exhibits for over an hour and a half (which included viewing a brief film on Freud). As I walked through the gentleman's salon, I felt the fatigue building and I was aware my walking was beginning to waver. *Oh-No!- I thought. NOT NOW!!* But it was too late!

I felt my brain begin to unplug as the loss of mental focus took over. I was losing spatial orientation and reluctantly kerned onto a nearby ottoman. I closed my eyes, as much to escape capitulating to the reality of the situation, as to also try to escape the dizziness that had overtaken me. I remained conscious, though. Thankfully, thus far none of these episodes ever directly resulted in my passing out. But the report from bystanders was often very different. Over ninety-percent of the time, people who witnessed my condition and saw me kearn or squat to a laying position on a floor also reported to authorities, incorrectly, that I had fainted- which really didn't happen. I'd spoken to my vestibular therapist about the experience of how people reacted and he admitted that it was in fact some sort of odd bystander reaction- a bystander "pathology, I wondered?

The Vienna ambulance sat outside on the street in front of #19 Bergasse. In it, the two paramedics who attended me were concluding their check of my vital signs. "Well, you seem OK except maybe for some slightly higher than normal blood pressure," the one with the slightly fuller build was explaining.

Yes, I thought to myself. *I am fine- at least 'Normal' for my condition.* And I couldn't risk any unnecessary hospitalization in Vienna. Nothing could be permitted to delay my flight to Israel the next day. I responded to the paramedic's observation, "No, I am fine," this time in a much stronger healthier voice than the mumbling I'd managed back in the salon.

"You sure? We think maybe you should come with us to

the hospital. You fainted back there."

"No," I assured them," that was what was reported, but I never lost consciousness. I'm staying at a hotel near here- The Hotel Imperial on Kaerntner Ring 16. I'll be fine."

"Do you have any family here?", the same paramedic asked.

"No, I'm traveling alone."

Both paramedics paused a beat. The other, younger and thinner man spoke." We can't force you to go to the hospital, but we think it may be a good idea for you to get checked out more thoroughly". I thought about a similar instance in France, four years ago in which I had gone briefly to a hospital. It had wound up involving several hours, and been interesting at the time, but here and now, I couldn't afford the diversion, either financially or in terms of time. I tried to explain to the two men with me that this was unfortunately normal for me because of my condition. But the concern did not leave their faces and I understood their skepticism from their position of being responsible care workers.

I looked at my watch. It was just 11:30am Vienna local time — about 5:30am on the U.S. east coast. I took a chance and dialed my Aunt Joyce, who knew somewhat of my condition.

"Hello," my Aunt answered. I quickly explained that I needed her to assure these two men that I was OK. After querying me if I knew it was 5:30am and acknowledging that I was lucky to get a hold of her because she was up early that morning, she did speak with the more senior paramedic.

After speaking with her, both paramedics relented in their concern, and had me sign a waiver of liability that I was rejecting health services on my own recognizance. They removed the EKG sensor tags from my body, as well as a PICC catheter from the top of my left hand and wrapped a light layer of guaze to speed formation of a scab. They then released me onto the street, but only after I promised that if symptoms reoccurred, or worsened, that I would call and accept further treatment.

As I crossed the street to look for a cab, or request an Uber from my phone, I noticed the blood beginning to soak through the gauze where the catheter had been removed. They'd apparently not removed it carefully enough, and certainly not wrapped it well enough. A proper band-aid may have helped, beneath the gauze, I thought. Hopefully, the hotel would have first-aid supplies- and disinfectant. The streets were unfamiliar to me- but eventually I made a connection and sat in the speeding taxi, staring at my bloodied hand as the car brought me back to the hotel.

1
EARLY LIFE

Existence

– Peter Weller:
The Adventures of Buckaroo Banzai
Across the 8th Dimension (1984)

Wherever you are as you read this—wherever in your lifecycle or aspirations, wherever in your relationships—you are constantly adapting to the changes in your life and around you. You are continually assessing your surroundings and tweaking your navigational guidance. Life simply necessitates that we respond as things happen.

In the process, we also haul a lot of past baggage around from both the best and the worst of our ongoing experiences. It's hard to escape all of that! Some of our experiences open us up to being receptive to new things. Alternatively, some stresses and bad experiences are too overbearing to our natures, and we become closed off. Still...wherever you go, there you are!

Perhaps, as you age and assess your own journey, you will decide that there are relative and enduring truths you've discovered through experience. It becomes natural to want to share those truths, to better the lives of friends, colleagues, and yes, even the next generation of loved ones who will one day replace us. Even the mysteries of existence to which we've found few personal answers are worth presenting to those who would benefit from our experiences. Why not? Share it! Pass it on!

That's my intent in sharing my story with you. As far as stories go, it's a little different. But then, so are we all.

Beginnings

My mother's parents had both come to the US around 1936.[1] They left Germany as the Nazi persecution of Jews was ramping up but before things had truly worsened. My maternal grandmother's family included a kosher baker— my Uncle Herman.

My father's family had emigrated from Russia, somewhere

around what is now Ukraine. My father's father had been a teacher, a kosher butcher, and a grocery store owner. My father and his twin brother were the youngest of four sons. Their family couldn't afford much and lived in a small home attached to grandfather's butcher shop (later grocery store) located in the Logan area of Philadelphia. They couldn't house all four boys comfortably, so the oldest, my Uncle Seymour, wound up staying with other family. As a result of their upbringing, he was the only sibling to become very religious and spend time studying Torah and Talmud.

(Right to Left) Brothers: Seymour, Jules Haskell & Nathan (Sahnie) Rickles.
Strawberry Mansion, Philadelphia-circa 1933

The twins went to pharmacy school at Temple University in Philadelphia. After pharmacy school, my father spent several months working as an assistant pharmacist at Gallaudet Pharmacy in Washington, DC.[2] He returned to Philadelphia in 1952 and began working as an assistant pharmacist at Axelrod's Pharmacy, located at 8317 Stenton Avenue in the Mt. Airy section of the city.

(1959) Haskell & Nathan "Sahnie" Rickles at an open house event hosted by drug wholesaler, Shoemaker & Busch. [3]

My father was a loyal and capable employee for ten years. When Sam Axelrod retired, he offered to sell the business to my father. Dad and his twin brother, Nathan, bought the pharmacy and renamed it Allens Lane Pharmacy after the side street northwest of the store.

(1960) Axelrod Pharmacy; 8317 Stenton Avenue, Philadelphia, PA. Source: book on Business Practices by Harold M. Lambert.

(~1964) Twins Haskell & Nathan ("Sahnie") Rickles as pharmacists & co-owners

(~1980) Exterior storefront

Unfortunately, in 1966, Nathan passed away at aged thirty-eight due to complications of rheumatic fever he'd had as a child. It left my dad as sole proprietor of the pharmacy. This was my first confrontation with loss. My "Uncle Sahnie" had left an indelible imprint on me that would last the rest of my life and inspire me to be the best uncle I could be later in life. When a few years later, in 1969, my parents would have their fourth child, a boy, they named him Nathan, perpetuating the memory of the wonderful brother with whom Dad had shared childhood and aspirations for a community pharmacy.

My parents were married at the Germantown Jewish Centre, a conservative synagogue in Philadelphia, where my mother's family had been members for years. I was born in January of 1963. Lori, my sister, came along a year and a half later, followed by Sara, in 1966. My brother, Nathan, was born six years after me.

Dad worked hard to provide for us. He spent most of his time at his pharmacy, but he made an effort to do "fatherly" things to express his love. He took me to ball games, but I was more of a "museum kid." I never quite fit the "typical boy" mold.

My family observed the holy days, but we weren't a kosher household. (My mother once attempted to buy filet mignon at a kosher butcher shop. She had to be informed that kosher Jews don't eat that cut of beef. It contains "forbidden" fats and nerves nearly impossible to separate properly from the meat.) My family had a sense of gratitude and respect for our Jewish heritage, but I also learned a certain distrust toward the "very religious" sects of Judaism. As a young child, I didn't really understand what it meant to be Jewish, but I experienced my first anti-Semitic incident when I was about five years old.

We lived on McPherson Street in the Mount Airy section of northwest Philadelphia until my brother was born in February of 1969. The home on McPherson was located only a few blocks from my father's pharmacy at the intersection of East Allens Lane and Stenton Avenue.

The Oxford Presbyterian Church property abutted the back yards of the houses on the east side of McPherson Street. I didn't understand it was a Christian church; my child brain conceived of it as an enormous, pointy-top house with a vast, open green space like a park.

One day, Lori and I went through the back yards of a row of homes and onto the church grounds to play. We ran around the open field and played without a care until four older boys found us there. They set upon me, pushed me to the ground, hit me, and kept repeating things like, "Jew! Jew! Jew! Get out of here!"

Scraped up and bleeding, my sister led me back toward home.

Hebrew School

In elementary school, I was a good student. I enjoyed reading and writing, but I was never quite as good at math. I liked to read about science and was especially drawn to astrophysics. I wanted to understand how an interstellar starship, like the USS *Enterprise* from *Star Trek*, might travel through space.

My parents sent me to Hebrew school twice a week, on Tuesdays and Thursdays. The architecture of the synagogue interested me, but I had no interest in learning Hebrew. I often played hooky from the classes, finding hidden places and little nooks and crannies to hide. The synagogue's library had many books, in both English and Hebrew, about great Jewish figures and philosophy. Sometimes I wandered into the main sanctuary, and I wondered if G-d was aware I was there. Was He angry I was skipping my Hebrew classes?

My mind tended toward more rational and scientific ideas. The idea of G-d seemed to be a concept incompatible with logic, and I didn't think there was any way to prove or disprove that G-d existed.

Science and reason seemed to explain the world more fully than belief in a monotheistic deity and an ancient tradition. To me, G-d was an unlikely and unreasonable explanation for the existence of the universe and life as we know it. Billions of years of evolution made more sense than an omnipotent Being who was the Creator of all things.

There were trillions of stars in the universe, and it was highly unlikely Earth was anything special.

Additionally, I bristled at the idea of the Jewish people being "the chosen" people of G-d. It seemed self-important to make such a claim, and it made me uncomfortable. From a very young age, I experienced a strong aversion to people telling me how to think or what to believe. Even more, I held the opinion that the Jewish people were perpetuating the stories, traditions, and myths of a 5,000-year-old culture, but those things had little relevance to my modern life.

Star Trek, Science Fiction, and Other Influences

As a young child, I'd been entertained by cartoons and other television shows. I had a special affinity for the cartoon skunk Pepe Le Pew and his romantic pursuit of the female black cat, Penelope Pussycat. I also really liked the cartoon adaption of Rudyard Kipling's *Rikki-Tikki-Tavi,* and the mongoose was my favorite animal.

Star Trek first aired in 1966 and ran for three seasons. In the 70s, the series ran in syndication, and I became a big fan of the show. In fourth grade, a school guidance counselor asked, "If you could be anyone when you grow up, who would you want to be?"

My answer was simple: "Captain Kirk." (I even had some dreams over the years where William Shatner, as Kirk, was my father, and he took me aboard the USS *Enterprise*.)

Other boys my age were into cars, but I was interested in space. I imagined the concept of a fleet of interstellar spaceships conducting science missions and discovering new worlds throughout the galaxy would some day come true.

It would have been impossible to articulate at the time, but what attracted me to the *Star Trek* stories were the themes of advancing technology's effect on the development of civilization. I gravitated toward the idea that new technologies and ideas would provide mankind with tools to solve the world's problems and further the evolution of the human race. I admired *Star Trek* creator Gene Roddenberry's creativity and prescience, and I hoped to one day write stories of my own.

Star Trek may have set me apart from a "normal" kid, but there was one aspect of the show that united me with other boys my age: I became aware of the attractiveness of the opposite sex. I specifically remember actresses Grace Lee Whitney's performance of Yeoman Janice Rand and Mariette Hartley's portrayal of Zarabeth as being moments of awakening.[4]

Reading was very important to me. I devoured books about the Mercury and Gemini eras of the US space program and was, of course, tuned into the Apollo missions happening throughout my childhood. This fascination, combined with the concepts inspired by *Star Trek*, helped me develop an ongoing interest in scientific inquiry.

In 1968, Erich Von Daniken's book *Chariots of the Gods* was published, and a movie based on the book was released in 1970. I don't remember which one I encountered first, but the premise—that ancient aliens had visited earth and seeded life here—really resonated with me. It seemed a technologically advanced alien race was a better explanation for Easter Island, the Egyptian Pyramids, Stonehenge, and the Nazca desert lines in Peru, than any anthropological, human-based explanation I'd seen. When I expressed these thoughts to my parents, we would end up arguing about my "wild ideas."

Another story published in 1970, "The Fatal Fulfillment," would influence my philosophical development.[5] This was writer Poul Anderson's contribution to a science fiction anthology, *Five Fates*. In the story, the main character, Bailey, is trapped in a repeating time loop where he keeps dying and cycling back to the start of new permutations of the loop. The story concludes when Bailey's experience ends, and he recalls his true identity as a sociologist who had been experimenting with a virtual reality generator to test alternative solutions to social problems.

The Anderson story was the start of my interest in sociology and the idea that research and study of human behavior, societal relationships, and aspects of culture might lead to improvement of the human race.

This led me to refine my critique of religion. Rather than "just a story" or a myth to be dismissed outright, I began to

Within this volume is "The Fatal Fulfillment" by Poul Anderson (Doubleday, 1970). It sparked my commitment to sociology.

be open to religion's practical utility in establishing norms for society and the encoding of those norms into civil law. Religion of some form was a constant in all great societies in the East and the West, and it seemed to be a necessary step in the evolution of society and culture. Religious adherence led to valuing laws and establishing family structures necessary to progress beyond small, tribal, nomadic clans and into a more civilized, technological society.

Also around this time I was first introduced to the author Michael Crichton. His 1969 book *The Andromeda Strain*—and the 1971 movie of the same name—was the first of his works I consumed. Soon, I was reading everything Crichton had written. Crichton's novels addressed the intersection of technology and governmental bureaucracy in ways I found compelling. His writing caused me to think deeply about social and technological changes to civilization, social norms, and ethics.

Anything Crichton wrote, I just gobbled up. When he released a new book, I was there within the first few days to buy it, then I'd spend the next three days devouring it! I admired his writing, but I also appreciated his life. Crichton had trained to become a medical doctor but had walked away from that practice to become a writer and thinker. He was handsome and smart, and I wished for a life like his.[6]

Knowing my affinity for *Star Trek,* my mother took me to a toy store when I was about nine years old. Leonard Nimoy and Deforest Kelley—*Star Trek's* Spock and McCoy—came to the store and interacted with the kids and parents. Deforest Kelly went up a different aisle to interact with other kids. Leonard Nimoy spoke to my aisle for a few minutes before leaving. It was the first time I'd met someone from television, and it started a lifelong interest in interacting with the creative people who were responsible for the shows, movies, and books I was deeply interested in.

When I was twelve, my mother took me to one of the first original *Star Trek* conventions of the 1970s. It was at the Commodore Hotel in New York. I was so excited, and I dressed up as Captain Kirk. The problem was, we had a Sony color TV that didn't do very well with giving "lifelike" color. I thought Kirk's command shirt was made of a greenish fabric, so my shirt did not match the gold other Kirk fans were wearing.

One of my fondest memories from that convention was meeting actor Robert Lansing.[7] Lansing appeared in some great films, including *12 O'Clock High*, and I thought he was a great character actor.

He appeared in the final episode of Season Two of the original *Star Trek* series, titled "Assignment: Earth." Lansing played Gary Seven, a 20th century human, whom the Enterprise accidentally intercepted during a historical mission to 1968. I was always interested in time-travel stories, so this was a favorite episode. (The episode was also supposed to serve as a pilot for an ongoing spin-off series featuring Robert Lansing in the lead role.)

Left: Me & Lori at the 1975 Star Trek Convention.
Right: A youthful Majel Barrett Roddenberry signing at a con table.[8]

At the convention, I had a chance to ask Lansing a question. "Mr. Lansing," my twelve-year-old voice trembled at the mic. "In 'Assignment: Earth', you were trying to rewire the navigation system of that big rocket. You were laying on the gantry, working inside the rocket. Were you scared to be so high up there?"

The entire convention broke into laughter, but I wasn't sure what was so funny.

"It looked like I was really high up," Lansing said. "But, I was on a set in a studio. They used painted backdrops and props, but I was only a couple of feet off the ground. I didn't have to be scared."

Even though I was embarrassed by my naiveté about how TV and movies were made, I have always cherished that memory.

Ghostly Encounter

In late 1969 our family moved out of Philadelphia to Cheltenham Township. Our new home in Laverock was a few blocks from one of the largest cemeteries in the area, Holy Sepulchre. The cemetery had been established in 1894. Around age twelve, I began to read books on psychic phenomena and paranormal activity. I was curious about ghosts and other evidence of a life beyond the perceived realm of existence.

I hadn't been sleeping well for a few nights. It felt, to me, like there was some sort of presence in my bedroom—like I wasn't alone. By the fourth night, I even had the sensation of being watched and I was frightened.

I finally fell asleep somewhere around two o'clock in the morning, and I experienced one of the most vivid dreams of my life. It was less like a dream and more like someone had switched the channel of my life and plunged me into a parallel reality. As my new environment took form around me, I knew I was still asleep in my bed, but I was experiencing something outside me. The walls of my room were gone, and I was outside, at night, in a wooded and hilly area.

I had sensations and experienced the dream as if I were awake. The air was cold against my skin, and I could hear the rustling of leaves that had fallen from the bare trees. There were hills around me, and a ridge overlooking the area where I stood. I felt isolated and alone. In the dream, I knew I was still asleep and in bed. Yet, even down to the sensory level the dream landscape was so real, I was very frightened.

From the ridge above me, I heard voices of a man and woman. "I thought I saw a cougar back there," the woman said, "or a mountain lion."

"There's nothing to be worried about," the man assured her. "There aren't any cougars in this area."

Suddenly, I was lifted up from the valley and found myself up on the ridge, following behind the man and woman. I could see them continuing to walk along toward the entrance of a cave. When they got to the cave opening, the man walked a few feet ahead of the woman. From my vantage point, I saw him disappear into the darkness of the cave. The woman hesitated and then began to follow. Just a few steps into the cave's entrance, as she was about to dissolve into the darkness, she suddenly (as if instinctually) turned to look out the cave's entrance, seeing … SOMETHING??

From my viewpoint, I couldn't tell what she saw, but the look that washed over her face was horrifying. The woman fainted, and the man reemerged where I could see him. He was also distressed, and I knew something very strange was happening. At first, my vantage point was only at ground-level, watching the clicking of his shoes on the hard ground as he re-tread his steps toward the cave's entrance. Then, I was following his sightline, and there, framed between two bare bushes, was the transparent, smokey silhouette of a cougar staring back at him.

Suddenly the dream ended. I was back, alone in my room, with the inescapable feeling of being watched.

Frightened and disoriented, I covered my head with my bedsheets and hid there for 30 minutes. The feeling didn't pass, and I was terrified. I needed to feel some human connection, so I forced myself out of bed with the intention of waking my brother, who was about six years old at the time. I knew it wasn't really what older brothers should do—wake their younger sibling because they were scared by a dream—but I couldn't shake the feeling of dread and loneliness.

Nathan's bedroom was about five feet beyond the turn in the hallway. Just as I rounded that turn, a premonition came to me: I was about to see something miraculous that I might never see again in my whole life!! Framed in the open doorway to Nathan's room, was the figure of a transparent man, in the same coherent white-smoke outline as the cougar had appeared in my dream! The young man looked to be seventeen years old, and he wore farm overalls. His face and hair were well kept, and he looked like an all-American guy, but from another era. Like a photographic negative, I could see through him—my brother was asleep in his bed—but the translucent figure had form and substance. I had the impression he was a living, breathing presence.

Our eyes met, and I could tell he saw me. In shock, I opened my mouth to scream, but no sound came out. My parent's room was right there—if I had yelled, they would have come quickly—but my frightened shout didn't materialize.

The man wasn't moving. We looked at each other, and I could sense some sort of sadness in him. It was as if he were pleading for me to help him in some way, though I couldn't imagine any way I could help.

It dawned on me that I was having a unique experience: This was the physical manifestation of a soul. I didn't know who he was or where he was from, of course, but I had the impression he was a farm worker, or he'd been part of a farming family.

My initial fear calmed. He lifted his arms toward me, as if reaching out for help. I stayed still for several seconds, unwilling to move because I didn't want to lose this experience, but this apparition's forlorn, silent pleas were overwhelming. I wondered if there was some way to communicate with him. Eventually, I decided I would try to step closer to him, but even as I made my first tentative movement to lift my foot, the man's form began to dissipate like a cigarette smoke ring losing its coherence and drifting off.

Just like that, the ghostly figure was gone.

I woke Nathan up. We went to the kitchen, and he listened to me tell this crazy story about what I had dreamed and what I had seen from the hallway. (Later, Nathan even had a similar dream, though it may have been a result of me telling him what had happened to me.)

I became convinced that certain places and things contain a psychic energy and that there is something more beyond this earthly life, but I had no idea what any of it might mean. I told a few other people, but my story was met with skepticism. My parents said, "Oh, it was just a nightmare. We don't even know if ghosts are real!"

Some people might say it was just a young boy's active imagination, influenced by books about paranormal activities. Others might say my reading had opened me up

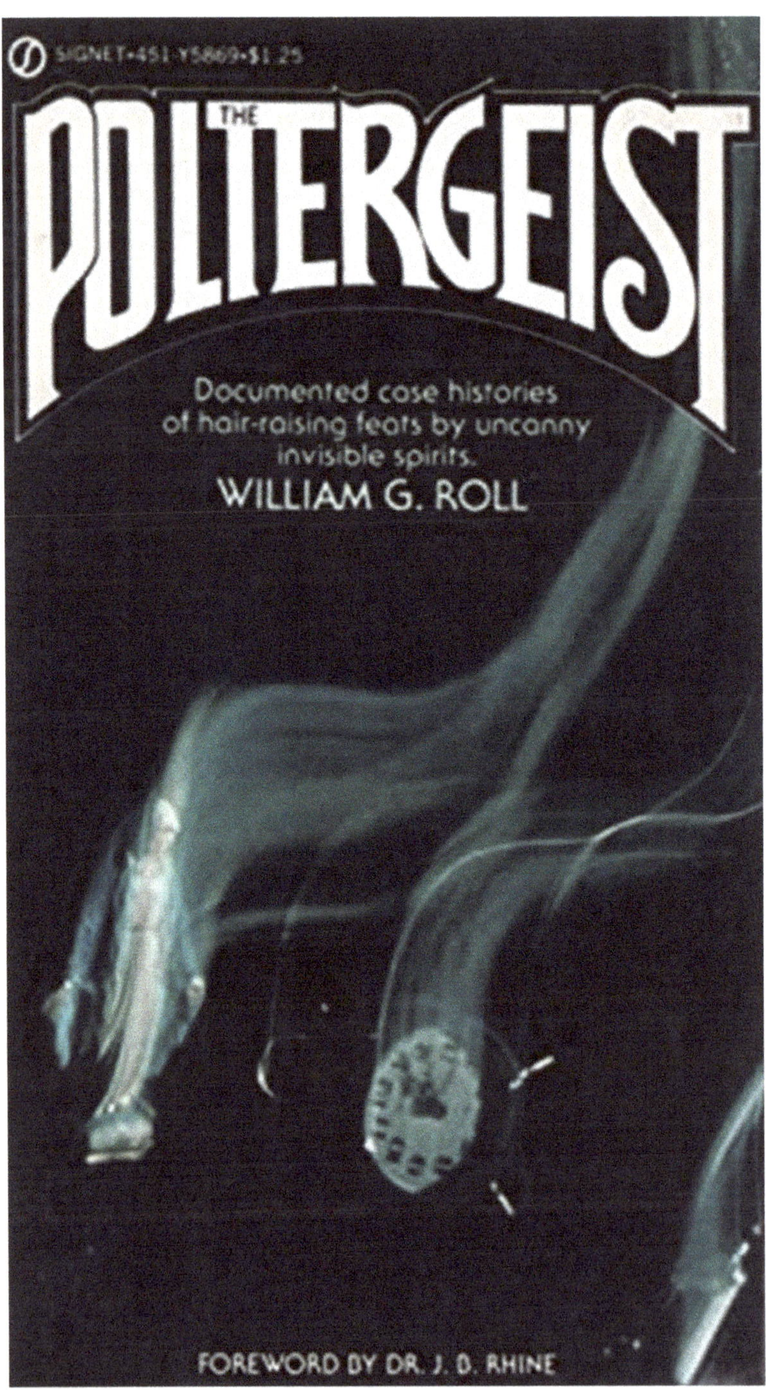

The cover photo of "The Poltergeist" (1972) aptly portrays the coherent white smoke and transparent features I witnessed.

to an experience that is more common and real than most people believe. All I know is, that was the first time I had an experience which exposed me to the idea of something beyond this physical world.

Later in life, I would read *Hamlet*. The line, "There are more things in heaven and earth, Horatio, than are dreamt of in your philosophy," reminded me of this first incident of becoming aware of "more things" beyond what can be easily explained by logic and reason.

In the aftermath of this experience, I did stop reading books about ghosts. So little is actually known about what happens after we die, I felt I might drive myself crazy asking questions with no answers. I wasn't sure why this experience had happened to me—and to this day, I am troubled by the question of what the farm boy wanted and how I might have been able to help him—but I was wary of pursuing these unknown, unexplainable phenomena in a deeper way. It felt too risky.

I continued to be interested in any scientific studies that attempted to understand or quantify incidents we perceive as paranormal. My disbelief in G-d pointed me toward some academic and scientific explanations for what I—and others—had experienced as a "spiritual" phenomenon.[9]

2

TEEN YEARS

Middle School

My Bar Mitzvah was held at the Germantown Jewish Centre, the conservative synagogue where my family prayed and where my parents had been lifelong members. We weren't an overly religious family, but there was a desire to keep a certain level of Jewish influence in the household, which I, of course, didn't relate to at that time.

My teenage years were often marred by adolescent conflict. I was bullied or harassed by other kids. I questioned the process of "socialization," even as I was immersed in it. My ambivalence towards the "norms" of society and my own sometimes awkward tendency to say the wrong thing probably didn't help. I liked to provoke a response in others, questioning their reality or shaking up their "normal" life in some unexpected way. I thought of myself as a free spirit, but I was also shy. It was difficult to connect with those around me, and my attempts to shake things up doubled down on my feeling of not fitting in.

It wasn't all bad. While I was attending Cedarbrook Middle School, I was invited by my teacher, Mr. Williams, to go to Florida as part of a regional science tour.[1] My mother and my sister Lori accompanied me. We traveled by train, which was a long trip between Philly and the Space Coast.

This included a visit to the Kennedy Space Center in the time between the end of the Apollo era and the ramp up to the Space Shuttle program. The Vehicle Assembly Building—which was usually a beehive of activity preparing launch vehicles for blastoff—was not in use, so NASA had painted the building with red, white, and blue for the Bicentennial and put some museum-quality pieces on display inside the big building. We got to see things not normally accessible to the public, which was a treat and a unique experience.

While we were in Florida, we also visited Disney World. (The first of several visits for me.) At one point, a tour guide pointed out a construction zone outside of the Magic Kingdom. "See that deep furrow in the ground? That's the future site of Disney's Experimental Prototype Community of Tomorrow." So I was able to see the newly broken ground of what would later become EPCOT, a place I would enjoy spending time.

Tour bus View of NASA's V.A.B.

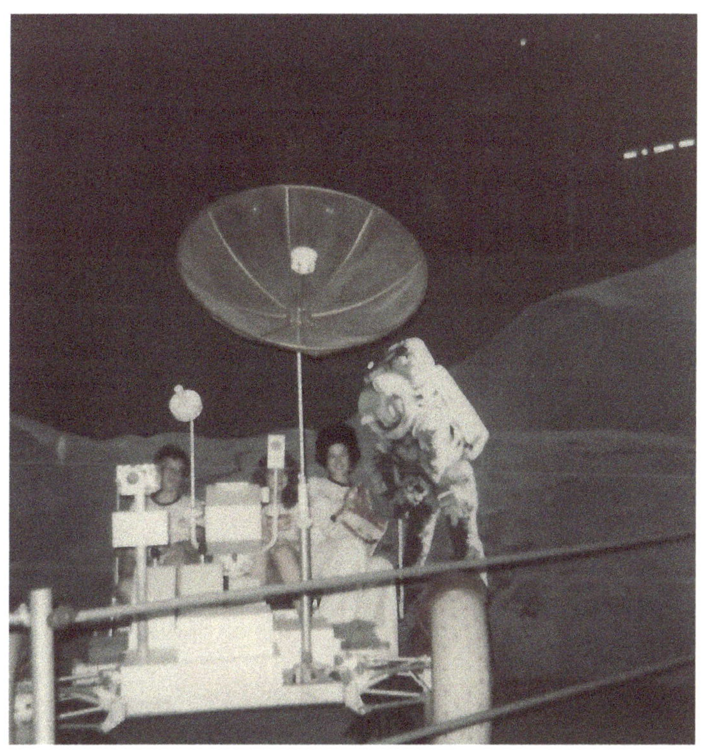

Mom, Me & Lori in a mock lunar rover inside the V.A.B. (1976) Cape Kennedy

Boundary Issues

I had an issue setting and maintaining boundaries. I found it hard to see the serious side of things and acted out against norms. From an early age, I almost always refused to tie my shoelaces, and that was just the start of it. If I couldn't see a good reason for an expected behavior, I would often act out and do the opposite. Frequently, I wanted to gauge the reaction of others. Would my behavior alter their response? Would it alter their thoughts or actions?

I began working in my father's pharmacy in my teens. My parents thought it would help me build a work ethic. Prior to being legally eligible to work, I did little chores around the store. I dusted shelves or helped my father count inventory. (All of my siblings worked at the pharmacy at some point. My sister Sara worked with Dad the longest, right up until he sold the store and retired in 1997.)

One bonus of working there was the corned beef sandwiches at Roxy's, a small supermarket next door. Another benefit was having early access to the store's magazines. I was responsible for processing the weekly delivery from the distributor—United News—which meant I never missed an issue of my favorite DC Comics: *Superman, Batman,* and other heroes of the Justice League.[2]

When I was old enough to be an actual employee, I was trained to run the cash register. The work was supposed to give me a sense of discipline, but I had a hard time taking it seriously. I was bored by it.

Since it was my father's store, I could get away with things other employees might not. Or, at least, I felt I could. For instance, while manning the register on hot days, I took off my sneakers and put them in the bottom of the roll-top freezer full of frozen treats. I'd bury them in the bottom and cover them with boxes of ice cream cones and sandwiches. People opened the freezer to make a selection, never knowing my shoes were cooling underneath. Later, I'd slip my feet into those cold shoes to get some relief from the heat.

I got a kick out of doing this, but it drove my dad a little crazy. "Don't you care about anything?" he would say. "You don't take your grades seriously. You don't take this work seriously."

His critique was partially correct: I was really only interested in the things I was interested in. Pressure from my parents, school, and society to "care" about what I perceived as arbitrary norms or expectations didn't compute. Partly, too, I was interested in seeing how people reacted to rules being broken. I got a kick out of how disproportionately some people would react to the most minor offense. I was curious why certain ideas had become "the norm," and deeply interested in exploring different ways of experiencing life.

As in other areas of my life, I had a hard time figuring out boundaries with the opposite sex. I remember thinking a girl named Margie was cute in elementary school, and I would follow her around and tried to be in the same places she was. I felt like, beneath her shyness, she and I had some sort of kindred sensitivity to life. Of course, I was curious about sexuality and romance, but my fixation wasn't motivated by the possibility of physical contact. I just wanted to be near her. With Margie—and subsequent crushes I would develop throughout my life—my desire was for proximity and recognition.

My intentions were never to harm or make anyone uncomfortable, but my actions likely caused distress in the objects of my affection. I didn't have the self-awareness to realize what I was doing was more likely to be seen as creepy than it was to endear me to my crush. It would be many years before I understood this.

Different Kinds of Friends

One of the ways my pushing against society's norms played out was in my selection of friends.

My junior year at Cheltenham High, I took French as a second language. I wasn't really interested in French, but I had to take a language class. I didn't do my homework most of the time and just zoned out.

I sat about six rows back from the front. There was a guy in the class with long curly brown hair who sat closer to the teacher, Ms. Hunt. One day, I watched that guy draw the entire periodic chart, upside down and from memory.

Lee Kaplan as he looked during the time I knew him (1980-'82).
We met as students together in Cheltenham High School.

This seemed like an interesting kid, so after class I approached him and introduced myself. His name was Lee Kaplan, and he lived in Elkins Park.

"Did you really draw the periodic table from memory? And upside down?" I asked.

"Yeah."

"So, I guess you're into science?"

"Yeah," Lee said. "I guess so."

Lee and I started talking and became friends. I told my parents I'd made a new friend and asked if I could go home with Lee after school one day. I rode a different bus and went with him to his house.[3] In his basement, Lee had an extensive chemistry lab set up, with beakers and test tubes. I was impressed. Lee was smart, and chemistry was his favorite subject. He had worked out a way to refine trinitrotoluene. TNT.

Lee's home life wasn't so great. His dad had left the family, and Lee's mom was—I would later figure out—an alcoholic and very depressed. I started to visit after school quite often, and she'd usually be stretched out on the sofa, oblivious to what we were doing.

I was introduced to two of Lee's friends from Melrose Park, John and his younger brother Lincoln. They were transplants from Georgia, with a southern twang. They were supposed to go to Cheltenham High, too, but I never really saw them there. I think they played hooky. Their single mother was focused on completing her dissertation in sociology and paid little attention to their comings and goings. Over the next months, I spent a lot of time with them.

My three new friends introduced me to a strange but interesting life I found very appealing for a while. Lee, Lincoln, and John would save up their money to buy commercial fireworks—cherry bombs, M80s, firecrackers— and metal piping from the hardware store. With Lee's ability and basement laboratory, they refined the ingredients to make effective pipe bombs.

I began asking to stay over at Lee's house. I told my parents we were studying for school, so they agreed to let me go. Elkins Park was about four miles from where I lived in Laverock, but it was over an hours' walk, and I didn't know that area well. Lee and I would hang out at his place for the afternoon and early evening, then go out, late at night to meet the others and walk around. After the passenger trains stopped running around midnight, we roamed the desolate tracks between Melrose Park and Jenkintown. We spent the wee hours of the morning wandering, and the next day, I'd be dead tired at school.

A couple times a month—after they'd gathered enough raw materials for Lee to work his magic in the basement— we'd set off one of the pipe bombs in the middle of the night. We'd place the bomb on the railroad track, light the fuse, and run like hell. The explosion was loud, but it didn't seem to cause any damage to the track. I'm sure the *bang* woke some folks from a deep sleep though.

The boys taught me how to chew tobacco, which gave me a chemical buzz on top of the adrenaline rush of traipsing about and setting off explosives. (The chew also upset my digestive system.) We sang crazy songs as we trudged along the tracks; they were ditties like bawdy limericks or sea shanties, and I really liked this new experience. It was the beginning of my relationship with Elkins Park.

Inviting Paul Over

In high school, I had a biology lab partner named Paul Kellerman. Paul and I worked well together, and he was a nice guy. Attempting to broaden my friend group, I asked my mother for permission to invite Paul to our house. She said it was fine, so I suggested Paul come hang out with me. He came over and I introduced him to my mom, then we left the house to walk around the neighborhood. I wanted to impress Paul and cement our friendship, so I hatched a plan for our afternoon together. "Let's make the afternoon interesting. How about we walk to the Pick-A-Deli. Maybe we'll get some beer?"

Paul looked incredulous, but I was pumped to see if we'd get away with it.

"You wait outside," I told him. Between the two of us, I looked significantly older. Paul had acne and looked younger. "I'm pretty sure they'll sell me a six-pack of beer."

I hadn't done anything like that before—I didn't care much for violating the taboo of underaged drinking—but I *did* like the idea of presenting myself as an adult and getting away with it.

I emerged with a six-pack dangling from my fingers, feigning a practiced nonchalance. I popped the tab and took a big drink while we walked along. There was a stranger passing by, and I casually offered the guy one of our beers. I reveled in the whimsy of the moment, but Paul wasn't too happy about my generosity. "You just giving away our beers?"

"I have one in my hand," I said, "and I gave one away. I still have one left. The other three are all yours!"

We got to the intersection of Willow Grove and Flourtown Avenue, and I could hear music from a party somewhere down the road. "Let's go crash the party!" I suggested.

Paul wasn't so sure. "You can't just crash someone's party."

"Let's just see what happens," I said.

Paul followed me as I turned down Flourtown, and as luck would have it, a police cruiser was coming up the street right toward us. I was pretty sure the cop had already seen the beer in my hand by the time I'd noticed him slowing his car to a stop.

Having the beer on me was bad enough, but I also had explosives in my pockets. A couple nights earlier, I'd been walking the tracks with my bomb buddies, and they'd given me a couple cherry bombs and an M80 of my own. If I was frisked, I'd be found out, so I decided to play it safe.

As the officer was getting out of his car, I said, "I guess you want these?" and held the beer out toward him.

"Yeah," he said. "I'll take that." The policeman asked us a bunch of questions. Who are you? Where are you from? What are you doing over here? My mother had instructed me that if I were ever stopped by the police, I shouldn't tell them where I live, so I responded I lived in Elkins Park, rather than a mile away in Laverock.[4]

The cop said, "I'm gonna take this beer. If either of you are standing here when I come back around the block, you're gonna take a trip with me to the precinct. Understood?"

The cop was giving us a chance to walk away, so I nodded along. Paul, on the other hand, wasn't feeling the same way. As the cop walked back to his car, Paul was mumbling under his breath, "We paid for that beer. If you want to give your beer away, that's fine, but I want my beer back."

"Don't worry about it," I said. "It's not worth it."

"But we paid for it," he said, getting louder. I tried to get Paul to hush, but he kept complaining. The cop was just about to slip into his car and drive away when Paul said, "Hey! Mister Policeman, Sir. Can we have our beer back?"

"No, no, no," I said, stunned by Paul's inability to appreciate the situation.

The officer took a deep breath and did a slow turn back towards us. He lifted the remains of our six-pack and said to

Paul, "You want this back?"

"Well, Mr. Policeman, I figure you can get your own beer. That's our beer, and it would be nice if you gave it back, since we paid for it."

The cop looked at me and made the same offer. "What about you? You want this back?"

"Nope," I said. "No, no. I'm good. I don't need it back. All fine."

"But you," he said to Paul, giving him one more chance to wise up. "You still want this?" He closed the distance between us and offered the beer for Paul to take.

Paul accepted it and said, "Yes, thank you very much." As he handed the beer to Paul, the officer reached for his handcuffs and opened them for Paul's wrists. That's when Paul had his lightbulb moment. "Oh, oh! Never mind. I changed my mind."

As I watched Paul being cuffed and guided into the patrol car, all I could think was, "Great job, Ted. The first friend who comes to visit, you manage to get him carted off to jail!" I knew Mrs. Kellerman was gonna be mad, even though, if Paul had just been cool, we'd have been fine.

Paul and I didn't hang out together outside of school after that, though we were still friendly and worked together in class.

Another Troubled Youth

My mother and father had concerns about how much time I spent with Lee and the boys. Mom grounded me and told me I couldn't hang out with them any more, but I snuck out of the house a few times late at night and made my way to Elkins Park for our late-night roaming anyway. One time, I snuck out my second-story bedroom window and forgot to unlatch the hook-and-eye lock from my door. When I returned home, I was stuck, and we had to break the lock from the hallway side.

I tried to do better in school, at least in the areas I found interesting. While writing a paper on the McCarthy era, I started to study at the Temple University library, where they had more resources to assist my research.[5]

The university campus beckoned. It seemed to be a more cosmopolitan society. The diversity of students gathering outdoors, studying, and interacting in that environment was more compelling to me than the fixed high school classroom. I encountered various groups and people with different ideologies, which I found interesting. It was a prime place for me to observe others who were trying to chart their own course through the world.

It was 1979 and The Hare Krishnas were highly active in the area between Paley library and the student activities building on Temple's main campus. They offered me magazines and pamphlets, which I took and read. I was trying to foster an attitude within myself that even though I didn't really believe in G-d, religions of the world had something to teach me, so I read their materials, including a copy of the *Bhagavad Gita*.

My mother was troubled when she saw that book. "What are you doing with this? You know you're Jewish, don't you?"

"Of course," I said, "I realize that. But I don't feel exclusively Jewish. I want to explore other ideas."

This was a straw-that-broke-the-camel's-back moment for my parents. In their eyes, their son wasn't serious about school or his Jewish heritage, his friends were trouble, and he had no regard for civil society and rules to live by. They saw me as a troubled young man, and it worried them.

My parents proposed a solution: They would send me to Israel. They had some friends who had sent their wayward daughter to Israel on a similar trip, and the experience had worked miracles, in their eyes.

I didn't think a trip to Israel would change my belief in G-d, or suddenly make me a better person in my parent's eyes. On the other hand, I hadn't traveled much—except for some trips to Atlantic City and that trip to Florida—and that was something I wanted to do. I also thought it was a good opportunity to learn more about Jewish history and culture, so I agreed.

So, in August of 1980—between my junior and senior years of high school—I packed my bags, got a passport, and signed up for a two-week trip to Israel with a tour group from Congregation Adath Jeshuran.[6]

Science Fiction and Movies

My school performance was uneven. I certainly wasn't stupid, but I had a problem putting forth effort in areas that didn't interest me. And the truth was, most of what interested me wasn't taught in school. I was easily distracted and would inevitably turn in term papers and other assignments late. Teachers often made a note that my work was excellent, then would strike through the A+ grade and mark me down to a B for lateness. Often, I was unprepared for tests, but in areas of English and history, I managed to somehow pull off an above-average grade.

As I had in my early adolescence, I continued to read a lot of science fiction and books about technology. In those books, I found information that intrigued me and sparked my interest and imagination. I also liked to read magazines with a focus on scientific discoveries.

I would procrastinate school work to watch television shows that captured my attention: *Star Trek*, *The Twilight Zone*, *The Outer Limits*, and *Mission Impossible*.

My family acquired one of the first commercially available video cassette recorders in 1978. It was a VHS format recorder by Magnavox. Unlike the nearly disposable VCRs of later years, this first video recording system was a substantial machine. It had beautiful Mahogany wood-paneled sides and took up quite a bit of space.

I began to collect movies and videos, and my family recorded a lot of television programming. Of course, I had boxes and boxes of *Star Trek* episodes and other science fiction movies and shows. I liked to record documentaries from PBS, especially shows about physics and outer space.

I also began collecting hard-to-find video copies of movies. In the early years of personal video machines, the available selection of feature films was limited. Even when a favorite old movie was made available on VHS tape, it often came with a prohibitive price tag. My copy of the 1966 classic *Fantastic Voyage* on VHS cost me around $100.

Science fiction and sociology seemed to go hand in hand. Sociology allowed me a perspective and intellectual path which incorporated my interests in technology, social norms, and the development of human society. Technological developments of the '70s and '80s promised a "brave new world," and I was deeply interested in how humanity would navigate it. How would we adapt to what lay ahead? How would technology reshape human behavior? Would we use these new tools for good?

In my teen years, I started attending the Philadelphia Science Fiction Society's annual convention, PhilCon. PhilCon was held in Philadelphia in those years, though it later migrated to New Jersey. It is the oldest SF convention in the US, its first meeting being in 1936.

I didn't go to the convention every year, but I certainly tried to go as often as I could. I had some great experiences. One stand-out memory was when I briefly met Isaac Asimov.

In November of 1980, one of the featured speakers was Ben Bova, a well known science fiction author and the editor of the prestigious *Omni* magazine. It was the kind of magazine I really enjoyed—a mix of hard science, investigation of parapsychology, and short stories of science fiction.

In 1979, *Omni* had run an interesting interview with psychologist and behaviorist B. F. Skinner.[7] That article about a social philosopher was right up my alley, but I felt it had ended too quickly. It was like a snack when I would have preferred a four-course meal. Skinner was a fascinating figure who believed free will was an illusion. His ideas gave me a lot to think about.

When I saw Ben Bova at PhilCon, I approached him and said, "Mr. Bova, I'm just curious. Why was the interview with B. F. Skinner so short?"

"There have been a lot of interviews with Skinner," Bova said. "His ideas are everywhere. Anyone can read more about him, if they want to."

Bova's answer annoyed me, but I went on with the convention activities.

I didn't have money for a hotel room, and I didn't want to go back to Laverock from the city, so I found an empty ballroom to sleep in. There were several rectangular tables set up with long, white tablecloths that draped to the ground. I crawled under one of the tables and fell asleep.

The next morning, I was disoriented when I woke up. The light was streaming in through the white tablecloths, and as I came to consciousness—flat on my back, surrounded on all sides by this white luminescence, and with a solid top above me—I momentarily thought, *Oh my G-d. I'm dead. I'm in a coffin and I'm dead!* Even worse, if I wasn't dead, there wouldn't be much oxygen left for me to breathe, and being buried alive seemed like a lousy way to go.

It took a minute to remember I wasn't in a coffin; I was sleeping in the convention center ballroom. Relieved of that panic, I climbed out from beneath the table and gathered myself for the day.

I went to the elevator, and who did I meet in there? "Good morning Mr. Bova," I said. He didn't respond. I guess my questioning of his editorial decision had annoyed him as much as his answer had annoyed me.

3

ISRAEL AND BEYOND

First Trip to Israel

The first days of the Israel trip were spent in Jerusalem. We stayed in the historic King David Hotel. We went to the site of the ancient temple and the Cotel Hamaaravi, the Western Wall. I knew this was a holy site for Judaism, but I didn't yet comprehend the whole history of the Temple Mount. There is a saying: When G-d created the world, he bestowed nine-tenths of the holiness of Creation upon Israel, and nine-tenths of Israel's holiness was centered in Jerusalem. And while I didn't believe in a Creator deity per se, there was a certain spiritual energy I could feel lingering in that revered and holy place.

I decided, impulsively and almost irreverently, to put the idea of G-d to the test. They had just hosed down the floor of the Cotel plaza. Everything was damp and glistening. I stood in that holy place—shoelaces untied, the stone tile wet from cleaning—and challenged: *If there is a G-d, He will protect me as I run across the plaza and right up to the wall.* If I hydroplaned and wiped out, I would have my proof against a loving G-d.

Off I went, barreling across the plaza. I made it all the way to the wall without falling. I didn't slip. I didn't crash.

I immediately talked myself out of the bargain with the Divine I'd just made. Surely that was too little proof to change my mind. G-d would have to work harder than that to convince me!

After Jerusalem, our tour group visited other areas of Israel, eventually heading north to Tzfat, a city near the Lebanese border. The air in Tzfat felt different. It was a mystical place, which I recognized immediately.

It was the middle of a hot August day when we entered the Rabbi Yosef Caro Synagogue. Walking through the doorframe, white light poured in through the windows illuminating the blue cushions of the bench seating area. A noetic thought came to me—not a voice, but I knew the thought originated outside of me because it was so opposed to my own thinking—that said, *You think science and technology have taught people how to live? That isn't true. People knew how to live more sensibly and they understood the world far better 500 years ago.*

This was deeply antithetical to my personal philosophy, but it stuck with me. I began to consider different ways of knowing and understanding the world. From that day on,

Portrait (2018) by an unknown artist of Tzfat, Israel: Rav. Yosef Caro (1488-1575)
In front of the synagogue of his name

Tzfat and the Caro Synagogue have been very special to me. I've returned many times.

The last couple of days in Israel, I returned to the Western Wall. A young man helped me put tefillin on my forehead and left arm to complete the mitzvah of praying at the wall. Afterward, he asked if I'd like to see the yeshiva where he studied. I was nervous—afraid he was trying to recruit me into a cult—but I decided it might be interesting. He showed me around Aish HaTorah and the yeshiva there. After, I rested in the area where the students took their meals.

This was a couple years after a famous *Rolling Stone* magazine article titled "Next Year in Jerusalem." The writer, Ellen Jane Willis, had penned a long essay about her brother's embracing Orthodox Judaism and the Baal Teshuva movement of the late '70s, which saw a lot of secular Jews becoming religiously observant. There were dozens of that issue of *Rolling Stone* scattered around the yeshiva's cafeteria area.

I grabbed a cup of coffee and scanned the dining area. There was a woman who appeared to be in her seventies, and I asked if it was her first trip to Israel. She said, "Oh, no. This is my eleventh trip. My husband brings me back every other year." Oddly, this was the first moment where I realized my first trip to Israel didn't have to be my last.

There was one other person in the seating area: a tall, lanky young guy with cropped curly hair, glasses, and a lot of freckles. He seemed like a typical student, and I wanted to see what kinds of things he was learning in the yeshiva.

"Hi, I'm Ted."

"Hello, Ted. I'm David."

"I'm from the United States."

"I am too."

"Oh yeah? I'm from Pennsylvania."

"Really? So am I?"

This seemed so crazy. Here I was, 6,000 miles from home, and the one student I talk to is from Pennsylvania? "What part of Pennsylvania?" I asked.

"Elkins Park," he said.

I told him I was also from Cheltenham Township and we laughed about it being a small world. David had been studying in Israel for several years, but it made an impression on me that we had more in common than I would have imagined.

During the return flight to the US, most of my group was seated in one part of the plane and I was separated from them, seated beside a rabbi who wasn't part of our tour. He and I talked, and I told him about my trip. I'd just been through an ineffable experience and was having trouble putting it into words. Without realizing it, I began to refer to G-d as, "The Name". It was difficult to grasp the idea of G-d as unknowable, but to say, "The Name," made sense to me. The rabbi told me that was how many Jews spoke of G-d. In my conservative Judaism, this wasn't common, so this was interesting to me.

"How do you say it," I asked, "in Hebrew?"

The rabbi said, "Hashem. The Name."

That felt right.

We landed at Kennedy airport and took the group bus back to Elkins Park. I stepped off the bus to greet my waiting parents wearing an Arab shirt and a keffiyeh. It was a planned prank to lead my parents to think that, once again, I'd gone in an opposite direction to what they'd hoped—but in reality, in my heart and in my mind, the gears of change toward a belief in G-d were already engaged.

Things Escalate Back Home

Fall of 1980 saw the beginning of my senior year of high school.

After returning from Israel, I reunited with Lee, Lincoln, and John after months apart. I could immediately sense things had changed. The group now had a name—Tactical Guerrilla Command, or TGC—and a "new mission."

When I asked what their mission was, I was told, "We're gonna get rid of all the freaks."

I didn't like the sound of that. "What's a freak?"

"Anyone who does drugs or smokes weed," they said. "We're gonna get rid of them."

"What are you talking about?" I asked.

"We think we found this freak hangout. We'll show you." The guys led me to a place along the railroad where there was a ravine. It was late at night, and I couldn't really see much, but there was some sort of lean-to or shack structure in the railroad bed. "We're going to blow it up."

My thoughts were that roaming the tracks and setting off explosives was a little crazy, but it was just recreational and hadn't hurt anyone. This was different.

"You can't blow that up," I said. "What if someone is in there."

"It doesn't matter," John said.

John was the oldest of the group, and he had a leader's charisma. Lincoln pretty much did anything John said, and Lee seemed on board as well.

Counter to my concerns, they detonated the explosive and we ran. I don't think anyone was hurt, but the idea of injuring someone changed the way I viewed the newly christened TGC. I began to make excuses and limited my time with them.

About a month later, I did go out with those guys again. We met up around eleven o'clock, and the night started normally. It was dark, and I didn't know my way around Elkins Park, so I just followed along wherever they wanted to go. On one of the side streets, the cars were parallel parked so tightly, we stepped up onto the back bumper of one car, then climbed—trunk, to roof, to hood—before stepping over onto the next car. We could go most of a block without touching the ground, which was kind of fun. While I stepped carefully, the others were more prone to jump and dent the cars as we walked.

We stopped at the corner of another street where John and Lee talked conspiratorially.

"What do you think?" Lee said. "Here?"

"Yeah," John said. "Let's do it."

I started to say, "What are you guys talking about?" when Lee pulled out a pipe bomb. They ran up the steps of one of the houses and put the bomb between the screen door and front door. The fuse was lit, and someone shouted, "RUN!"

We scattered and my heart was pounding. What was happening? Why would they do this to this particular house?

I was alone and lost, and didn't know where to go or what to do. Somehow I found my way to Curtis Park and hid out there for a while. I heard cop cars circling. I didn't want to get caught on the streets, but I wasn't even sure how to get back to Laverock from there. Eventually, I ended up back in Melrose Park, where John and Lincoln lived, and all three of the guys were there. Reuniting with them helped me reestablish my bearings, and I made my way back home.

After that night, I made any excuse I could to not hang out with the TGC anymore.

Eight Weeks of Miraculous Events

Up until I took that first Israel trip, I hadn't felt much interest in my Jewish heritage. After I returned, all of the sudden, I was being barraged by Judaism. I couldn't turn it off.

After school started, my friend Ellie Biernbaum, who lived on the corner, called me and said, "Guess what? I just became president of KIFTY!"

"That's great," I said. "What's KIFTY?"

Ellie explained that the Keneseth Israel Federation Temple Youth was a Jewish youth organization associated with the reformed synagogue in Elkins Park. "You're a good writer," she said. "I was wondering if you'd be the editor of the youth group newsletter?"

I'd always had a crush on Ellie. This opportunity seemed like a good way to impress her and spend time with her, so I agreed.

I became involved in KIFTY events in Elkins Park, and over the next year, we published about a dozen newsletters that received some great recognition.

Shortly after Ellie had invited me to KIFTY, David Indik—a Junior at Cheltenham High—approached me. David was also Jewish and a very intelligent guy. He said, "There's a new synagogue forming in Elkins Park. They are going to start meeting next month. Why don't you come? It could be interesting."

I went home and told my parents, and they questioned me about the new synagogue. When I told them it was an Orthodox synagogue, they pushed back. "You don't want to do that! You're going from one extreme to another. Before, it was Hare Krishnas, now you're going to be Orthodox? What's wrong with our conservative synagogue?"

I told them I really didn't know what path I wanted to take. I was exploring and gaining experiences with three branches of Judaism, and I wanted to see what this new synagogue was about.

"Ah, it's a cult!" they said. "You don't want to be involved with that!"

To appease my parents, I made a point of missing that first Shabbat service in October of 1980 of what would come to be known initially as "The Orthodox Minyan of Elkins Park." I also made sure that I attended Rosh Hashana and Yom Kippur services at Germantown Jewish Centre to assure them that we were still all a family and practicing our Judaism together. But even while I prayed with them, I felt I was striving for something more.

Orthodox Minyan of Elkins Park

Attending the new congregation in Elkins Park was one of the most important decisions of my life. The Orthodox minyan that was forming was an offspring of Adath Jeshurun—the conservative synagogue on Old York Road—

after some of AJ's members decided they wanted more traditional worship. The group was led by its first president, Sidney Bernstein, and his wife, Paulette. Within a year or so, a constitution would be developed. Dr. Frank Schwartz, who I liked immediately, would be elected as the minyan's second president (after Sidney), to be followed by a whole host of others.[1]

When I finally did begin to show up at the Shabbat services of the OMEP, it was around Passover time, in April of 1981. Those first few years, the group met for services during the week in a back-lot building of the former Cheltenham High campus at High School Road and Montgomery Avenue. The campus had been purchased and become the Beth Jacob Day School. An administrator of Beth Jacob permitted the new minyan to use that back building in which no classes were being taught, at the time.[2] However, on Shabbat and Holy days we were able to convene in the more spacious and better kept space in the front administrative building.

*From 1953-1959, this building served as the Cheltenham High School
and was also the birthplace of the OMEP*

*Prior to 1985 – 618 Spring Ave., Elkins Park was home to Sidney & Paulette Bernstein,
founders of the OMEP, later YIEP*

Dr. Peter J. Goldstone-friend, confidante, mentor & support in every way to the community of Young Israel of Elkins Park

Following that first Shabbat service I attended, I was invited to the Bernstein's home for a meal, where I also first met Dr. Peter Goldstone, a professor of philosophy at Temple University.[3]

I was drawn to Peter immediately. I admired his mind and education. He was newly religious and very thoughtful about the things he was experiencing. He became a great resource for me as I attempted to understand my own spiritual journey. I was still on guard, since my parents had warned me this new group might be a religious cult. Peter's participation helped me keep things in a proper perspective.

Peter lived in Glenside, between my home in Laverock and the synagogue. In order to attend services in Elkins Park— and observe the Sabbath rules—I walked from my home to Peter's home in Glenside, or we'd meet at Cedarbrook Middle School), and we'd walk together the hour to Elkins Park. We did this for many years, and our conversations were enlightening. I learned so many things during those walks. Peter treated me with kindness and generosity.

Peter told me about growing up in Chicago, and I learned about his career and family. He invited me to his home for Shabbos, and I met his wife and children. He mentored me in many ways, and I am grateful for that.

The founding members of The Orthodox Minyan of Elkins Park were fairly diverse, but all united by a common interest in the traditional service with Hebrew liturgy. We had the required ten men for prayer and public worship, including: Sidney Bernstein, Peter Goldstone, Jon James, David Indik, and his father, Mark Indik, Sam Mazursky, Howard Snyder, Paul Breslow and his son, David. Rhea Blackman was initially the only woman in the congregation aside from Paulette Bernstein, but they would later be joined by Joye Schwartz, Cathy Snyder, and the wives of so many others. In a short time, these women formed the Sisterhood of the OMEP.

My parents questioned my new-found dedication. I had gone from casual indifference about my Jewish heritage to walking an hour and a half each way to pray in Elkins Park on Saturdays. "You go there a lot more than you ever went to Germantown," was their general complaint.

"I'm learning a little bit," I told them. "And I like it there."

My mother was thoughtful about this and felt that if I was on this path, it might help to have a discussion with the conservative Rabbi of Germantown Jewish Center, Rabbi Elias Charry. Rabbi Charry had married my parents, my Aunt Joyce and Uncle Harvey, and had in recent years retired to the position of "Rabbi Emeritus" of our synagogue. It had been a number of years since I'd heard Rabbi Charry's wisened words echo in the main sanctuary at Germantown on a Shabbat morning. He moved more slowly and his gray hair was beginning to bald, but his office was filled, floor to ceiling, with shelves of books. With my mother present, he spoke and advised that if I was really going to go toward the path of traditional orthodox Judaism, that it was a decision

I should not take lightly and should pursue responsibly. I thanked him and considered the weight of his words.

I also told my parents I was still "experimenting" and trying out the different branches of Judaism. KIFTY was a reformed Jewish organization, my parent's congregation was conservative, and the Elkins Park congregation was Orthodox, so I was getting a wide-ranging experience with the faith. In order to further appease my parents, and to honor them, I began to make more of an effort to attend services with them at Germantown Jewish Centre. I didn't find the services to be as compelling, but I was glad to attend occasionally to make my parents happy.

KIFTY Activities

As editor of the KIFTY Bulletin, I had a staff of six, including an artist. Ellie and I came up with the idea of focusing on the ongoing issue of Jewish people—especially Jewish youth—being lured away by other faiths. Many young Jews were being tempted by the Hare Krishnas, the Moonies, and various Christian denominations.

During the 1970s (and into the '80s), there were several Christian organizations that specifically targeted Jews. These domestic missionary groups promoted the idea that people could "stay Jewish" even though they "accepted Jesus as the Messiah," and in doing so, they would become a "completed Jew." This appealed to people in the growing number of interfaith marriages looking for ways to maintain some of their Jewish heritage.

Many of these groups adapted Jewish customs and practices, incorporating Jesus into their worship. I attended a meeting of one of these "Jews for Jesus" type organizations led by a man named Martin Chernoff. They held a Shabbat observance, but in the reading of the Friday night Kiddush, they replaced the references to G-d (HaShem) with the Hebrew word for Jesus (Yeshua). (Jesus was thanked, for example, for the commandment to light the Shabbat candles.) They also incorporated Holy Communion into the sanctification blessing of the wine. I found this appropriation of sacred Jewish customs frightening.[4]

I wrote a multi-part series for the KIFTY Bulletin about these Christian missionary groups and other cults luring young Jewish people from the faith. It was a well-received series. Several people approached me to say, "Are you the young man who is the editor of the newsletter? You're doing a great job. Those articles are so well written and informative. Keep it up."

Ellie was happy with the articles as well. So it was a double bonus for me.

It would be dishonest to pretend that trying to impress Ellie wasn't a big part of my involvement in KIFTY. I did reap spiritual benefit from my time in KIFTY, but I was also trying to convince Ellie to be my girlfriend. I'd even brought it up several times.

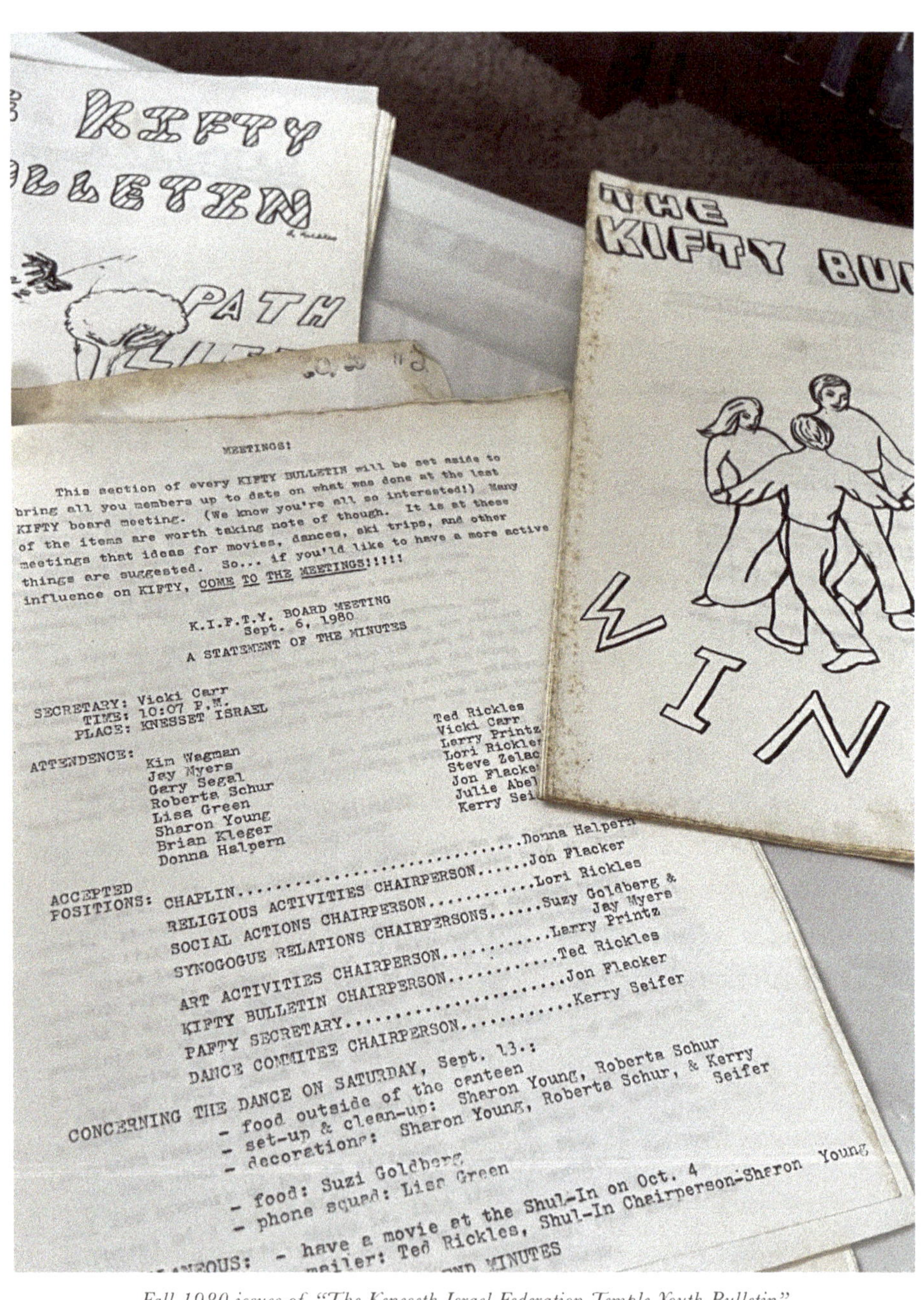

Fall 1980 issues of "The Keneseth Israel Federation Temple Youth Bulletin"
which included poetry, art, articles & more

"I like you, Ted," she would tell me. "But I don't know how I'll feel about you tomorrow."

I knew Ellie had dated a few guys casually, but at the Winter Pennsylvania Federation of Temple Youth (PAFTY) retreat in December of 1980, I found out she was dating Larry R. Larry was in a different youth group, and I hadn't met him before. He was a nice guy and a good guitar player, and it was obvious their relationship was leaning toward the more serious side.

During the weekend, Ellie's allergies were acting up. As usual, I tried to be of service to her. I offered her some of the Benadryl I carried for my own, ever-present allergies. I gave her two pills from my bottle.

Unfortunately, I hadn't thought that through very well. Ellie was slim, and shorter than me, and my usual two-pill dose was more appropriate for a larger, heftier man. Ellie fell into a deep sleep, and the adult advisor had trouble waking her up. Everyone was worried about her, and I was especially despondent: What if something bad happened to her because of my incompetence? What if my stupidity would have killed her? I was in tears and worried like crazy until Ellie recovered.

Thankfully, Ellie's deep sleep was temporary. When she woke up, she was a little annoyed at me for giving her too much of the allergy medicine, but she didn't hold it against me. I felt more bonded to her than ever. So did Larry. The PAFTY retreat had brought Larry and Ellie closer together and strengthened their relationship. (They married, eventually, in the following years.)

Continued Spiritual Growth

In March of 1981, I was part of a trip to Borough Park in New York with Mordechai Katz, who had authored a Jewish book titled, *Lilmod Ulelamade*. I met a Gadol Hador—that is, one of the great Torah scholars of his generation—Rabbi Moshe Feinstein. Rav Feinstein gave me a blessing in Hebrew. I didn't understand the words, but the act had a powerful effect on me. In subsequent years, my friend David Toplin and I would make trips to Crown Heights, New York, spending Sabbaths and holidays in the bustling services at 770 Kingston Avenue. And YES! We met the Lubavitcher Rebbe on more than one occasion.

My interest in Judaism continued to grow, so when I had a chance to attend Torah workshops in Moodus, Connecticut, I took it. With the help of the Ohr Somayach yeshiva in Jerusalem, Rabbi Yaakov Rosenberg had purchased an old hotel complex, where they were offering a six-week Torah summer study camp for Baal Teshuva (people returning to Judaism). In addition to learning from the rabbis, there were recreational opportunities and wonderful Melaveh Malka (post-Shabbat meals) for socializing. I met good people there, and I experienced a warm, rich, spiritual connection, similar to the mystical connection I'd felt in Tzfat, Israel.

I wanted to return to Israel, eventually, but with my freshman year of college upcoming, that was put on hold. I felt like a very spiritual thing was happening to me. It was mystical. I wasn't looking for it, but it kept coming to me.

I discovered new respect for things I had dismissed earlier in life. The rules for what a Jew can and can't do on Shabbat, for example. I didn't think I necessarily needed to be overly strict about the Shabbat laws, but during this period, it seemed like every time I tried to do something counter to the rules, I would have problems. If I skirted the law against doing work on the Sabbath—reasoning that making copies for the KIFTY newsletter was at least doing G-d's work— the copy machine would break down or something would go wrong so I couldn't complete the task. It was like G-d was sending me a message. I began to believe—very slowly, and often incompletely—that whenever I did something wrong, G-d pointed it out to me, and He protected me in ways that defy rational explanation.

The Hebrew language also took on a new vibrancy with me. When I was younger, I struggled with learning and decoding Hebrew writing. (That was one of the reasons I skipped out on my Hebrew classes.) I learned the alphabet and pronunciation, but I didn't know what the words meant.

After this period of spiritual awakening, the language somehow became transformed in my consciousness. I saw Hebrew words in a prayer book, and while I still didn't know what they meant, the letters vibrated with me in a mystical way. They almost danced on the page. The letters possessed a deep history and a richer meaning than I had discerned before. This experience gave me a connection to the language I didn't necessarily understand, but it ignited a desire to interact more with Hebrew. Over time, I also came to appreciate the symbolic and numerological significance to the Hebrew alphabet.

I developed a particular affinity for the letter lamed (ל), but all of Hebrew seems alive and multidimensional in ways I don't perceive with English letters.[5] Lamed seems to vibrate on a different frequency. It seems to jump out at me. I see ל everywhere. Lamed has a spiritual meaning of learning and the source of all learning, the Torah. (In Israel, student drivers are marked with a ל on their car to signify they are still learning!) This special relationship to lamed seems appropriate to me: I feel like I'm being perpetually encouraged to learn.

In Israel, the letter lamed (ל) when visible on top of a car, indicates that the person driving it is a student driver.

CIA Headquarters

In March of 1981, I was invited to participate in a program called Presidential Classroom for Young Americans. The organization's goal was to take exceptionally bright and motivated students from high schools across the United States and give them a week of speakers, tours, and experiences in Washington, DC.

While I struggled with some aspects of academic life, I was always interested in the social sciences. My favorite high school teacher, Mr. Joe Stefanisko, told me there was an opening for me to participate in the week-long experience.

It was my first visit to DC. There was a day for general sightseeing and a jam-packed itinerary for visiting many historical landmarks in the nation's capital. This was my first opportunity to see the Air and Space Museum, a place I would visit many times in my life. I was excited to see the original filming model of the starship *Enterprise* hanging high above our heads.

I found out many of the other students had gone through a rigorous application process to earn their spot in the program. It made me feel uncomfortable that I'd been placed in the Presidential Classroom without any real effort. Knowing that secret made me feel self-conscious around the bright, dedicated students.

While we had a lot of freedom during the week, we were still high school students, and the program leadership was very clear there were rules of conduct we had to abide by. There were security personnel on hand from one of the military branches, and if we got out of line, we'd be kicked out of the program and sent home.

We met representatives from various branches of the government and many government agencies. We were even invited to the CIA building in Langley, Virginia. On the bus ride to the CIA, the program leaders sternly told us what was expected of us. No cameras were allowed, and we had to be on our best behavior.

Seated in the big auditorium, Paul Chretien, a senior briefing officer, addressed us from the podium. He started the presentation by passing around "edible paper" he claimed spies used when they were in dangerous situations. If the field agents were discovered, they could eat their notes and destroy any evidence of spying. The student seated next to me passed me some paper, but after I ate a bite that same student revealed he'd been pranking me, and his was just regular paper.

Chretien spoke about some of the Cold War-era concerns of US intelligence agencies. The floor was opened to student questions, and most of the queries concerned events in Central America and America's involvement with the Sandinistas and Contras.

I had another topic on my mind. I'd been reading some of the declassified information about a secret US operation called MKUltra, which tested the viability of mind control

CLASS VII, Number 6   Thursday, March 12, 1981   MARRIOTT TWIN BRIDGES HOTEL

THURSDAY'S ACTIVITY SCHEDULE

7 a.m.   WAKE UP

7:30-8:15 a.m.   BREAKFAST
    PLACE: Commonwealth Ballroom
    NEEDED: Coupon #13

Buses leave for Capitol Hill at 8:15 a.m.

9-10 a.m.   SEMINAR: The House of
                                Representatives
    SPEAKER: The Honorable Louis B. Stokes
    PLACE: The House Chamber

10 a.m.-3 p.m.   LEGISLATIVE ACTIVITIES
    Lunch: Dirksen Cafeteria 11 a.m.-noon, 1:30-3 p.m.
           Longworth Cafeteria: 11-11:45 a.m.;
           after 1:15 p.m.
           NEEDED: Coupon #15
You may have lunch only at the Dirksen or Longworth
Cafeteria. Your coupon will not be honored at any
other cafeteria or carry-out service to the Senate or
House.
  Buses depart at 3:20 p.m. from First and
    East Capitol Streets.

4-5 p.m.   SEMINAR: Foreign Policy:
                               Its Making and Execution
    SPEAKER: Mr. L. Paul Bremer III
    PLACE: Acheson Auditorium
           Department of State

5:15-6:30 p.m.   DINNER
    PLACE: State Department Cafeteria
    NEEDED: Coupon #16
Buses depart at 6:30 p.m. from the main entrance of
  State Department on C Street.

7:30-9 p.m.   SEMINAR: The Role of Intelligence
                                in Foreign Policy
    SPEAKER: Mr. Paul Chretien
    PLACE: Central Intelligence Agency, Langley Center

9:15-10 p.m.   NIGHT TOUR OF WASHINGTON
10-11 p.m.   DISCUSSION GROUP: CIA
    MODERATOR: Mr. Paul Chretien
    PLACE: Salon C

11:30 p.m.   CURFEW

THE HOUSE OF REPRESENTATIVES THE HONORABLE LOUIS STOKES

Congressman Louis B. Stokes has represented Ohio's 21st Congressional district since 1969. The first black Congressman from Ohio, he held many influential positions on the Hill. He sits on the powerful House Appropriations Committee and three of its subcommittees. In the early 1970's he served two consecutive terms as President of the Congressional Black Caucus; since last September he has been President of the Black Caucus Foundation. In 1977-78, he chaired the House Select Committee on Assassinations, which investigated the deaths of President John F. Kennedy and Dr. Martin Luther King, Jr. And on January 28, 1981, he became Chairman of the House Ethics Committee.

Representative Stokes was born in 1925. He received his Doctor of Jurisprudence degree from Cleveland Marshall Law School. During the Second World War, he served in the Army.

Before his bid for Congress, which was his first campaign for public office, Congressman Stokes practiced law in Cleveland for 14 years. He argued several cases before the United States Supreme Court.

Representative Stokes has received many awards for his service in Washington, including the Certificate of Appreciation from the United States Commission on Civil Rights and the Distinguished Service Award of the Cleveland Branch of the NAACP. Last September the Black Caucus presented him the William L. Dawson Award for his leadership in the development of [illegible].

THE ROLE OF INTELLIGENCE IN FOREIGN POLICY PAUL CHRETIEN

Paul Chretien's duties as Senior Briefing Officer at the Central Intelligence Agency include briefing ambassadors, diplomats, senior officials, and select university groups. He joined the agency in 1950. During his career he has served as the CIA's official spokesman, as a member of the agency's Executive Committee, and in 1963 he was appointed Assistant to the Director.

Mr. Chretien holds a B.A. from Assumption College in Worchester, Massachusetts, and an M.A., Ph.D., and J.D. from Catholic University in Washington, D.C. Before joining the CIA, he worked as a prep school track and football coach, a public opinion pollster, and an economist at the Department of Labor. He has also taught college sociology and university philosophy.

Please Note

Pens, notebooks, cameras, and tape recorders are not permitted inside the CIA headquarters at Langley Center.

Daily briefing to students-Thurs., Mar. 12, 1981.

CIA veteran Paul Chretien holds photo taken high over the Soviet Union by aerial reconnaissance.

A B&W scanned mimeograph image of Paul Chretien

during the 1960s and '70s. To determine if rumors of Soviet "mind control" were plausible—and to figure out ways to loosen the lips of spies, military prisoners, and political opponents—the CIA had experimented with electroshocks, hypnosis, sensory deprivation, isolation, verbal and mental abuse, and drugs, especially LSD—but performed it on innocent unknowing Americans.. However "noble" their reasoning, I was offended that some of these experiments had been conducted on unsuspecting, vulnerable, and "disposable" people, without consent and without regard to how they might be harmed. CIA had used subjects overseas, which was bad enough, but the secret operation had also targeted the mentally ill, addicts, prostitutes, and prisoners in the United States.

Though I was very uncomfortable, I approached the microphone and asked, "Mr. Chretien, if the United States ever found itself in a similar situation to the Korean and Vietnam Wars, when our soldiers—as prisoners of war—might be subjected to the enemy's use of new drugs or mind control to dupe soldiers into revealing classified security information, would the American government ever again stoop to sanctioning the exploitation of innocent, unknowing Americans, on American soil, in operations like Project MKUltra?"

Chretien responded, "Yes. If it were necessary."

My question was the last student question, and I was devastated by the answer I'd received. To me, something big had just happened. I was mortified, and I felt alone in my reaction. Everyone else just filed out, got on the bus, and went about things as if nothing had happened.

I'd already felt uneasy about unbridled patriotism. As early as fifth grade, I'd questioned the daily Pledge of Allegiance as I envisioned US planes raining bombs on the people of Vietnam. But that moment in Langley, I realized my government didn't protect "people who could not fight back," and I lost all faith that my government would actually stand up for me. If push came to shove, my rights meant nothing. On top of that, I was discouraged no one else seemed to have taken note of the revelation that had just occurred.

At the end of the week, the program held a big dance at the hotel for the 400 students in attendance. I wasn't feeling sociable and didn't want to be there, so I quickly found an opportunity to slip out of the ballroom and make my way the short distance outside, back to the hotel room. There were some high school assignments I pretended I needed to work on before returning home, but really I just wanted to get out of there, get some sleep, and go home.

My roommates returned around 2 a.m. and woke me from sleep. "Where were you?" they asked.

I told them I was tired and had decided to come back to the room, but I was also surprised anyone had noticed I was missing.

"The program director called out your name several

times, and you weren't there!"

I found out the evening had concluded with an awards presentation. They had announced the students who had asked key questions or otherwise stood out throughout the week. I had been selected for an award based on my question at the CIA, but I hadn't been there to receive it. Apparently, my question hadn't gone unnoticed, as I'd feared.

Choosing My Path Forward

In the spring of 1981, I was set to graduate from Cheltenham High. I applied to three colleges: Syracuse University, Temple University, and Penn State. I was a C student and didn't have a stellar academic record. My social studies teacher, Mr. Gyenes, liked me, though, and he wrote a letter of recommendation to Syracuse on my behalf.

I visited the campus at Syracuse that spring and found it overwhelming.[6] The campus was so big and busy, it felt like a major metropolitan city all its own. I'd had very little experience outside of the Philadelphia area. I didn't want to be so far from home, and something about the Syracuse campus made me feel like I would lose myself if I went there.

Penn State wasn't any better, really. It was still fairly far from home, and I didn't feel like I would ever be comfortable there.

For my Temple University tour, I visited the Ambler campus. Ambler was about six miles from my parent's home. It was further from the city, so it had a more rural feel that suggested a sedate atmosphere where I could do a lot of thinking and learning. I read through the literature for Temple and saw the University offered a kosher meal option, which had become important to me.

My mother and I went back to Ambler campus for an open house. While we stood in the long line to get checked in, my mother said, "Look over there. There's Chuck Blumberg." Chuck had graduated from Cheltenham ahead of me, and his parents and my parents were friends. "Go over and tell him you're coming here. Maybe you'll have a friend on campus when you get here."

Even though our parents were friends and we'd gone to the same school, Chuck and I weren't really familiar with one another, but I approached him anyway and told him I was planning to come to Ambler the following fall.

"You are?" Chuck said. "Why?"

"I have three schools I'm considering," I told him. "But I think Temple Ambler is the right one for me."

"You don't want to do that," he said. "Coming here would be a big mistake."

Chuck told me he needed to go to class and took off. I walked back over to where my mother was still waiting in line.

"How'd it go?" she asked.

"It was a little weird," I told her.

Despite Chuck's warning, I decided Temple's Ambler

campus was the best option for me. Mr. Gyenes wasn't happy with this news.

"I wrote you a great recommendation!" he said. "You're going to choose Temple? Good luck with that. Go be one of *those* people."

Mr. Joe Gyenes: "…Go be one of those people." – World Cultures teacher, Cheltenham High School, May, 1981.

4

LOWS AND HIGHS

Freshman Year at Temple Ambler

Early September 1981, my parents drove me to the curb outside the dorm, I extracted my two suitcases from the trunk, and off they drove. I walked into the F Wing dorm and was immediately struck by how different everything seemed compared to the campus tour.

This was three years after the movie *Animal House* had been released and had set a precedent for rowdy college behavior. The dorm was really noisy; I couldn't even hear my own thoughts. Everyone was boisterous and clamoring around the hallways. It was immediately clear: this would not be the sedate, contemplative college life I had imagined. Within minutes of my parents dropping me off, I knew I had made a huge mistake.

Realizing I had done this to myself—that I'd made this decision—saddened me. I didn't want to admit to my parents I'd made a mistake, and I had already said no to my other college options. I had to try to make it on my own. I had to live with my naive mistake.

I tried to plow forward, but life on Ambler's campus didn't improve much from that initial experience. It was immediately clear there was not a kosher food option for me after all. The description I'd read in the Temple brochure was for the main campus, and it did not apply to Ambler.

I felt very much alone, and I stood out because I wore a kippah and tried to remain religious. The university gave me a little room where I could put on tefillin and pray in peace, which was one respite from the cacophony around me.

I didn't see many other Jewish students. My roommate, Neil Goldman, was Jewish, but he was not religious. We were like the characters from *The Odd Couple*. Neil was the fastidious and orderly Felix, and I was the messy and disheveled Oscar.

There was also a guy there, Chris, who found special pleasure in intimidating and harassing me. I had hoped to move beyond the teasing I'd experienced in middle and high school, but here I was, on a college campus, trying to avoid a bully.

It wasn't just the social and dormitory aspects I found disappointing. I really didn't enjoy my classes. The teachers were dull, and the courses seemed less rigorous than my high school classes. My teachers at Cheltenham had been more stimulating and committed to the curriculum and education.

Campus was a nightmare during the school week, and I couldn't imagine staying there over the weekends. Thursday evening, I'd leave campus and take the SEPTA train from Ambler Station to Elkins Park, where I took a class on "Moreh Nevukim" (Miamanides 'Guide to the Perplexed) at the Beth Jacob school supported by congregants of the OMEP, then my parents would pick me up.[1]

Back home for the weekends, my mother would do my laundry. I walked to meet Peter for Shabbat, and we would go together to pray. Then Sunday night, I would head back to campus, as late as I could.

I dreaded Sunday night. I never knew what I was going to face when I returned. New holes in the dorm walls? Uncleaned messes from the weekend? Noise and chaos were a given, but how crazy would it be when I got there? One night, Chris—the bully—spotted me as I was returning. He came down the hall, making sexual comments. He had his hand on the zipper of his jeans, and I was scared he was going to do more than just suggest lewd acts. When he cornered me, he laughed, pushed me, and walked away, but I was always afraid the bullying would escalate.

One place I found some peace was the library, and I spent a lot of time there. I left the dorm when things were too chaotic, and I'd wander the area near the library, praying to G-d to send someone into my life so I wouldn't feel so alone.

Meeting Laura

The first semester passed slowly. I was depressed and floundering. When November rolled around, I went to the administrative building to pick up the course offerings for spring. As I struggled in the tight confines of the building to grab my copy of the spring course bulletin, with a copy of the Tuesday New York Times wedged under one arm, a girl stopped me!

"Excuse me," she said. "Do you have a car?"

"No," I said. "Sorry."

"I can pay you. I need a ride."

I told her I would like to help, but I didn't have a car.

"How did you get here, then?" she said.

"I live on campus. In the dorms."

"Do you know anyone in the dorm who might have a car?"

I found out her name was Laura Kessler. Laura was three years older than me and took classes in early education on campus, but she had a job doing advertising copy for Progress Newspapers. We walked a little while together, but I needed to go a different direction, so we parted ways.

A week later, Laura spotted me on campus, once again walking along with the *Times* tucked between my arm and body.

"Don't you remember me?" she said, after she said hello and I seemed confused that a girl was talking to me.

Temple University Ambler Campus, showing Administration Bldg.

"Oh sorry," I stumbled. "We met last week, right?"

Laura and I began to spend more time together. I learned a lot about Laura's life. She was Jewish, but not religious. Her work at the newspaper was paying for her tuition, but to make ends meet she was also living at home. That home life was dominated by a difficult sister as well as working parents. To avoid some of those home issues, she would often stay late on campus, or at work at the newspaper as late as possible.

She seemed interested in me, but as a newly religious person, I was attempting to live a chaste lifestyle. It was clear that we were attracted to one another. Still, one day as we we seemed to be becoming more comfortable with each other, she began to reach to unbutton her blouse as if we might share more. At that point, I demurred and said, "No, I just want to be friends."

One particular night, Laura and I wandered the campus, trying to kill time. We found an unlocked door to the girl's gymnasium, and we snuck in. In the locker room, I saw one of the women's coach's jackets hanging on a hook, so I took off my high school jacket and put on the women's jacket. I sort of danced around and tried to make Laura laugh.

A campus security guard noticed the lights in the locker room, and he confronted us. "What are you two doing in here?"

"We're just hanging out," I tried to explain.

"In the girl's locker room? Go on. Get out of here."

We left before there was trouble, but Laura wasn't ready to go home. I was torn. Even though she was 22 and an adult, I didn't want her to get into trouble with her family, so I thought she should go home, but I also didn't want her to have to be in a place where she felt unsafe. I didn't know how to help.

We were walking the back trail between the gym and the dorm when a student I barely knew said, "Hey Ted, there's a big hulk of a woman looking for her daughter. You know anything about it?"

Then another student followed saying basically the same thing: There's a large, angry woman demanding to see her daughter.

Laura exclaimed, "It's my mother!"

"Just stay here," I said, with more confidence than I felt. "I'll go talk to her."

I trudged out from the path area and found Mrs. Kessler, silhouetted by the light coming from the library, like the Colossus of Rhodes with the moon and library spotlights rising behind her. When I approached, she said, "Where is my daughter?"

"Laura is fine," I told her. "But she doesn't want to come home."

"What do you mean? She has to come with me. You don't have a say in this." I tried to reason with her, but Mrs. Kessler cut me off. "Get away from me you little pip-squeak."

Campus security came along to see what the fuss was.

They took Mrs. Kessler's side. "If you know where this woman's daughter is, you better bring her out here."

Laura came out from the wooded area and went with her mother. All of this drama was depressing. I didn't know how to deal with it, and I had no experience of this kind of family conflict. Plus, although I sort of had a girlfriend in Laura, the situation was more agitating than it was consoling. This, added to my other negative experiences on campus, was really weighing me down.

The only real relief from my depression was my friend Harvey, who also lived in F Wing. He'd gone to Cheltenham High, but he was a year ahead of me, so we hadn't known each other real well. But even in high school, I had liked him! We reconnected at Ambler, and he was the only person there I could really talk to. Harvey was funny and good-natured. He sort of took me under his wing, and I could talk to him about anything. Harvey wasn't a big fan of my relationship with Laura. He advised me to stay away from her, but I obviously didn't listen.

He and his roommate lived a couple rooms down from me, so after this encounter with Laura's mother, I wound up at their door. They were drinking beer and offered me one. I was down in the dumps, and I drank a six-pack. I can't hold my beer, and I ended up passed out in their room. Harvey was a big guy, so he carried me down the hall and put me on my own bed.

I woke the next morning and couldn't find my eyeglasses,

but I really needed to urinate, so I shuffled down the hall toward the bathroom, hungover and half blind. Other students in the dorm had, apparently, had a crazy night because there was broken glass in the bathroom I couldn't see, and I cut my feet.

When my head cleared a little, I remembered I'd left my jacket behind in the girl's locker room. That was an awkward conversation when I went to ask the staff there if I could have my jacket back and had to explain why it was in the girl's locker room in the first place.

One positive connection came when I met a young man at the classes I took at Beth Jacob. He introduced himself as Lou Kessler, and it turned out he and Laura were cousins. Lou was religious, with a solid Jewish education, and he was interested in science fiction, like me.

My relationship with Laura continued to evolve. Even though I was pursuing a chaste life, things between us eventually did become more physically intimate.

Reaching a Breaking Point

Sometime in March, Harvey and I were in line in the cafeteria to get breakfast, and I was staring down at an egg salad platter; I was thinking how this was my ninety-seventh egg salad meal alternating with my ninety-sixth tuna salad meal. I was fed up. It wasn't just the food but the whole Ambler experience that had me deep in a funk.[2]

"I wish I could wake this campus up," I said.

"I know what you mean," Harvey said.

"No, really. I want to do something to shake this place up. I almost want to call Lee and get a pipe bomb to set off the last night of finals, or something."

"Yeah, sure," Harvey said. "Why not?"

Harvey later told me he'd thought I was speaking metaphorically and that he'd been playing along, but I was serious. I'd had enough. In that state, I couldn't think of a reason my idea was a bad one. I'd put the bomb in an open space where it wouldn't hurt anyone, but the sound would shake people out of their beds. I'd wait until after finals so it wouldn't harm anyone's academic performance, and I would detonate it at three in the morning so no one would be around to get hurt.

I hadn't talked to Lee since I'd stopped hanging out with the TGC, but I called him and said, "If I paid you, would you make a pipe bomb for me?"

After I told him what I intended to do, Lee said, "You're crazy."

"We used to do this all the time," I said. "You can put it together for me, can't you?"

Lee told me he could, and I said I would be in touch when the time was closer.

I was curious how people would react to my plan, so I spoke to a guidance counselor, the dorm's resident coordinator, and a few other people. They asked why I felt like I should do something so dramatic. When I told them, they had a sort of sad look on their face, but not one of them ever said, "Hey Ted, this is a bad idea."

As the semester progressed into April, I knew I should get ahold of Lee and finalize a plan to get the pipe bomb, but I found myself dragging my feet. I had an internal dialogue with myself: *Why are you hesitating? You said you were going to do it, so if you can't see a reason not to do it, why aren't you doing anything?*

I realized, deep down, I actually did have reservations. If I deconstructed my plan, there were things I took for granted that might not be solid assumptions. I didn't really know how far the shrapnel might fly, or even in what direction, and I couldn't be sure some late-night wanderer wouldn't come along at just the wrong time. Instead of a late-night bang to wake people up—literally and symbolically—my plan could actually hurt someone unintentionally. Once I realized that, I lost interest in trying to wake people up that way.

The problem was, I never went back to all the people I'd told of the plan to inform them I'd come to my senses. I had made another faulty assumption: I didn't think anyone had taken me seriously.

The night before my last final, I was trying to figure out if my time would be better spent working on a late term paper or studying for my math final the next day. My mother called and asked if I knew there was a meeting scheduled with the dean of students and the school psychiatrist the next day.

"Did you know you're being expelled?" she said.

"No." This was news to me.

"Is it true you were planning to blow up the campus?"

"Well. Yes and no," I replied. I explained that I had come to realize my idea was a bad one, I wasn't blowing anything up, and I really needed to study. She relayed the details of the meeting the next day, and I told her I'd see her there.

After my final, I turned up at the appointed time and place. My parents, the dean, and the psychiatrist were all waiting for me. I was exhausted after a night of cramming for my test, and I just wanted the whole thing to be over as quickly as possible.

Dr. Kravitz took me into a room and said, "Tell me, Ted. Why did you want to blow up the campus?"

I was tired and grumpy. My answer was improvised on the spot and meant to be dismissive, "I don't know. I guess I'm just a paranoid schizophrenic."

As tired as I was, I was incredulous that Dr. Kravitz simply and immediately recorded my response and used it moments later to conclude the meeting with my parents and the Dean. That was pretty much all there was to it. I was expelled from the campus and told I was not permitted to return without a note from another doctor.

For years after my experiences at Temple's Ambler campus, I held a deep grudge. I hated myself for being so stupid to attend the Ambler campus; I hated the campus for the experiences I'd endured there; and I hated the town of Ambler itself for offering no relief. When I couldn't find any solace on campus, there was no escape to be found in town. The sidewalks rolled up at six o'clock every night.

After leaving school, I needed to reset. Thankfully, I had a trip to Israel planned.

Strange Forebodings

Upon my return from the first Torah camp in August of 1981, I had experienced the first of what would be a recurring string of foreboding experiences.

After the camp, my parents met me at 30th Street train station upon my return. As we walked to the car, I was overcome by a strange feeling upon seeing *The Philadelphia Bulletin* newspaper building from the station's parking lot. I'd seen the building many times, but in this instance, I had a deep, visceral feeling something was not right about the appearance of that building. I had the experience of *feeling* or sensing something different from what my eyes could perceive.

A year later, in the summer of '82—after the difficult year at Ambler, and before my trip to Israel—I was able to go to Moodus again to repeat the Torah instruction. When I returned, it was like an odd repetition of the scene from a year earlier, with one major difference: *The Philadelphia Bulletin* had closed. The paper had published its final edition earlier that year. The newspaper that once had the largest circulation in Philadelphia—their slogan at the time was, "Nearly everybody reads the *Bulletin!*"—had ceased to exist, and with it, the marquee that had adorned that building a year earlier. It was as if that previous summer, I'd had an impression of the coming change and the future absence of the marquee

It was as if back then, I had been looking through the eyes of myself a year later and feeling a tactile disconnect between that point of view and what was the perceived "reality" in front of me. This wouldn't be the last time I felt something like this.

Return to Israel

After my inglorious finale at Ambler, Laura and I continued our relationship, mostly via telephone. I was gone to Connecticut for several weeks, and when I returned, I was preparing for my second trip to Israel.

My feelings regarding our relationship remained conflicted. Laura was beautiful and, unlike the girls I'd known up to that point, she was willing to share herself and her life with me. She was my first girlfriend, and I cared for her deeply. I felt bad for her home life, and I recognized she had issues that made things difficult for her. I wanted to be a positive force in her life, but there was also a lot about our relationship that made me uncomfortable.

Laura Kessler and I together, posing on the Atlantic City beach, New Jersey, circa 1983-'84

Salisbury Plain, England- Visit to Stonehenge mere days after summer solstice 1987
on my way to Israel for the 3rd time.

Laura wasn't happy I was leaving. She thought I was leaving *her*, but I assured her I needed to discover more of my Jewish identity. I promised I would return in January.

After a stop in London, I was in Israel before Rosh Hashanah. I was all set to study at Ohr Somayach in Jerusalem. As I was settling in, I made the mistake of talking to one of the junior administrators, Reuven, about my semester at Ambler and my relationship with Laura.

Reuven went to the higher-ups and said, "I don't think Ted Rickles belongs here. He seems pretty messed up. I don't think he's a good fit."

So, there was a move to kick me out of the yeshiva. I defended myself by saying, "Any number of other students probably have horrible stories about their lives, too. I shouldn't be singled out for being honest about what happened in my life this year. Why discriminate against me just because I made the mistake of telling something to the wrong person?"

They agreed, and I was allowed to stay as long as I continued to take classes and participated. That worked for a while. I was paired with a more experienced yeshiva student, and we had a detailed schedule of study and prayer from first thing in the morning into the evening.

Talmud study was difficult, but I enjoyed it. I was slowly learning to read and understand more. Rabbi Cardoza taught a class in medical halakhah that I found fascinating, and there were other great teachers there as well. That was the first time I slept in a sukkah during Sukkoth.

Every Thursday, I made two phone calls: one to my parents and one to Laura. Long-distance calls to the States were expensive—something like $5 a minute.

My calls to Laura were discouraging. She told me she was going out with other guys, and some of the stories she told had me questioning her judgement. On one hand, I felt like she needed me around to protect her—from her family and herself—but on the other hand, I was questioning the commitment I'd made to return to her.

I realized four months in the yeshiva was insufficient. I would need to stay a year, at least, to get the full experience, but I'd made a promise I didn't intend to break. The longer I was there, the more I wished I'd never made that promise.

While I was in Israel, my parents came to visit. They were on a tour of Israel and Egypt offered to my father by a wholesale pharmaceutical company. I had a copy of their itinerary, and I surprised them at their hotel in Tel Aviv. We toured together for a few days. One of my favorite memories was returning to Tzfat—this time with my parents!

After they returned to the States, I continued to wrestle with my pledge to return to Laura. I couldn't come to an answer. Both options seemed wrong to me. I didn't want to break my promise and abandon her, but I didn't want to leave the yeshiva. My indecision led me into a deep depression. I stopped going to classes, and when the leadership found out, they asked me to leave.

Dad, me & Mom in Jerusalem, fall 1982 with the Cotel HaMarivi (Western Retaining wall of the Temple) in background.

I had nowhere to go, and I needed time to arrange travel back to the US. I had visited the Aish HaTorah yeshiva in Jerusalem during my previous trip, so I went there and asked if I could stay while I sorted myself out. They agreed to let me room in a shared apartment in the Old City with several other young guys, as long as I attended classes. Rabbi Noah Wienberg was teaching from his *48 Ways to Wisdom*, and for several weeks I lived there as I continued to wrestle with my future.

My experience at Aish HaTorah made me wonder, *Was I making things more complicated than they needed to be?* I enjoyed the yeshiva life—as I had at Ohr Somaych until I'd let depression get the best of me—and I was very doubtful that going back to college and having a life with Laura was the best path. The yeshiva path seemed to be the right direction for me, but I'd messed things up.

I decided to give Ohr Somayach one more try before I left. I met with a Rabbi there and explained all that had happened and all of the conflicting thoughts and feelings I'd had. The Rabbi listened carefully and said, "There is a yeshiva in New York. I think you would fit in very well. I will make a phone call and speak to them on your behalf."

I thanked the Rabbi and took the information for the yeshiva. Soon after, I boarded a plane back to the US, and I felt a deep sadness at having to leave Israel. When I arrived home, I had made up my mind that the New York yeshiva was the correct path. I planned to settle in for a few days, then tell my parents I intended to move to New York to continue my Jewish studies.

Mislaid Plans, New Beginnings

I was back home, and after rest and recovery from the jet-lag, I felt ready to rejoin the family. At dinner, my parents asked what I was going to do, now that I was back from Israel. Was I planning to go back to college? I told them what had happened in Israel and that I was thinking about going to the yeshiva in New York.

"Yeshiva in New York? That's not for you."

"Maybe it's good for me," I replied. "Yeshiva is interesting and I enjoy it."

My family was confused by my news and didn't know what to say. "Think about it," was their advice. "You don't have to decide right away."

Next, I needed to inform Laura of my plans. I called her, but as was usually the case, Laura did most of the talking. I couldn't get a word in edgewise. I finally managed to say there were some serious matters I wanted to discuss, and she said, "Oh, just tell me when we get together. *ET: The Extraterrestrial* is playing. Let's go see that!"

I'd imagined a quiet, private conversation about my future, but Laura insisted we go see the movie.

"Meet me at the theater," she said. "We can talk there."

My parents dropped me off at the theater, and Laura and

I reunited. We got our tickets and found a seat. Laura put her arm around me and held my hand. After all the things she'd told me about seeing other people while I was gone, this physical intimacy surprised me. Also, knowing I wanted to tell her I was planning to leave—basically breaking up with her—made the whole situation awkward.

Fifteen minutes into the movie, I couldn't take any more. I got up, walked out, and sat in the lobby.

"What is wrong with you?" Laura asked, after she came to find me. "We're missing the movie."

"This isn't what I wanted. I have some important things to tell you."

"You can tell me," Laura reassured me.

So I did. I told her what I was planning. "Besides, you don't need me. You told me about seeing other guys, anyway. You'll be fine without me. This is something I need to do for myself."

"You mean, you're not going back to college?"

"I think maybe that part of my life is over," I said. "I got kicked out of Ambler."

"Just because you can't go to Ambler," she said, "doesn't mean you can't go back to Temple. Go to the main campus."

I hadn't thought of that. I tried to argue that it was probably too late to get into Spring semester classes. She responded I wouldn't know if I didn't at least try.

"Why are you just giving up?" she said. "Go down to main campus tomorrow and see if you can register."

We went back to watch the movie, but my mind was racing and I didn't actually see *ET*, even though it was playing on the screen. My resolve for following my plan to go to New York evaporated. Laura had a point. I hadn't even tried to figure out my standing at Temple. And, apparently, she wanted me around more than I had anticipated.

Even though I figured I'd surely been flagged as "unwelcome" at Temple, I figured I might as well at least try. The next morning I went to Temple's main campus. Spring classes hadn't yet begun, and I signed up to restart my college career. No one stopped me from registering, and I listed my major as sociology.

5

TEMPLE UNDERGRAD YEARS

Return to College

When I told my parents I had enrolled at Temple's main campus, they were relieved I had "come to my senses" and abandoned my plan to go to the yeshiva. I wasn't convinced I was yeshiva material, anyway, so moving to New York would have been a big risk. Plus, if I stayed at home, I could continue to pray and learn with the Orthodox Minyan of Elkins Park. The congregation there was growing. They had evolved their constitution and were on their way to becoming a recognized synagogue. I felt good about being around to be a part of that. It was getting into January, and by the end of the month, I was to turn twenty!

Having a second chance at Temple was a good thing. I had always had an interest in sociology, and earning a degree in that field remained attractive to me. I also learned

I could get college equivalency credits for the studying I'd done in Israel, which was a nice surprise.

Almost immediately, I started making new friends in the undergraduate sociology department. One of the other students was Judy Lutz. Judy's mother and my mother had shared a maternity room, and we'd been born about a day apart. It was a strange coincidence to run into Judy at Temple and have classes together.

I also met Ben Silver, Steve Hirsh, Vince Singleton, Mark French, and Harold Rose. They became valued classmates and friends over the years. Ben and I met in Larry Rosen's freshman statistics class, and we studied together often. Ben and I became good friends, much like my friendship with Harvey.

Laura and I were still rebuilding our relationship. Some days seemed good. Some days weren't. She liked the attention of different men, and I worried for her safety. It felt like she was playing a game.

One evening, she called me at home. "Where are you?" I said. "I was going to get a cab and come see you."

"You have to guess where I am," she said.

"Guess?"

"If you want to see me," was her coy response, "you'll have to figure out where I am."

Suddenly, I had a clear vision of Laura, as if a video connection had been hardwired into my brain. "You're standing in the telephone booth at the Benson apartment building at Township Line Road." And I described the dress I saw her wearing.[1]

"How could you know that? That's crazy."

I couldn't explain it. Laura and I had been to the restaurant in that building, but it wasn't a "regular" spot for us. There were many places that would have been a "better guess," but I wasn't guessing. Somehow I saw exactly where she was.

Student Activism

Steve Hirsh had gone to Central High School. I didn't know much about Central, though my father had graduated from there, as had my friend Seth from Germantown Jewish Center, who worked at my father's pharmacy. In the summer of 1979, a riot of Central High students had broken out at the Olney subway station. In the aftermath, Steve and another Central student, Greg Sock, had met with the Philadelphia Council on Human Relations. They created a high school organization called Students United to Provide Transit Action to be an advocacy group for high school students, with a focus on better experiences with public transportation. (The group's acronym, SUPTA, was a play on the acronym for Southeastern Pennsylvania Transit Authority, or SEPTA.)

Steve was active in student government at Temple, and he had gone through the student affairs office to establish a college-level version of SUPTA to help Temple students have better, cheaper access to public transportation. He encouraged me to get involved, which I did.

Steve was working with SEPTA to extend their corporate discount fare program (ComPass) to college students. The ComPass program provided commuters with a 10% discount on passes and tokens to take public transit to and from work. The employee's company paid five percent of the difference, with SEPTA taking a loss on the other five percent.

Steve's idea was to convince SEPTA and Temple to partner together to develop and fund a similar program for student commuters. There had been some preliminary meetings before I got involved, and there were still hurdles to overcome.

First, in the corporate world, there is less turnover and more stability. A college student might be enrolled one semester, then gone the next. We needed a way to ensure only actively enrolled students could get the discount.

Second, Temple had to be convinced to spend the money to underwrite the program. To determine if the program was needed and would be of value to students, the university and SEPTA had developed a survey of the student body to assess commuting habits and student interest in a discount fare program.

When I started helping Steve with the project, I asked to see the survey questions. He showed me the blue, five-question card used to collect responses. I asked how the responses would be gathered, and he said SEPTA and the university were taking care of it.

"We gotta get involved in this," I said. "If we leave it up to the university and SEPTA, we won't know how good the data is. Who are they asking? Is it a representative sample? Are they going to ask people at each of Temple's campuses? We have a responsibility to not let them fuck this up."

"The survey is already happening," Steve said.

"Is there someone we can talk to so we can slow this thing down or get some control over it?"

Steve said there might be someone who could help, and before I knew it, he and I were walking into the office of the university's vice president, H. Patrick Swygert. I was impressed, until I found out we were meeting with Swygert's executive assistant. I reasoned that if we were meeting with an assistant, two things were true: We weren't high enough in the food chain to warrant the VP's time, and the assistant had likely been instructed to listen politely, then tell us things were too far along to change course.

Steve and I walked into the assistant's office, and he said, "Ted, this is Kristl Mehnert."

Kristl invited us to sit and tell her what was on our minds. She was very cordial, and she welcomed me to the project. We explained our concerns for 10 minutes as she listened attentively.

"The survey is already in progress," she said, "why not

just let SEPTA go ahead with it?"

"I think they're going to mess it up," I told her. I was worried SEPTA or the university would use the survey as a convenient reason to veto the program.

"You don't know what their results will be," she said. "It might be just fine for your proposal."

As I suspected, the VP's assistant was giving us lip service, and it didn't look like there was much we could do to change the project's course. What I hadn't expected is what happened next.

Because I am often outspoken and not always wise with my words, I said, "I suppose we could steal the completed surveys and conduct our own independent analysis."

Kristl paused for a moment and said thoughtfully, "Yes… You could do that. But you realize, if you conduct your own analysis and it contradicts the survey report, you'll be taking on the responsibility for the success—or failure—of the project, right? If you mess up, the blame will be on you. It could go either way, so consider what you do carefully."

Her response caught me off guard. I'd just suggested apprehending the survey responses, and she hadn't batted an eye. Instead, she'd simply laid out a clear understanding that we would be responsible for our actions.

Steve and I left the meeting. I remember looking back at Kristl as I left, and I realized I'd just met someone who was different, in a good way. She didn't ruffle easily, and she had a practical, prudent, and sincere approach to her interactions.

Later that semester, Kristl was promoted to become the dean of students. I was fascinated by her and wanted to be in her presence as often as possible.

Steve suggested I get involved with student government. I was reluctant, at first, but when I realized, as dean, Kristl would be actively involved with the General Assembly meetings, I decided to join. She also lead student leadership seminars, which I regularly attended. The more I listened to her speak and spent time in her presence, the more I wanted to be around her.

Survey Says!

The SEPTA surveys were completed. They collected about 1,000 of the little blue cards. I thought the questions were weak and weren't sufficient to gauge student interest or the potential usage of the discounts, but that was the data we had to work with. I convinced Steve we should steal the cards, so on a Sunday, we snuck in to the student government offices, took the box of cards, photocopied them, and then returned them before they were missed.

In addition to the SEPTA-approved survey, we developed a longer, more detailed survey to collect more data from Temple students. Then, we combined the information we had into a report detailing the benefits of extending the ComPass discount to students. We distributed copies of the report to decision makers and had a presentation meeting with university and SEPTA representatives.

At that time, Temple was more of a commuter school than it is today. As Dean of Students, Kristl's mission included supporting the mostly commuter population in their efforts to engage with campus activities. Our plan would, hopefully, help with those initiatives.

Overall, we handed out about 100 copies of the report, and the program was adopted. Temple students who registered in the program each semester could get a ten percent fare discount for public transit. The university never promoted the program properly. I think they liked the idea, but didn't like spending money on their five percent underwriting of the discount. Steve and I wrote another report a few years later to evaluate the program. Both the original report and the evaluation were added to the Urban Archives collection of the university library.

<u>THE COMPASS PROGRAM:</u>

<u>A TWO YEAR EVALUATION OF SEPTA's COMMUTER PASS PROGRAM AS ADMINISTERED FOR</u>
<u>TEMPLE UNIVERSITY STUDENTS</u>

BY

STEVEN A. HIRSH

SETH J. ITZKOWITZ

THEODORE M. RICKLES

A Program Evaluation Conducted by:

Students United to Provide Transit Action
in conjunction with the
Department of Commuter Affairs of the Temple Student Government

1990-The 2nd Compass Report detailing a 2 year evaluation of the program.
Both reports on file w/Temple-Urban Archives

B&W reproduction of brochures of each of the 4 semesters of the first 2 years of the SEPTA Compass program for Students

Deeper Obsession

My fascination with Kristl intensified, mirroring some of the behavior I'd exhibited in my youth. Physical proximity was paramount for me. The nearer I could be to Kristl, the more I experienced her energy; and the more I experienced her energy, the more I wanted to be in her presence. I felt a powerful desire to observe and emulate her character, wisdom, and approach to communicating and supporting others

With Kristl, I started loitering in the Grand Court at Mitten Hall.[2] Her office was on the second floor, and I could see her coming and going, or maybe bump into her and say hello. On the best days, I'd walk along with her as she was going to another building on campus.

I got to the point of feeling anxious and uneasy if I thought I wouldn't see her, even at a distance. I'd be depressed if I went too long without interacting with her. I started writing poetry about her.

I felt bombarded by feelings I didn't understand and couldn't categorize. Was it a romantic or sexual attraction? Did I see her as a maternal figure? I couldn't disentangle the web of emotions I experienced. She had a certain physical beauty, and her unique and captivating personality made her even more attractive, but she was also not a realistic romantic possibility. She was a few years older than me and an established professional with so many talents and skills.

I was a poor, awkward, college student.

At one point, the geological association had a crystal and geode sale fundraiser near the bell tower. I saw a beautiful piece of amethyst—a quartz stone said to "encourage connection and love"—and I bought it. I stopped in at the dean's office for some legitimate reason, and while I was there, I asked to see Kristl. (I still remember the KLM Dutch Airline poster she had on the wall. KLM were also her initials: Kristl Lynn Mehnert.) I gave her the amethyst and she thanked me. For a fleeting moment, I was tempted to try to kiss her, but that moment passed and I appreciated not having crossed that boundary.

In the General Assembly meetings, I couldn't concentrate on the business at hand. I focused on her. She was like a narcotic, and I was addicted. Everyone in the TSG Assembly knew I had a problem. They couldn't utter her name without my head snapping around to take notice of what was being said.

On one occasion, I pushed things too far. I was in Mitten Hall, lingering on the ground floor of the Great Court, below Kristl's office. She exited her office to go down the hall, and when she saw me, despite the distance, she quickened her pace. There were two campus security guards who had probably noticed how often I lurked in the building, and they had seen how Kristl reacted to seeing me. When she came out, the guards asked Kristl if they should remove me from the building. She calmly said, "No. That's OK."

The Great Court of Mitten Hall, Temple University. In the 1980s the 2nd floor housed the Office of the Dean of Students.

Top Left: me, Kristl & Steve Hirsh.
Interior: Temple News articles.
Bottom: Kristl family photos; B&W VP Temple P. Swygert.

Her calm demeanor was an integral part of Kristl's being, as well. She had a nearly unflappable nature and seemed to understand the dynamics of every situation. She could facilitate a chameleonic approach in adapting to those situations. She was a leader who possessed charm that went hand-in-hand with diplomacy. One of the nuggets of wisdom she had imparted during a Student Leadership seminar is that, "Conflict is only adversity that has not yet been overcome."

Living With Laura

As much as I obsessed over Kristl during the week, I endeavored to direct myself to my duty to G-d on the Sabbath. I continued to pray at the synagogue in Elkins Park. My weekly walks with Peter continued, and he would sometimes invite me into his home.[3]

I still struggled to figure out what the future held for me and Laura. Our relationship was rocky, full of ups and downs, but I wondered if Laura was the person I was meant to marry and have children with. I never felt the kind of emotional draw to her that I did to Kristl, but unlike Kristl, Laura was closer to my age and Jewish.

Laura battled bipolar disorder. I didn't know what that meant at the time, but there were many rough times when she was crying and despondent and inconsolable. The only thing I could do was hold her.

Even though I knew it would be "living in sin," I convinced Laura we should move in together. I thought it would be better for her than her tumultuous home life, and maybe if she felt more comfortable and safe, it would improve our relationship.

One aspect of living together that concerned me was my religious observance. Laura was Jewish but not observant. I had started to adopt being kosher, and there were many things I could not do on the Sabbath. I made a list of 25 potential problems with cohabitation. The list detailed the laws of Sabbath I observed and how to maintain a kosher kitchen. She was hesitant, but she agreed. We moved into the Park Spring Manor apartments in Elkins Park on May 10, 1983.

Living together had its own set of ups and downs. Sometimes the beds were pushed together, sometimes they were apart. We were physically intimate, up to a point, but she was leery of intercourse. I cared about her and wanted her to be okay, so I did whatever she wanted, if it helped her feel safe.

We had fights over the way she managed the apartment. She used the oven any way she wanted, regardless of my requests for keeping kosher. I came home from Temple to find she'd rendered the oven non-kosher by baking an uncovered macaroni and cheese dish in an oven set up for meat preparation. I reminded her of the agreement we'd made and again explained that if a dairy dish wasn't completely covered, I had to redo the oven. A few days later, she made the same mistake. Clearly we couldn't make agreements she would stick to, which was incredibly frustrating to me.

In hindsight, I realize trying to enforce Sabbath and kosher rules on someone who is not religious was a bad idea. Laura and I had different priorities, and we were incompatible. But at the time, I thought maybe we would find a way.

The longer we lived together, the harder it got. Our arguments were more frequent and more heated. I spent hours pacing the laundry room, where I escaped to cool off.

It wasn't all bad. I have one lovely memory of a late spring morning, bright sun filtering in through the window. Neil Diamond's "Song Sung Blue" was playing. I looked into Laura's eyes, so blue and beautiful, and I could only think, *I love you. Despite all the craziness, I love you.* In that moment, I imagined having a child with Laura. The baby was a little girl, and she was beautiful.

It was a fleeting thought, but one I've remembered all my life.

There would be no baby. I was an unemployed college student. My parents paid my tuition and half the rent for the apartment. Laura paid her half from money she made working at Progress Newspapers. I had a couple of campus jobs during my undergraduate years. I worked in the circulation department of the campus library for a while. Later, I worked in the alumni relations department, telemarketing to Temple alumni and encouraging them to donate to the university.

Laura suggested I might make a more favorable impression on her father if I had a couple more "selling points" for what a boyfriend should be. Her parents had no respect for me. Her mother didn't like that she had less control over Laura, and they viewed my attempts to maintain a more religious household as manipulative and draconian. Plus, Laura was working while in school, and I did little to provide financially. She was getting pressure from her parents, so I agreed to try to help them feel more at ease with their daughter and I cohabitating.

I got my driver's license and started working a part-time job. Laura was working in advertising, and the sociologist in me was interested in the psychology of advertising. She taught me some of the principles of marketing, and I found the work sparked my imagination a bit, so she helped me to get a job working at Intersearch in Horsham, PA, doing marketing research calls.[4]

Another big change in 1983 was that Harvey decided to move to California. Harvey had been a wise and valued friend for several years. I hadn't realized how difficult his own family life was, and it was good for him to put some distance between his family and himself, but I was sad to see him go. We would maintain our friendship at a distance in the decades to follow, but I missed having his calming influence and counsel.

Thankfully, my friendships with Steve Hirsh, Ben Silver, and Vince Singleton were filling the void left by Harvey's departure. We would often get together to study and quiz each other over the social psychology and social networking topics we were learning with Dr. Robert Kleiner. The three of us all really admired Bob Kleiner, and we were energized by his passion and dedication to the subject matter.

Math wasn't my strongest subject, by far. One thing that stuck with me from my freshman college math class was the day the Hindu teacher came in and said, "I'm a born-again agnostic!" which I thought was funny. I was still struggling to figure out my own on-again, off-again relationship to Judaism, and I appreciated his humorous declaration.

Poof, She Was Gone

Even though there were many downsides to living with Laura, I liked living in Elkins Park. Despite the cockroaches, I liked our apartment.[5]

There was a presidential election that year. The Elkins Park library was our local polling place. When I came home from Temple around twilight on election night. I walked toward the library and, all of a sudden, there was a *whoosh* sound. As in any unusual situation, my brain attempted to process what was happening through a lens of the everyday, but nothing computed. In my periphery, I saw what my brain perceived as a plastic sheet or a vinyl car roof spinning through the air. It arched upward and then fell with a *thud*. Immediately, a group of people rushed to the spot, and my brain caught up with the reality of the situation.

It hadn't been a sheet of plastic tumbling through the air. It had been a person. An off-duty policeman who'd volunteered to provide security at the voting precinct was helping people cross a busy intersection when a car full of kids had gone speeding through and hit him. The ambulance came to help, but I was shaken by what I'd seen.

That night, I couldn't sleep, thinking about the man who'd been hit. I felt such deep sadness, even though I didn't know him personally. Around two in the morning, I sat up with the thought, "Oh, no . . . he's died." Something had happened, and I just knew he was gone. I felt it.

The next day, I scoured the newspaper to get more information on the accident. The article gave the man's name and that he'd been a father. He'd been transported to the hospital but had died in the overnight hours. How strange that I had been awake and sensitive to his passing, despite not knowing the man and being miles away from the hospital. That incident had a deep effect on me.

My life during that year was a mix of good and bad. I was enjoying classes and making friends with students and faculty in the sociology department, but my fixation on Kristl was a drag on my energy and time. I was involved in student government and activities at Temple, but my long-established pattern of procrastinating and turning in work late continued. And, on the home front, I was still swinging back and forth in my feelings for Laura. We were constantly at odds, and yet, I was still not sure whether or not she was the woman I was supposed to build a home and family with.

One afternoon, in December of 1984, I came home and Laura was gone. Her belongings were gone, along with the tablecloth I used for the Sabbath and holidays I found a brief note saying she was leaving, but with no details. That was it. Laura had left me.

I was hurt and confused. After all we'd been through, she'd left—poof!—with no conversation, no apology, no explanation. For the first time in my life, I was completely alone.

I went to the building superintendent, Wade Hitchings, and explained what was going on. I said, "If I can find someone to share rent with me, can I keep the apartment."

"We'll see," was his response.

I knew Ben Silver and his girlfriend were looking for a place to live. Ben and Lois moved in, and they took the main bedroom while I stayed in the reconverted guest bedroom which Laura and I had previously used as an office. Everything seemed to be working out until the end of the month when Wade came by.

"You're going to have to leave," he said.

"You said if I got someone to share rent, I could stay."

"I said we'd see," he replied. "And the rental company doesn't want you here. You and that girlfriend caused too much trouble. People complained about the noise."

"Have you heard a peep out of us in the last month? She's not here any more."

"Doesn't matter."

I was mad and upset, but it didn't matter. I was booted from the apartment in January of 1985, and I moved back to my parent's house in Laverock. My mother—aware of the cockroach problem—was adamant all of my belongings had to be boxed up and stored with Borax powder for a number of days.

I lost track of Laura for a while. I did, eventually, find out that on the last morning we were together, Laura's mother came to the apartment and convinced Laura to leave. Her sister, Sandy, had—for many years—been operating a business buying and selling toy robots and other collectibles she purchased privately and at flea markets.

Apparently, business was booming, and Laura's mom and sister needed a third person to help at a flea market that same day! Parental pressure had been applied to Laura to get out of a dead-end situation and help the family— pressure Laura gave into. She'd packed her belongings, but before she left, her mother had seen my nice Shabbat tablecloth and said, "We can use this for one of the display tables," and just took off with it.[6]

*Laura's sister, Sandra (Tamler) Kessler in aqua blue dress & mother Mildred Kessler
at a flea market selling toy robots.*

Spiritual Things

With all I had going on, I wasn't as involved with the Orthodox Minyan of Elkins Park. Having made continued refinements to their constitution, they were on their way to becoming a Young Israel synagogue. A synagogue constitution would enable them to democratically and procedurally appoint a rabbi. Up until that time, at least a couple charismatic individuals had vied for possible spiritual leadership of the fledgling community. Rabbi Aryeh Botwinick, another Temple University professor was one, the other was Rabbi Shmuel Eisenberg, a Lubovitch Rabbi.

Searching for a rabbi apparently sparked some division among the minyan's original founders. Synagogue politics had led to a split, and when I returned to regular attendance, many familiar faces were gone. Sam Mazursky, David Indik and his father, and Rhea Blackman had left in protest. (Had I been involved in the internal struggle, I might have left too. I aligned with those who had left on many topics, and I felt their loss.)

One familiar face was still there: Peter Goldstone. As the new synagogue started to grow under the leadership of Rabbi Dov Brisman , Peter and I shared a bond over being two of the few "early members" still left. Thankfully, there were many people among the new arrivals that I got to know and care for over the years.

Me & Rabbi Dov Brisman. Across 3 decades, Rav. Brisman has served Young Israel of Elkins Park w/wisdom & dedication.

Rabbi Brisman was a funny man. When we first met, he asked me my name, and I told him, Theodore.

"Ah," he said. "So you're a gift?"

"What do you mean?" I asked.

"Theodore," he said, "means, 'Gift of G-d. 'So you're a great gift!"

My English name is of Greek origin. My Hebrew name, Eliezer (אליעזר), means, "G-d is my help. I hadn't appreciated my Hebrew name when I was younger, but as I got older, my fondness for it grew. Throughout my life, G-d *has* been my help. The differences are subtle, and I appreciate the English version of my name, but אליעזר seems a more perfect fit.

One of the ways Rabbi Brisman helped me was when I told him about my ongoing obsession with Kristl. Other than Rabbi Zelig Pliskin in Israel, Rabbi Brisman was really the only Rabbi I really talked to about it.[7] He listened attentively to everything I told him, and from time to time, he would check up on my mental state. "And how is Reb. Kristl?" he would ask. He knew of my fondness for her, of course, but also the incredible wisdom and character I observed in our every interaction. In short, Rabbi Brisman had understood that underneath all the obsession, I was truly trying to learn from her and wanted to emulate her practices and ways of working and communicating.

As my Judaism was growing, I began to acknowledge the commandments and that I was bound by the teachings of the Torah. For many years I'd harbored the idea of wearing a charm of the Egyptian ankh, symbolizing "breath of life." As my Jewish faith grew, I knew the Egyptian gods had been false idols for the Jewish people, and it wasn't a good idea to wear jewelry with the Egyptian symbol.

I also had felt energy from certain gems and stones and believed there was some validity to crystals having restorative or invigorating effects. But I did not know from where such "power" might come, and, with few exceptions, I decided to not wear crystals, no matter what positive effect they might have.

Italian artist Paolo Serpieri created a comic called *Druuna*, and I longed to have a tattoo of Druuna on my calf. If I didn't have responsibilities to G-d, I would have gotten the tattoo, but it is against the Torah for a Jewish person to get a tattoo, so I didn't do it.

There were a number of spiritual or mystical experiences in those years. After my adolescent experience with vivid dreams and an encounter with an apparition outside my brother's room, I'd restrained my pursuit of knowledge of parapsychology, but there were times when I didn't seem to have much choice. I found myself experiencing things that clearly felt "other worldly" regardless of my willingness or belief.

I began to feel more and more that G-d was protecting me. There were many instances when I felt an internal prodding to quicken my pace, or take a different turn, or that I wasn't supposed to be in a certain place or situation so I should leave. Even with a lot of the crazy—and even wrong—things I've done, the feeling of G-d's love and understanding continued to grow.

One powerful instance happened when Lou Kessler's father died. Lou and I had become good friends, and we maintained that friendship even after Laura and I were no longer living together. After Lou's father passed, I visited the house during the Shiva period of mourning following his burial. I felt the strong, inescapable feeling that Bernard Kessler was present in the house. Not just a memory of him, but his soul was actually present.

This would happen to me several times in the coming years. Sometimes, I attended a funeral or burial and wouldn't have that feeling at all; other times, I had a distinct experience of the person's soul lingering. I developed a theory about the afterlife, and I believe there are certain steps for the soul to be released after death. I believe the soul remains close to the people and places that were most important in life, and then that tie begins to loosen and widen until, eventually, the soul is freed.

I would later learn this is similar—if not parallel—to the customs of Jewish mourning, which commands the severest, most intense mourning to the first week, and then a less imposing mourning for the first month, followed by even less restrictive mourning that concludes at the one-year remembrance of the person's death. I don't pretend to understand the metaphysics of my belief, or that I know all the answers, but my experience has been consistent enough throughout my life to believe. As much as I want to know and understand the world, the Shakespeare quote I mentioned earlier reminds me: There is more in heaven and earth than any philosophy can contain.

From Laura to Andrea

In 1986, Ellie hosted a reunion for those of us who had been involved during her tenure as KIFTY's president. She was studying at Beaver College (now Arcadia University), and she invited us there. We had a model seder for Passover, and afterward, Ellie introduced me to her friends Andrea Sakim and Jerry Weinger.

Andrea and I began to spend time together. I think she liked me as a romantic possibility, but I wasn't attracted to her in that way. I enjoyed spending time with her but just didn't see her as a romantic partner.

Andrea had a car and didn't mind driving us places. Plus, she liked hanging out with me and my friends. She also found my sometimes off-putting sense of humor to be funny. She was a good audience for my antics, and I enjoyed making her laugh.

One day, as we were riding the train back from the city, she said, "Oh, by the way, I met your friend Laura."

I hadn't heard from Laura and had no idea where she

was, so I asked Andrea where she had seen her.

"She lives in my building now," Andrea said.

Andrea lived in an apartment right near the Jenkintown train station. When I found out where Laura was, I went to see her. Her father came to the door and said, "What are you doing here?" He was nicer to me than Laura's mother, but he wasn't happy to see me.

Laura came out and said, "You have to leave."

Not long after that, Laura moved into a different apartment, down the street, and when I visited her there, she invited me in, which I was grateful for. I still harbored some idea Laura might be the person I was supposed to have a conventional life with: Marriage, children, a "normal" life.

Inside her apartment, it was dark and there was no furniture. She had a job with an office machinery and telecommunications company, but her living conditions were stark.

"You have a good job," I said, "and it looks like you're trying to get yourself settled. Why don't you have any furniture?" My critique upset her, and we ended up arguing, so I went home.

Later that night, Laura called and we patched things up. But the call went on and on, late into the night, and I—embarrassingly—fell asleep while she was talking. I woke the next morning with the un-cradled receiver beside me, and I realized what I had done. I felt really bad, and I tried to phone her right away.

I kept calling her house and never got an answer, so I eventually called her work number and asked to speak to Laura Kessler. I was told, "She hasn‘t shown up for three days. She‘s been fired."

Once again, Laura disappeared, and I had no idea where she‘d gone.

Strangely enough, I got a phone call from Laura‘s sister a couple of months later. Sandy and I had never gotten along—the one time we‘d spent any time together, she‘d called me "the slow one" because I wasn‘t quick enough to make a backgammon move—and I genuinely disliked the way Sandy mistreated Laura and ruled like a dictator over the family. For whatever reason, Sandy called and said, "I found out where Laura is. Are you interested?"

Apparently, Sandy had used phone records to track Laura to Florida, where she was living with a guy named Gary. I‘d briefly met Gary during my year at Ambler campus. He and Laura had gone to Abington High School together, and apparently she‘d been interested in him romantically for a long time. Now, they were shacked up in Florida.

Much like when I‘d been in Israel and she told me she was seeing other guys, I had a moment of clarity: *She‘s made her decision, she‘s with someone else, she‘s a thousand miles away. Time to jump ship, Ted!*

As always, a part of me was reluctant to let go. I wanted to know if she was OK. I wanted to know this was the right guy for her, and that she would be safe and happy. I ended up calling her in Florida and telling her I wanted to come visit, which I eventually did. (That was a messy, big mistake on my part.)

I was as confused about my feelings as ever, but I tried to get on with my life. Although during the week I was at school, Wednesday nights Andrea would drive us to University of Pennsylvania, where they had weekly lessons for people interested in learning Israeli dances.

When I visited Andrea, I would enter her apartment, give her a hug, then bend down to pet her cat, Lucky. There were a number of times when Lucky would sniff me, then immediately turn around and pad off to his litter box to relieve himself. This happened often enough, I joked that maybe I should rent myself out as an "all-natural cat laxative." Andrea thought that was funny.

Andrea and I enjoyed laughing together, and I have fond memories of sitting in her car at the end of a night out, laughing and laughing together for 20 or 30 minutes. As we got to know each other, I also learned some of the sadness in Andrea's life. She was very sensitive, and sometimes she would cry while I tried to comfort and console her.

We became closer, and I felt Andrea's soul had touched me in some mysterious way. I hadn't initially been attracted to her physically, but the more I got to know her, the more I felt a physical desire beyond the friendship we'd established. While I was growing in my Jewish faith and trying to be more religious, the sexual component of that was always

Andrea Sakim (left) w/me at a 30th year birthday party at Williamson's Restaurant, Philadelphia arranged by Steve Hirsh.

a struggle. I wanted to do the right thing, but I also had sexual desires I wrestled with. Andrea's position was more conventional than mine; "I love you as a friend, and we have a lot of fun together, but I'm not getting in bed with you unless we are married."

Unfortunately, I did not see Andrea as wife material. Things with Andrea were nowhere near as volatile or unstable as my relationship with Laura, but I wasn't convinced we were a good long-term match.

Barbara

During our trips to University of Pennsylvania for Israeli dancing, Andrea introduced me to her friend, Barbara Lewandowski. Barbara was cute, had a good sense of humor, and was of Polish Jewish descent. She had a great smile, which I enjoyed encouraging. The three of us hung out together, and it became clear Barbara was interested in me. We talked a lot and spent time together, and eventually we were officially dating.

Barbara attended Penn, and we were a good match on an intellectual level. We had stimulating conversations, and she could hold her own when discussing ideas. She also had an artistic side, writing poetry.

She lived in a tough area of West Philadelphia, and I visited her there. One Sunday night, Lou, Andrea, and I were at Barbara's place having such a good time, I wasn't paying attention to the time. The last train left central Philly for the suburbs at 12:15. Without a cab, it was clear we weren't going to make it to the station on time.

Leaving Barbara's apartment, the streets were deserted. It was Sunday night in a rough neighborhood, so finding a cab seemed like a long shot. Suddenly…out of nowhere, a cab came around the corner. We all piled in and made it just in time to get the last train out of the city.[8]

One unique aspect of my relationship with Barbara was that she was aware of my obsession with Kristl. Barbara's obsession was a little more conventional. She had a thing for Peter Tork of the band, The Monkees. If we were out together and I started going on about something Kristl had said or done, Barbara would launch into a soliloquy about Peter Tork to make a point.

(In an odd intersection of our two obsessions, I have a memory of walking and talking with Kristl during the 1985 Temple Spring Fling, which featured The Monkees—minus Mike Nesmith—as a musical act.)

At one point, we took the train to Greenwich Village in New York to see Peter Tork in concert. In the Village, who did we happen to run into as we exited onto the subway platform? Peter Tork himself! Barbara was beside herself with excitement, babbling and nearly hyperventilating with glee.

"It's OK," Peter told her. "I'm just a normal person. I put on my pants one leg at a time just like everyone."

The idea of Peter Tork putting on his pants probably wasn't the right way to calm Barbara down. We went to the performance that night and had a fun evening. And Barbara had gotten to meet the object of her obsession.

I liked Barbara a lot, and we had a good relationship, but it seemed like she was feeling the pressure of the "biological clock" more than I was. She confronted me, "So, where is this thing between us going?"

I wanted her to be happy, and I understood why she wanted something beyond just dating and having fun, but I also knew I was a broke college student who didn't have much to offer. We got along really well, and Barbara was stable and seemed like a solid candidate for long-term commitment. I wasn't head over heels for Barbara, but there was a practical and reasonable argument to be made for marrying her. I was 25 and knew I wanted to have a family at some point. When would I meet another cute, intellectually stimulating, funny, and charming woman like her?

Kristl's Marriage

Kristl was in a relationship and engaged to be married. Even though I knew the small, romantic hope I'd harbored for her was unrealistic, the thought of her marrying someone else was terrifying. Kristl was a Christian, and I knew it would be improper for me to marry anyone who wasn't Jewish. She was the Dean of Students, and she deserved more than I could offer her, anyway. I'd come to care for her deeply, and I wanted her to have a good life and family, but the thought of not having her presence in my life made me nervous.

The closer her wedding got, the more anxious and distracted I became. I wanted to talk to her about it, but I was also scared to. One Sunday, shortly before her scheduled wedding, I was at the campus library doing research. Thoughts of Kristl kept me preoccupied, and I decided to ring the dean's office to see if she was there, as unlikely as that was. I stood in the rain and dialed from the payphone outside the library.

It was around five o'clock, and I was surprised when I heard her voice on the phone. "Ted, what are you doing calling the office on a Sunday?"

I said I wanted to talk to her and that I'd had a feeling she might be there. We ended up meeting on Berks Mall, the main pedestrian thoroughfare on campus, near the bell tower.

As I confessed my love for her, I started to cry. I said, "I know you're getting married. I'm happy for you, but I don't want to lose my connection with you." I explained I wasn't trying to get in the way of her happiness, but I couldn't imagine not having her in my life. "If we could be in each other's lives somehow. Even if it's just on my birthday or your birthday. I need to know we will still see each other."

Kristl was very compassionate. "OK, we can do that. We'll get together twice a year."

And we did. We established a pattern of meeting near my birthday in January and hers in June. I would take her a little gift, and we'd meet for a meal and catch up. We shared wonderful lunches—for over 33 years!—and I got to even know her family a bit better.

In that moment, though, I was still depressed.

Steve Hirsh and I went to the Eastern Sociological Society's annual conference in Boston the weekend of Kristl's marriage. We presented a paper on the sociology of student transportation. With Steve's company and the activities of the conference, I was able to put Kristl somewhat out of my mind. Steve and I roamed Boston and went swimming at the hotel. I was also able to meet Robert K. Merton, one of the greatest sociologists of the twentieth century.[9]

Back at Temple, for a while, I felt mostly excluded from Kristl's life.

Me, Sociologist Dr. Robert K. Merton and Steve Hirsh. Eastern Sociological Society Conference, Boston, MA. 1987.

6

TEMPLE GRADUATE YEARS

Third Israel Trip

I n 1987, as I was finishing the requirements for my bachelor's degree, I sought admission to Temple's graduate program in sociology. I was excited to continue my education and get my master's degree.

That summer, I returned to Israel for the third time. Bob Kleiner had recommended me to be part of a summer social work course led by Rutgers Professor Paul Shane. The course was co-facilitated by Rutgers University and Hebrew University in Jerusalem.

In addition to the classes, we also went on field visits. As part of the course, we visited the "triangle" towns, where a high concentration of Israeli Arabs resided. One of the Arab leaders shared that things were really stressed in the Arab territories because the Israeli government was providing too limited resources. I was disappointed by this information. I understood the country was governed by the Jewish people, but I felt the Israeli government had a responsibility for equitable distribution of resources to everyone, including the native Arabs. (Later that year, after I'd returned to the US, tensions between Arab Israelis and the government boiled over and the First Intifada protests and riots began.)

That trip was the first time I dreamed of a working career in Israel. If I finished my sociology education and moved there, I might become a social worker in the Arab communities, helping guarantee their fair access to food, water, transportation, housing, and other basic necessities. Had I been more focused academically, I might have tried for a dual major in sociology and social work. I never followed through on that idea, but it was something I considered.

While there, I hoped to reunite with Lou Kessler, who had left for Israel a year earlier to live on a moshav, a religious settlement run by Shlomo Carlebach. Before I left the US, I reached out to Lou's mother and asked if there was anything she wanted me to take to Lou. She gave me money and some clothes for him, which I packed in my bag.

What I found in Jerusalem was troubling. Lou was in bad shape. Whatever he'd hoped to find at the moshav had obviously not worked out, and my dear friend was basically homeless and out of touch with reality. He was living on the street, eating from trash cans. I gave him the money and clothes, but Lou needed more help.

This caused deep conflict inside me. I was living in nice student housing on campus at Hebrew University while my friend was suffering in the streets. I tried to help him while I was there, but my six weeks of classes were ending, and Lou wasn't willing to come back to the US, where his family or I could help him.

I told one of the Hebrew University liaisons and Paul Shane, the head professor from Rutgers, what was happening. They urged me to have Lou committed to a psychiatric hospital in Jerusalem. I was confused and anxious about this. Lou certainly needed an intervention, but I wasn't sure a psych hospital in Israel was the right path. They suggested I have Lou meet me somewhere near the hospital, and they would arrange for his care.

I asked Lou to meet me, and I think he had an idea of what was happening. I told him I was worried and that I had to return to the US in a few days. "I can't force you to go in there, but I'd rather know you're safe. These people will take care of you." Lou refused, so I pleaded with him, "If you won't get help here, then come back to the States. If you come back, you know your mom will help you. I'll help you. You can't keep living like this." Again he said, no.

When I left Israel, I had no idea what would become of my friend. I was desperately worried for his health and well-being, but I was powerless to help.

I was relieved when, a month or so later, I heard Lou had come back to his mother's house. He spent some time

Reunited w/friend, Lou Kessler the summer of 1987 while taking a course in social work at Hebrew University, Jerusalem.

in psychiatric care at Friends Hospital in Philadelphia, and he did get better.

I began graduate school in the Fall of '87. Steve and I began to work on the second ComPass report, which was an evaluation of use and benefit of the student discount program. I had a teaching assistantship with Dr. Turner as a lab assistant in the sociology lab. I don't think I was very good at it, but at least I got paid. I was even able to put some money into the credit union.

Big changes were also happening at that time for my congregation in Elkins Park. The Beth Jacob School system went bankrupt and ceased operating the school at the conclusion of the 1986 spring semester. With their departure, the O.M.E.P. now had the regular use of the bigger building throughout the week, in addition to Sabbaths and holidays!

Rabbi Brisman, retained his residence in northeast Philadelphia, but would occasionally be accompanied by his wife and children during those Sabbaths and holidays. When they stayed over, they would occupy a room on the upper floors of the main building, while the services were conducted in the main space of the first floor.

As opportune as it was to have a regular and dedicated space, it was a short lived benefit. With the departure of the day school, even less maintenance was occurring to the building. It was freezing cold in the winter (we survived using space heaters) and oppressively hot in the summer. The community also grew, and with the growing attendance by women and young children, we needed a new, proper, safe, and comfortable building to inhabit. The solution was the purchase of a house at 503 Spring Avenue, across the street from the Elkins Park train station. So, sometime around the Fall of 1987, the YIEP congregation moved into that house where it remained for nearly 6 years.

Loss of a Classmate

My high school graduating class was late in celebrating our first class reunion. In fact, nearly seven years had gone by! That first reunion was held in center city Philadelphia on Thursday, March 24, 1988. I hadn't been notified of the event—likely because my phone number had been unlisted in the school directory—but I happened to run into a former classmate, Neal Brody, while I was in Center City that very day, and he told me about it. After that first reunion, I got involved with the reunion committee and have been part of every reunion committee since 1988.

I found out my classmate at Cheltenham High, David Dornstein, had been killed in the terrorist bombing of Pan Am flight 103 in December of 1988. David had been returning from Israel when the plane exploded over Lockerbie, Scotland. David's brother, Ken, wrote a book in 2007 called, *The Boy Who Fell Out of the Sky*, about that incident.

Brief Engagement

My mother and I went to the jewelry store and bought a modest diamond ring, and Barbara and I were engaged. We began to plan the wedding. I was still unsure about the decision to marry. On one hand, Barbara was a good option, and a smart choice if I wanted to have a wife and family, but I also just never felt the reality of marrying her. At the time, because I genuinely appreciated Barbara, I chalked this up to "wedding jitters."

As time went on, my mother approached me with an idea. She and my father had been married on January 14th, 1962, and her parents had been married on January 14th, 1938. "Wouldn't it be nice," she said, "if you and Barbara were married on January 14th?"

I wasn't sure that was a great idea, but my mother said I could at least ask. I knew Barbara already felt like my mother had a disproportionate influence in my life—and, therefore, our relationship—but I bowed to the pressure of my mother's request.

When I went to Barbara's apartment, I brought up the subject. That request broke the dam. Barbara began crying and was inconsolable. There was no way to help her, so I left. We later talked, and Barbara broke off the engagement. We agreed it was probably better if we didn't have any further contact.

After that, I never spoke to her again.

End of the Temple Era

The master's program in sociology was supposed to take two years, but I continued the trend of not turning papers in on time. I also flunked statistics a couple times, which didn't help. I was, however, on track to complete my degree at the end of my fourth year.

For my last semester, I was fortunate to be placed at the Delaware Valley Regional Planning Commission as an intern. That experience was in line with my interests in the intersection of sociology and transportation, and I enjoyed those months as a way to cap off my master's study.[1]

I planned to pursue a Ph.D at Temple, but I didn't realize how much opposition there was in the sociology department to my continued study at Temple. At first, I was told, "You shouldn't get your doctorate from the same school as your other degrees. It's academic incest. Go somewhere else. Broaden your experience."

I was really only interested in staying at Temple. Bob Kleiner and Kevin Delaney were two faculty members who were willing to support me. Eventually, a third faculty member provided a referral letter as well.

However, soon after, the official word came from the department chair: "We can't have you as a Ph.D student. You require too many resources, and you're a drain on the department."

I was devastated. I had the bright idea to take some

doctoral-level courses, even though I wasn't an approved Ph.D candidate. I thought if I did well, I would prove they'd been wrong, and I'd reapply. Unfortunately, I didn't have the energy or drive to do the work, and I ended up taking "incomplete" grades. I felt defeated, and I walked away from the dream of achieving a doctorate in sociology.

I ended up being on Temple's main campus from 1983 to 1991. I had a lot of great experiences there, and I met some amazing people, including my classmate friends and the university's faculty and staff. I was also fortunate to meet and interact with some memorable individuals.

Bobby Seale, a founding member of the Black Panthers, taught at Temple during those years, and I met him several times. We had a couple of interesting conversations. I also attended a lecture by two other members of the Chicago Seven—who had been charged with inciting the protest riots at the 1968 Democratic Convention in Chicago—Abbie Hoffman and Jerry Rubin. (Afterward, I asked Hoffman for an autograph. He told me, "I usually don't do this," but then scribbled his name on a piece of paper for me.)

Lou Kessler and I attended a talk by well-known feminist journalist, Gloria Steinem. After her lecture, we approached her and we had a brief conversation.

B&W Photo Abbie Hoffman at the lectern: sourced Getty Images

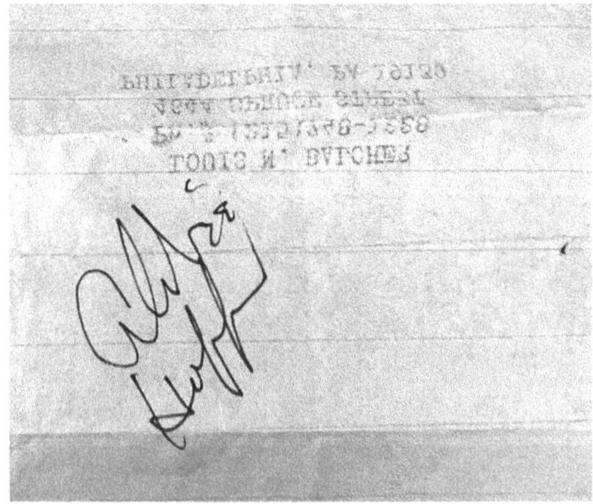

Hoffman's scribbled autograph at Temple U.

Post-College Job Search

With my master's degree, I thought I might get a job teaching undergraduate sociology. There weren't many teaching jobs available. I found one opening at the Community College of Philadelphia, but I didn't have a car, and the logistics of public transportation for that job weren't workable.

Bob Kleiner told me several of his former students had secured jobs with the Philadelphia Department of Mental Health and Retardation. Bob spoke to Larry Benner, the department's director, and I got an interview. I went down and took the civil service exam.

The next thing I knew, I was called into a meeting. Benner was there, along with several other people, including former classmates who were already working there. They congratulated me for achieving the highest score on the civil service exam. I was fully qualified for the position, and I had the job if I wanted it. I was told to expect an official acceptance letter with the information I'd need to come in and get started.

It was an honor to be given the opportunity, but I was hesitant. My statistics skills were weak, and I was worried about running programs with clients. Another problem was that I lived in Cheltenham Township. My mailing address was a Philadelphia address, but I actually lived in Montgomery County. It was a stretch, but I considered listing a friend's center city address for a month or two until I got my own apartment in the city.

Several weeks passed and I hadn't received the letter. I could have called to find out what was going on, but I wasn't confident in my ability, so I didn't press the issue. Several months passed before I went back to the office. Their basic response was, "Who are you?" Larry Benner had died of a heart attack. He had been a good guy, and left a young family behind, and I was sad to find out he had passed.

I was hunting for a job when—out of the blue—Laura called. She'd returned from Florida after her relationship with Gary had bottomed out. She offered me a job at her business, Lead City. It paid very little, but I wanted something to add to my resume, so I agreed.

Lead City bought data compiled from magazine inserts and sweepstakes entries. Magazines from *Cosmopolitan*, to *Modern Bride*, to *Golf Digest* were packed full of perforated cards offering a chance to win a free honeymoon or dream vacation in exchange for filling out demographic data. (They were the pre-internet version of web browser "cookies" that scoop up data to sell.) Laura bought data sets from list brokers in New York for something like a penny per name and then re-sold the information to insurance companies for a dime per lead. Insurance agents were always looking for new clients, and Laura could give them information that was slightly more warm than a "cold call."

Laura's parents had bought Lou's family home after

Lou's father died, and we initially worked from there. We packaged up the leads based on the needs of the particular insurance company—Prudential, New York Life, etc.—and Laura would express ship them out to the agents, ready for them to make calls.

When I showed up the first day, Laura was outside the house, and we spotted each other from a distance. I hadn't seen her in years, but the old feelings came rushing back. I ran to her, and we rushed into each other's arms. We kissed. It was like a movie scene, except for what happened next: We both stepped back and seemed to have a simultaneous realization that we didn't actually feel the way we had in the past. That part of our life was over.

From that point on, Laura and I operated as friends and business associates. She showed me around, introduced me to the dozen other employees, and I settled in. The first thing I realized was wrong with the job was that Laura sold duplicate lists to agents representing the same company. Agent A from Prudential would call a potential customer and be told that Agent B from Prudential had just called. This was, of course, not what the agents had paid for. In some fairness to Laura, this was not entirely her fault—the agents generally purchased the data by zip code and their coverage areas did occasionally overlap.

A bigger issue arose when Laura shipped those leads to the various insurance company's agents. On their leads folder, she placed a company-appropriate graphic sticker. That meant that she put the image of a rock on the Prudential agents 'folders, and a Snoopy image on the MetLife agents 'folders (since Snoopy had an endorsement deal with MetLife in those years). When management at the insurance company heard about this, they called and told Laura she didn't have the rights to use Snoopy, and she should cease and desist using the logo.

Laura didn't take the issue seriously, and she continued to slap Snoopy stickers on the folders, and MetLife officials called a second time. "This is serious," I told her. "These big companies don't play when it comes to copyright infringement." She shrugged off my comment, and I said, "If you don't care about yourself, at least understand that if this all comes crashing down, the people who work here are going to be hurt, too." "I know what I'm doing. It's my business," Laura replied. "Go back to work." It was in fact Laura's business, and however she was running it, it was successful enough to prosper for several more years, as well as inspiring 'spin-offs' among her friends and colleagues.

Premonitions and Strange Dreams

One contributing factor that exacerbated my lack of motivation and inconsistency in my academic and professional life was a lingering, nagging feeling that had been ever-present since my teenage years: I had an instinctual belief something very big, and very bad, would begin in the

2020s. It was a resonant feeling I could never shake, and it sapped my motivation and drive. Why struggle—why work toward a house, a family, a good career—if it was all going to be destroyed or taken away?

It felt like a spiritual intuition, and it fueled a lot of my depression over the years. I didn't want it to be true, but it felt like something terrible was inescapable.

There were other mysteries that occurred in my life. From late 1991 to March 1992, I had a recurring, short and strange dream where I was seated in the cabin of a commercial airliner. The plane accelerated for takeoff, and I watched through the window as we climbed into the sky, where I observed the cloud cover from above. Then, the dream would end.

This was strange for a couple of reasons. First, it recurred night after night for weeks. Second, at that time, I hadn't traveled by plane often. And it was a short, pointless dream. It didn't go anywhere. Literally.

As weeks went by, I noticed slight changes to the dream. As the weeks progressed, the dream version of me was growing more nervous with each takeoff.

The few times I'd flown, I'd found the takeoff exhilarating, but dream me grew more and more anxious with each flight. By 7 weeks into this dreaming, my dream self was sweating, heart pounding, hands clenching the seat's armrests, legs locked as if bracing for impact. The dream still ended with me looking out at the clouds below.

And then, the dreams just stopped. It didn't make sense. The normal response to traveling or doing something new is you get nervous at first, but repetition makes you less anxious. My flying dream was exactly the opposite, and that confounded me.

Also in the 1990s, I experienced the first of a recurring sensation I find very difficult to describe. I was walking on the east side of Market Street in Philadelphia, not far from City Hall, where Macy's is now. I was overwhelmed with a weird awareness.

On one hand, everything was normal. Cars were rolling along the street; people were walking on the sidewalk. At the same time, I experienced another reality. There was an overlay—or a mental impression—of the city deserted, empty, and destroyed. Buildings were broken. There was rubble everywhere. If I closed my eyes, I was overwhelmed with the sensation of being utterly alone. I had the dual experience of walking down the street in the present and normal reality but receiving psychic echoes from a dystopian future.

It was similar to the premonition I'd had at the newspaper building. It was as if I were a bridge between two different eras.

Those impressions did not go away. Over the next 25 years, this same awareness would pop up. It happened irregularly, but when it did happen, it was very powerful. The strongest impression of destruction I had was on the east side of City Hall.

Over the years, I talked about this to therapists because when it happened, it affected how I lived my life. There were places I couldn't walk because the feeling was so intense and I had to alter my route. I could feel a giant hole in the floor a short ways into the entrance to the Pennsylvania Convention Center (formerly the Aramark Tower). If I used the lobby ATM there, I had to walk a wide circle around the perceived crater. At the 15th street east platform of the Market-Frankford Elevated subway station, I could sense collapsed girders.

It even happened to me in Washington, DC, in 2018. Leaving the Smithsonian on my way to the metro stop, I looked back at the Capitol. The building was there, but part of me sensed it was gone. Like it had been destroyed.

I've been reluctant to talk about my premonitions because I don't want to be misperceived as advocating for something I actually hope never happens. Despite my uneasy relationship to blind patriotism, I don't want to see the United States attacked and cities—and lives—devastated. I would mourn the destruction of the US, and I don't think war and destruction is ever a good thing for the world.

But these premonitions had a major impact on my life, so it seems appropriate to mention them here.

Standing near Macy's & looking back toward City Hall – Earliest "overlay/impression" (1992) of a post-apocalyptic Philly.

View South on east side Philla. City Hall. Alfredo's and my impressions strongest.

The 15th East MFL platform

Exterior & entrance to PA Convention Ctr.

Interior-5 ft radius before the ATM where we perceived a hole.

7

ENTERING THE POST-COLLEGE WORLD

Data Groupie

Around the time I wanted to get away from Laura's business, Steve Hirsh told me about a job with a marketing research phone company he worked for in Plymouth Meeting. I'd had some telemarketing experience in college, so I went in for an interview. When I was offered the job, I broke the news to Laura that I'd be leaving Lead City.

"You're leaving?" she said. "But why?"

I knew she wouldn't listen to my critique of her business practices, and I preferred to leave on good terms, so I stretched the truth. "It's a job with more opportunity for advancement," I said. "And more related to sociology."

Working at Data Group, I administered phone surveys gathering data for clients like Johnson & Johnson or Proctor

& Gamble. We were evaluated on how many surveys we could complete. I didn't think the surveys were very well designed, and it was difficult keeping people on the phone long enough to answer all the questions to get "a complete." My supervisor, Alfredo Valencia, listened in on the calls and critiqued me. He always complimented me on the things I'd done well before offering suggestions of how to improve. I respected and trusted Alfredo.

I was faced with an ethical dilemma when we made phone calls on behalf of a national investment and wealth management company. We were supposed to call their customers and ask a series of questions, which was pretty standard. The difference was, the company had supplied us with information about the individual client's portfolio of investments, which we could refer to while asking the questions. The amount of personal financial data we had access to was shocking.

Working as a market research call agent didn't require a college degree, and many people doing that work were not the most trustworthy. I was appalled that a such a nationally established company would be so cavalier with customer data. I understood why Data Group wanted the contract, but I couldn't fathom why we had access to so much private information. I wouldn't want that level of detail of my financial information shared with call center employees. Plus, I didn't want the responsibility of having seen that information.

I did whatever I could to secure other assignments so I wouldn't have to participate in something I considered unethical. I didn't care if it was baby food preferences, grocery stores habits, or whatever, I just didn't want to be working with the portfolios of unknowing investors who (in good faith) believed their holdings were kept private. Alfredo assigned me to other projects any time he could, which I appreciated.

It was a monotonous job but a steady paycheck. I still lived with my parents, and since I didn't have a car, the commute to Plymouth Meeting was laborious. I had to walk from Cheltenham Avenue, down Willow Grove Avenue to Stenton Avenue, then catch the route L bus up to Plymouth Meeting. Transportation on Sundays was always iffy, so if I had a Sunday shift, I was always worried I'd miss the last bus and be stranded.

There were other companies in the Plymouth Meeting Business Center where Data Group was located. In late summer of 1992, I had an employment opportunity with another company, World Marketing Services. I went to a group interview for entry-level applicants. About a dozen of us listened to the spiel about the company, what it was like to work there, and the expectations of the job. One piece of information I gathered was that as it was a 24/7 operation, working for World Marketing would require odd shifts.

I was honest about my reservations, and said I would not work Friday night to Saturday night since it would violate observance of the Sabbath. Next thing I knew, they were asking me and another applicant to leave the room; my presence was no longer required. World Marketing Services did not have a place for me.

Other people at Data Group were getting jobs with World Marketing Services. Eventually, in December of 1992, I decided to try again. This time I was hired.

I submitted my shift request to have off Friday and Saturday, and when I received my assignment, I was happily surprised. I had an 8:00 to 4:30 shift, with Friday and Saturday off. *Not too bad!* I thought, until someone pointed out I was reading it wrong: It was 8:00 pm to 4:30 am. But, at least I had secured the job *and* was able to meet my religious obligations.

The company involved a strange mishmash of activities housed in a large warehouse space, with different areas sectioned off for different business pursuits. One area was dedicated to travel and airline reservations, another section for Dutch Gardens flower orders. They took orders for the as-seen-on-TV Great Wok of China and other infomercial products. There was even a section of the company dedicated to fulfilling the "If you'd like a transcript of today's program" offers at the end of *Donohue* or *60 Minutes*. (We had a whole video tape library for this purpose.) There were too many other niche products to list, but anything you could order by phone in the 1990s, chances are the calls were routed through World Marketing Services.[1]

It was hard to describe what I was doing at my new job because it was so varied. I might spend five hours taking airline reservations—helping Joe from Boise decide between a cheaper flight with a long layover or a direct flight—then I might be told, "We need you in Dutch Gardens!" where I would have to help Myrtle decide between irises or tulips for her yard.

While working the phones, I developed a pseudonym persona: Max Hellstrom. I would answer, "Thank you for calling Travel Bargains. This is Max. How can I help you?" Max Hellstrom was an alias I used at various times throughout my life.

For a while, I kept my job at Data Group, part time. I worked there from 4 p.m. to 8 p.m., then I'd log off my phone and run down the hill to start my overnight shift with World Marketing. When I got off work, I had to kill time until the busses started running. My mother saw how hard I was working, and she often picked me up at the bus stop at Willow Grove and Stenton so I didn't have to walk the last couple miles home. I kept the overnight shift at World Marketing for two years but eventually moved into a daytime position.

A major part of the business was working the phones for a Trans World Airlines-related company, Travel Bargains (1-800-AIRFARE), which the airline utilized to capture a low-cost market segment. After three months' employment, I was able to get non-fare "Triple E" tickets to fly just about anywhere in the US roundtrip for $20, and international flights were $100.

We were also allowed to trade shifts with other employees—a blessing when I wanted time off to observe religious holidays—which allowed me to use a combination of vacation time and traded time to travel. I went to Carlsbad Caverns in New Mexico and visited my brother when he was interning at a job in Texas. I went to California a few times and visited Vancouver and Seattle.

My sister was in school at American University in Washington, DC. I visited her several times, staying in the dorms and exploring the city during the day. I always found my way to the Air and Space Museum, and would spend a few minutes watching the aging video loop of President Kennedy's 1961 speech to Congress in which he spoke passionately about the value of the Moon program to America's future. The Air & Space Museum on the Mall remains an all-time favorite destination of mine.

In DC, Lori introduced me to a great restaurant, Sequoia. Located on the Potomac, it has a great outdoor terrace and was a favorite of the Clintons when they were in DC. It was pricey, but it became one of my favorite restaurants in the States.

In addition to traveling to new places and regular trips to DC, I was not very careful with my money. I was working a lot and living at home, so my regular expenses weren't extravagant, but I spent a lot of money on other things— computer software, for example.

Lori & me lunching at Sequoia restaurant on the Potomac river in Washington, DC. Remains 1 of my favorite places to eat![2]

During my Vancouver trip, I was supposed to be watching my finances, but I lost my sweater on the ferry to Seattle. I went to the rotating top at the Space Needle—I've always had a fascination with rooftop restaurants as well—and I purchased a sweatshirt to replace my lost sweater. When I got home, my dad saw the souvenir and said, "Did you really have to buy that?"

I told him what had necessitated the purchase and ended with the punchline: "You didn't want me to be 'Sleeveless in Seattle', did you?"

I returned to Florida several times. My old friend Ellie was living there with her husband, Larry. She had a job with Disney, and she got me a pass. We had a lovely lunch at the French bistro in Epcot.

As the number of flights accumulated, I realized my dreams of a few years earlier were coming true. I was flying more often, but with each trip, my anxiety increased. I found myself gripping the armrest and sweating with nervousness with each takeoff. Statistically, I reasoned I was flying so often, my probability of being on a plane with a major issue was much higher. (I'm sure there were some stray thoughts about my classmate, David, who'd died in the Pan Am 103 incident, as well.) I thought, *Maybe I'm running out of luck!*

I started reading articles on plane maintenance, which didn't help. All it took was one bolt or one missed step in the maintenance routine for there to be a problem. I had no idea how often—or how competently—any given plane

Ellie and me dining at the French Bistro restaurant in EPCOT, Disney World, FL in the mid 1990's.

had been maintained. When I was flying, I had zero control over a whole host of factors, and I couldn't control the racing thoughts of impending disaster. However, just as in the dreams, the anxiety was mostly on take-off and landing, once we were stable in the air, I relaxed a bit.

Back in Elkins Park, change continued for the Orthodox Minyan. The congregation continued to grow, and by this time was inclusive of over fifty families. On Sabbaths and holidays, the house where we were meeting seemed even more crowded than the larger gatherings we'd had in the old high school building!

The corner house at 503 Spring Avenue was no longer a viable location. Several alternate plans were considered, including renovating extensions onto the existing building, or even purchasing an entirely new location. One congregant, Marvin Berman, suggested purchasing and renovating the old Bell telephone utility building at 7715 Montgomery Avenue. It had been empty and unused for many years. Armed with research, congregational president, Stanley Sved took the bull by the horns, and after several heated debates, that old warehouse building was purchased with a mortgage. The congregation moved out of the house and into the newly renovated building in 1993.[3]

Psychic Surgery

After not getting into the Ph.D program and struggling to find meaningful work, I was feeling depressed. I had a degree, but I wasn't working in a job that made use of my training. Plus, I was working long hours with very little social life. I still went to Elkins Park for Shabbos, which was a comfort, and I'd been seeing a therapist, but that didn't seem to help.

Walking in Philadelphia, I spotted a psychic's storefront and decided to go in. I commissioned Cindy, the psychic, for a tarot reading. As a practicing Jew, it wasn't the wisest idea, but I was in a rut and felt doomed to bad luck. Maybe I'd find some answers.

"What happened to you," she began, after I'd ponied up my $40 and after the reading," is that the right side of your aura is damaged."

I believed there was something to the idea of energy or auras and that some people could intuit things based on that energy.

"I can fix it for you," she said. She went on to explain I'd have to wear a crystal necklace, I'd have strange dreams, and I'd feel sick to the point of feeling like I needed to be hospitalized—all for a duration of three days. In addition to the physical toll, there was another cost to the procedure: "It will be $500."

That was a lot of money, but I was in a vulnerable place. I

wanted to believe there was something like psychic surgery to help get me un-stuck. This was a definite spiritual gray area, so I told Cindy I needed to think about it before committing to her cure.

"Don't take too long," she cautioned.

I spoke to Rabbi Brisman and told him what I was considering.

"I'm telling you," he said, "don't do it. You're asking for trouble."

His response annoyed me a little, and I was desperate to find a cure for my ongoing funk. I decided to gather up $500 and go back to Cindy.

Things progressed pretty much as she'd told me. There was a day at work when I felt nauseous and was afraid I would pass out. I had to rest, sitting quietly and couldn't work for a while. I didn't quite feel like I needed the hospital, but it was a significant wave of illness that eventually passed.

Additionally, I had several nights of vivid dreams, one in which I was chased across a rooftop by students who had bullied me in school. Only, in my dream, I turned to confront them and defended myself from their harassment. The next day, I woke up refreshed, with more confidence.

After all this, I had a tremendous amount of energy in my body. For a while, I could intuit people's thoughts and hear their feelings. It was an incredible experience that lasted a few days, until the energy dissipated, and I was left with a concentration of the energy residing in my hands; they felt as if they were glowing. It was overwhelming, like I needed to find a way to discharge the energy.

Why in my hands? I decided the energy was concentrated in my hands because I was supposed to tackle a creative writing project. I tried writing a little, and that helped. It had been an unconventional path to get there, but I'd found my way out of my depressed state. I had a goal and a path to travel that renewed me.

But there was a downside: Not long after my psychic surgery, I went to the synagogue to pray, and I realized I was experiencing a palpable disconnect between the left and right side of my body. When I prayed, it felt as if only my left side was in contact with G-d. No matter how hard I prayed, no matter my intentions, the right side of my body didn't have any spiritual connection. This was a lasting side effect I would continue to deal with for the next two decades.

I went back to Cindy and demanded to know what she'd done to cause this. "I helped you," was her answer. "I fixed you."

"Everything happened like you said it would," I said. "But now I can't pray to G-d right. What did you do?"

"I did nothing to you," she insisted, "other than give you a jump start." She told me the "fix" was only temporary, and if I didn't devote myself to a new path and honor the revelations I'd had about creative work, my soul would revert back to its depressed state.

After all that, I'd learned a couple of lessons. First, I

realized visiting a psychic was a denigration of Torah, and I regretted that. The ancient rabbis knew things like astrology and psychics might be real, but if so, they were deflecting the glory of G-d onto themselves and away from the source, like thanking the moon for its light, which is really a reflection of the sun.

Second, I learned to never ask a rabbi's opinion unless you plan to follow his advice. To ask a rabbi to make a judgement is the same as asking what the Torah says, and to ignore that advice is like ignoring Torah.

Finally, I had the conviction that I needed to channel my energy into something creative. I had a project in mind, the seeds of which had been sown in my childhood.

Genesis II

With the conviction that I needed to apply myself to a creative writing project, I considered the books, shows, and movies that had the most impact on me in my childhood. One idea that had really stuck with me was Gene Roddenberry's movie, *Genesis II (1973)*. Unlike the original *Star Trek* series that had exploded in popularity after it was cancelled—and spawned an ever-growing number of movies and spin-off series—*Genesis II* had slipped into relative obscurity after its release as a made-for-television movie in March 1973.[4] A majority of non-fans of *Star Trek* could identify Spock or Kirk. Only die-hard sci-fi fans would have recognized Dylan

Hunt, the main character of *Genesis II*.

I had a deep appreciation for the story and characters Roddenberry had created in the *Genesis II* world, and I began to ponder the idea of developing a comic book sequel to the movie. This was the kind of story world that would make a solid transition from television screen to the printed page of a graphic novel.

Buffy the Vampire Slayer was one of the touchstones I kept in mind. *Buffy* had started as a movie that inspired a critically acclaimed television series and had found additional life in the world of comic books. I was also inspired by DC Comics' more mature imprint, Vertigo. There, creators like Alan Moore and Neil Gaiman were raising the bar for comics.

I didn't think I was Gaiman or Moore, but I believed I had something to add to the elevation of comic books from something children read to a more refined, and impactful, art form.

World Marketing World Traveler

Having access to inexpensive plane tickets was a great benefit. It allowed me to reconnect with my old friend Harvey in California. He called with the big news that he was getting married, and I suggested I come for a visit to meet his intended bride.

My friend David Toplin—a cousin of my friend Steve— had become religious with me at Young Israel (though later he went a different route, becoming part of the Hasidic Lubavitch branch of Judaism). David's uncle lived in Southern California, near Burbank, so David and I arranged to visit him, check out Disneyland, then rent a car and head up the coast to meet with Harvey outside of Napa.

On the flight to LA, I developed a head cold. When David's uncle fetched us at the airport, I complained that my head hurt and I wasn't feeling well. He stopped at a drugstore so I could get some medicine, then took us to our accommodations. Turns out, David's uncle had a converted storage facility, so we ended up sleeping in a storage unit.

That night, I had a strange dream that affected me for the rest of my life. It was a like a kaleidoscope being rotated, images fractured and changing. The content of the dream spanned decades of my earlier life and into events that hadn't happened. Yet.

Even though I had only been working on the *Genesis II* idea for a few months—and hadn't made much progress— when the dream shifted into the future, I experienced myself walking down the stairs at my parents house, carrying a binder filled with pages from a graphic novel. (I knew this was in the future because my father—reclined in his Barcalounger—had much more gray in his hair.)

In the dream I also saw myself attending a number of fan conventions, breaking any number of Sabbath laws, and attempting to justify doing whatever I wanted to do.

The scene skipped to my family gathered around the

table, with one person I didn't recognize. There was a deep sense of loss and sadness. In the dream, I had the sensation I'd been pulled outside of my body, observing this scene from nearby, and I wasn't sure if I was alive or dead.

When I woke, I experienced a mixed reaction. The part about the graphic novel buoyed my enthusiasm, but the part about being displaced from my body was scary. Had I died? Had someone else died?

These things were on my mind as we continued our trip. David and I stopped at a Chabad community in Palo Alto, and I told a rabbi there about the dream.

"You have a choice," he told me. "The dream is showing you what life will be if you go down one path. But you can change it, maybe, if you observe the commandments and approach life in a more practical way."

After that, I did try, though I still often chose to follow my own path. I never forgot that dream, and in the coming years, I would be reminded of it often.

Other things however began to pass me by. The grind of working full time left me little space during the week to pay attention to events or changes in life around me. It's no surprise, then, that I didn't find out right away about a major incident in Elkins Park. In the early morning hours of January 11, 1994, a fire ripped through the old abandoned high school building! Fortunately, the buildings were empty and no one was injured, but it was the end of an era. The building was historically significant, not only as the earlier home of Cheltenham High School and the Beth Jacob Day School, but as the birthplace of the Orthodox Minyan of Elkins Park—soon to be renamed Young Israel of Elkins Park!

While working at World Marketing Services, I made a friend, Ted Perkoski. Ted had met my parents and we got along pretty well. He won a special trip as the "employee of the month" and invited me to accompany him to Yosemite Valley, which was a beautiful and fun excursion.

In 1995, I traded shifts so I could have a week to go to Paris. During my earlier Israeli trips, I'd traveled through London, but I'd always wanted to visit Paris. My sister Lori had been several times, and she suggested a specific hotel on the southern bank of the Seine. (Just for fun, I rolled up my pant legs and waded into the river. Why? Just to prove that I was in-Seine!)

I arrived in Paris on Friday morning and went to the Eiffel Tower to eat at the Jules Verne restaurant on the second landing. As I exited the first set of elevators, I noticed a very peculiar photograph on the wall. It was a black and white photo, approximately 12x18 inches, of two German SS officers posing and smiling in front of the Eiffel tower during the occupation of Paris in WWII. It seemed unconscionable they would have that photo of two Nazis standing shoulder to shoulder, grinning like they were on vacation. That image haunted me for a long time.[5]

That set a tone for the evening. The sun was going down,

and it was Shabbat, but there I was, breaking the rules, dining on salmon in a fancy restaurant instead of being in a synagogue for prayers.

The food was delicious, but as night fell, so did my mood. I was struck by the fact I was in the most romantic city in the world, in a fine restaurant, watching the lights of the Paris skyline flaring to life, and I was completely, utterly alone. It was such a beautiful moment, and one I wished I could share with someone I cared for—preferably an attractive woman who also cared for me—but I was experiencing it all by myself. It hurt, and the loneliness drove me to tears.

I hoped to rebound from that sadness by visiting Musee d'Orsay. It was spectacular and one of my favorite museum experiences of all time.

During that trip, I had a lot of run-ins with Parisians who were rude to me because I didn't speak French, and an equal number who were happy to overcharge me because I was an ignorant tourist. I realized I'd been paying between $8 and $10 for a bottle of Coke.

On Tuesday, I made it to the Louvre, but I arrived late enough in the day and realized I wouldn't have time to see the entire museum. I did make it to the Mona Lisa and asked someone to use my camera to take a photo of me standing there. Unfortunately, mere minutes after the photo was taken, the camera stopped working. (I later had it looked at but was told the camera was broken and the film unretrievable.)

Disappointed, I decided to check out the gift shop to see if there was a resource that would help fill in the gaps I would be missing due to my limited time. CD-ROM discs were a big technological advancement in those days, so that was my selection. But as I walked around the museum, I realized just how diverse the artworks were. And I realized the CD-ROM set I'd purchased only included the paintings of the Louvre, not any of the sculptures, artifacts, and other artwork on display. I hustled back to the gift shop and found a thick, heavy book filled with beautiful photographs that was more representative of the museum experience.

I took the book and CD package I had purchased to the sales clerk and indicated I'd like to make an exchange. The CD package was $80 and the book was $55, so I didn't think there would be a problem.

"No, no, no," the clerk said, dismissively. "You can only exchange for something more, not for something that is less."

I was so angry at being talked down to and taken advantage of, I marched to the Gare du Nord station and asked how much it would cost to take the Eurostar train to London. Before purchasing the ticket, I phoned a friend who lived in Manchester and said, "What are you doing tomorrow?"

He hadn't even known I was in Europe, but I told him I was coming for a visit. (I didn't realize it would take me longer to get to Manchester from London than the trip from

Paris to London.) I stayed overnight, saw his house, and met his mother, then returned to Paris the next day. My last stop in Paris was at Versailles, which was beautiful and peaceful, and I had a wonderful time there. It really helped salvage what had turned into an unpleasant French excursion.

On Thursday afternoon, I took a flight to Israel so I could spend Shabbat in Tzfat. I took a bus from Jerusalem late Friday morning and made it just before sundown. I was able to spend the night at Ascent of Tzfat, then headed back to the States the next evening.

Before that Israel leg of the trip, and at the airport in France, I'd overheard two FedEx employees who had just returned from the French Riviera, where they had gambled and partied. One guy said to the other, "Can you believe it? Seventy dollars for a Coca-Cola?"

I looked at them and said, "You just made my day. I thought I was getting suckered at $10 a bottle."

Bomb Squad

On days I worked, I called my mother during my lunch break. On October 10, 1997, it was my father's birthday. I called home at lunchtime, and my mother didn't answer. This was very unusual, so I tried again on my break. Again, no answer. That made me nervous.

When I got home, I learned of my parent's very eventful day.

My father had recently decided to sell his pharmacy and retire. Part of closing or selling a pharmacy is to make a detailed inventory that must be reported to regulatory agencies to ensure controlled substances don't get lost—or stolen—in the shuffle. My father had made the list of his modern-day pharmacy inventory, and he included details of items that had been stored—untouched—in the basement of the building since it had been owned by Mr. Axelrod.

My mother was my father's right hand; she took care of the household business and he trusted her with everything. She usually stayed out of the pharmacy business, but in this case, she had offered to call the agency and read the inventory to them, item by item. When she got to the line that read, 'picric acid, 'the agent on the phone said, "Can you repeat that ma'am?" She repeated it and he said, "We're going to have to send a bomb squad to that location."

Pharmacies at the turn of the century had kept picric acid on hand. It was used as a chemical testing agent and was useful for burns, malaria, herpes, and smallpox. According to internet searches, it was used to help burn victims in the Hindenburg disaster and as a treatment for trench foot for soldiers in WWI.

If not stored properly, it becomes crystalline and unstable, with a chemical structure similar to TNT. The picric acid in my father's pharmacy had been in the basement for decades. Dad may have literally been operating his business atop a powder keg!

My mother, always quick on her feet, heard 'bomb squad' and said, "Can you hold off ? That could cause a panic. I'll go to the store and my husband and I will get everyone to leave in an orderly fashion, then you can come in."

And that's exactly what happened. They quietly, but quickly, closed the store and got everyone out. The bomb squad came in full protective gear and removed the picric acid, without incident. There were several fire trucks on hand, just in case.

When the fire fighters found out it was my dad's birthday, they serenaded him and let him sit in the fire truck.

The story made the evening news telecast in Philadelphia, though a lot of people probably didn't see it. Yom Kippur started that night, at sundown.

Dad

Mom

Mom & Dad joined under the sign for the Pharmacy, at it's closing, fall, 1997.
It was in our family for over 35 years.

Comic-Con

I expanded my convention experience, traveling to my first San Diego Comic-Con. In addition to enjoying the convention, I was hopeful I could make connections and meet people who might be helpful in seeing the dream of the *Genesis II* project come to fruition.

That first Comic-Con was still mostly comic book vendors. Every year there were more toy vendors and media companies vying for attention. (By the time I attended my last Comic-Con in 2006, it had transformed into a pop-culture "Hollywood South" phenomenon!)[6]

On my way back to Philadelphia, my eyes began to bother me. They were teary and wouldn't stop watering. My mother took me to our eye doctor, who seemed unconcerned. "It's a stye, don't worry about it. I'm leaving for vacation, but here's the number of a colleague if you don't get better."

Well, it didn't get better, so I went to the other doctor. He called me in from the waiting room, took one look at me, and yelled, "Get out of my office, right now! I'm going to have to sanitize everything!"

It turned out I had viral conjunctivitis, which is highly contagious. The doctor was mad my eye doctor had referred me. For a whole month, I was isolated and had to be careful of anything I touched. I got treatment at Wills Eye Hospital, and I had to put drops into my eyes three times a day. It didn't clear up completely, but it was manageable and I was no longer contagious.

After a month away—and secluded from the world like a pariah—I returned to work. One of the employees said, "Ted, you haven't been around much."

I told them about my eye condition and Paul Bruno—who was also a trucker, in addition to working at World Marketing—piped up: "I had that. I tried everything. Even considered surgery. Tearing up all the time, couldn't get it to stop. They couldn't do anything about it."

"How long did it last?" I asked.

"Ten years."

Ten years? That was nuts! I believed Paul, but I also hoped he was wrong. (Turned out, he was right. My eye issue lasted almost exactly ten years, and then, one day, it was over.)

World Marketing Winding Down

TWA entered its second bankruptcy in 1995. After they restructured, our company received a letter from TWA that basically said, "Thanks to the wonderful work of World Marketing and Travel Bargains, we were able to sustain the airline for an entire month while we worked to reorganize."

Several of the vice presidents saw the writing on the wall, though, and bought the company from TWA. At that point, we still sold TWA fares, but we added other airlines to our offerings.

In 1996, Southwest Airline celebrated its 25th anniversary by offering really cheap airfares, promoted via newspaper advertisements. To counter their promotion, other airlines made matching offers, so for about a month, people could get ridiculously inexpensive airplane tickets from a number of competing companies.

During this hubbub, I was manning the phones at World Marketing. One gentleman who called said, "You're Travel Bargains, right? What's the best you can do for a flight from Cincinnati to San Antonio?"

"That fare is $50, round trip," I answered. "And I can book that for you right now."

"Fifty dollars?" he replied. "I can get that rate from any of the airlines. I thought you could get me a bargain! Thanks for nothing."

When he hung up the phone, I was struck by how people's perceptions could be a bit screwy. No matter what, you'll never make everyone happy.

The explosion of TWA 800 in July of 1996 was a difficult experience. I had flown that flight during my trip to Paris a year earlier. It also started TWA toward its third bankruptcy.

By 1999, things at World Marketing were not great. They were downsizing and reorganizing. It wasn't the best job in the world, but if I could stay there a little longer, I would be vested in the pension program. I tried to hang on as long as I could.

Then it was announced the whole operation would be

moving to New Jersey. Since I didn't drive, there was no way to make it work, so I didn't continue my employment after the move. (Unfortunately, the company went belly up less than a year later.)[7]

A Brief Diversion

June of 1999 I was unemployed. I worked on the *Genesis II* project and found a part-time job with Medical Phone Company in Bluebell. Again working the phones, I contacted doctor's offices and did marketing for various pharmaceuticals. We also did surveys on behalf of drug manufacturers.

The company really didn't have its act together, but one benefit of that job was that I reconnected with Alfredo Valencia. The Data Group had also gone out of business, and Alfredo was working at Medical Phone as a manager in the packaging room.

Five months into my time there, I arranged for some time off. I got a good fare and flew to Florida, where my friend Ted Perkoski had relocated. We went to Disney together, and I got a hotel in Orlando. I got a three-day stay for agreeing to hear a one-hour presentation. Unfortunately, it was one of those time-share situations, where we were pressured to buy into a vacation program. A free ride is never free.

Ted was perturbed, and I felt bad I'd put us in that

situation. I also felt bad for the lady pitching the time-share, because I wasn't buying anything.

I felt bad about taking time off, so I called work on Monday to check in. I didn't recognize the person who answered, but I said, "This is Ted Rickles. I'll be reporting for my regular shift on Wednesday."

The voice on the phone said, "What do you mean? Who is this?"

I repeated my name and said, "I'll be back to work Wednesday."

"Oh, really? When did you last work here?"

I was confused by the way the conversation was going, but I told him I'd worked there the prior week and had just taken a brief trip.

"Nobody's working here," the guy said. "The company's undergoing major renovations. They sent all the employees home. Didn't they tell you?"

No one had told me anything. In the span of a week, my job had disappeared. There was some chance they might call me back at some point, but at that moment, I was out of a job.

"Listen," I said. "If I file for unemployment, are you gonna fight it?"

The person I was talking to told me to hold on a second, then when he got back on the phone, he told me he'd talked to personnel and they wouldn't fight it if I filed for unemployment.

I went back to Philadelphia without a job. It wasn't a big loss. I'd been making way less money than I had at World Marketing. But it was still a blow.

Laura's father was in a nursing home and not doing well. Laura and I hadn't been in contact in a couple years. She'd married Gary, but that marriage had been annulled, and she was living in Florida with a man I didn't know, Richard.

She called and said she was coming to visit her father and wanted to see me. We met up, and while I didn't get to know Richard well, I immediately liked him better than I had Gary.

Laura and I went to visit her father. Her dad was frail but seemed stable and in decent health. Laura was returning to Florida the next day, but I told her dad I would come back for a visit after my brother's graduation.

My family celebrated my brother's graduation in Wisconsin. While we were there, I got a call from Lou, who told me Laura's father had passed away. I tried to get ahold of Laura to express my condolences, but I was unsuccessful. However, Lou had also given me a phone number to reach Allen Kessler, Laura's brother. I did speak with Allen briefly, and at least had the opportunity to express my condolences on the passing of their father. Bill Kessler had been a kind man. I'd seen much of his brightness and optimism reflected in Laura, as well.

Laura had told me Richard was kind of jealous, so I didn't pursue any sort of connection with her. Despite our rocky history, I still cared for Laura and felt I owed her some credit for my academic career and even getting me started in marketing, which had helped me professionally. I missed hearing from her and having that connection.

8

NEW MILLENNIUM

Progress and Setbacks

Thankfully, my unemployment was approved, based on my wages at World Marketing—rather than Medical Phone—which meant I had a bigger safety net.

I leveraged this to my advantage and focused on deeper development of the *Genesis II* project. In the summer of 2000, I took a trip to California to research and scout locations for the book.

In the original movie, the main character, Dylan Hunt, had been trapped in suspended animation in 1979 when his laboratory—deep inside Carlsbad Caverns, New Mexico—is buried in an earthquake. He wakes in 2133, in a post-apocalyptic world. Civilization has been mostly destroyed, and there are isolated colonies trying to rebuild.

Hunt is found by PAX, a group of scientists and

peacemakers who are attempting to preserve what little technology remains and restore a peaceful civilization. Through a series of twists and turns, Hunt is led to doubt the motives of PAX and tricked into helping an aggressive, power-hungry regime, the Tyranians. When Hunt realizes they want his 20th-century knowledge to try to activate nuclear missiles—and not to repair their failing power plants—he leads a violent revolt and sabotages their nuclear device.

Returning to PAX, Hunt reluctantly agrees to join their efforts to build an idealistic society.

My sequel would pick up where the movie left off, with Hunt working with PAX. I studied the Dramatica theory of story development and was trying to build a rich, layered story with complex characters and a gripping theme. I began to outline and write short pieces of the story.

I wanted it to be set in southern California, in the rural areas north of LA. I had done research and secured topographical maps, but I wanted to understand what that rural area of California looked like.

On my way to Comic-Con, I built an extra trip into my itinerary. I flew to Santa Barbara and arranged with Blue Sky Tours to have a driver and vehicle for the day.[1] I had an Olympus 35mm camera and plenty of film to document the landscape and have reference materials for the illustration of the graphic novel. Using a Magellan GPS device, I kept track of where each photo was taken so I could later look at the topographical maps and match the visual with the map.

The driver picked me up in the late morning, and we traveled toward Ojai. I took a lot of photos. Halfway through the route I wanted to photograph, the driver said, "Yeah, I have an appointment at four o'clock. I've gotta be getting you back."

This was news to me. "You didn't tell me this before," I said. "I thought I had the whole day."

"Yeah, well, I'm telling you now."

This guy was my only way back to the airport. What else could I do?

I started taking pictures more rapidly, trying to squeeze as much research out of the situation as possible, but the driver was more and more antsy. "One more picture," I said, and I ran down the road to get the last shot. After I took it, I realized I was 75 feet from the guy and his little bus, and I didn't trust him. I was afraid he'd take off without me, so I turned quickly, caught my foot in a break in the pavement, and started the slow-motion fall you experience when an "Oh, shit!" moment happens.

I twisted as I was falling to protect the camera, so my body took the brunt of the fall. My leg went numb, and I couldn't get up. I was immobile, in the middle of the road in Ojai, scared a car would come along and run me over.

The driver took a long time to notice I was down—he was sulking and "over it," I'm sure—but he finally rolled the minibus down to where I lay, opened the folding door, and watched as I crawled into the narrow stairwell.

By the time he got me to Santa Ynez hospital, my leg had blown up like a Volkswagen. It was so swollen, they couldn't get an adequate X-ray. They gave me a pair of crutches and a compression boot, and I went back to the airport.

One serious problem: I'd have to change planes at L.A. Airport. The plane to LA was a small "puddle-jumper," and the stewardess had to check my crutches. When we landed after the short flight, the pilot handed me my crutches at the bottom of the steps, but one side wasn't locked in. It collapsed under my weight and I fell again, on the tarmac, before boarding the next flight to San Diego.

I stayed at the Grand Hyatt in San Diego. The staff tried to help as much as they could. They brought me extra pillows to rest my leg on. In the middle of the night, I went down to the desk to see if they had a screwdriver I could use to tighten the crutches that seemed to always be collapsing. The staff jumped right to helping me get it fixed. It was the height of hospitality.

I spent most of Comic-Con in a wheelchair, which was a drag. It did help me get a little sympathy from Chase Masterson, one of the beautiful actresses of *Star Trek: Deep Space Nine* when I met her. I also met some well-known comic book artists and saw Will Eisner, a comics legend.

I struggled through and made it back home to Philadelphia. The staff at Santa Ynez had told me I should get my leg looked at by an orthopedist, so I made an

With actress Chase Masterson. San Diego Comic-Con 2000.

Cruising San Diego Convention Center. San Diego Comic-Con 2000.

At San Diego, Comic-Con. 1998 w/Will Eisner.

At San Diego, Comic-Con. 2002 w/Margot Kidder[2]

appointment. I wore the boot I'd been given in California when I went in. The doctor said he didn't think anything was broken, and I should keep wearing the boot and take it easy for a while.

About a month later, I got a statement from the orthopedist. They had billed my insurance company for the visit and for the boot I had already been wearing. I made sure to call the insurance company and let them know, "These guys are trying to pull a fast one on you!"

9/11 Aftershocks

When 2001 rolled around, my high school reunion committee was preparing for our 20th reunion celebration. A former classmate, Bob, and I were in charge of putting together a biography booklet to be distributed at the event. We sent a survey to the members of our graduating class to collect information like where they were living, what they did for their career, if they had a spouse and family, any traveling they'd done, and other "catch us up on your life" details.

We were late to send the survey out before the planned November reunion, so it was late August before we mailed the packets. We hoped to get them returned quickly so we could assemble the booklet prior to the event. They began hitting mailboxes all around the country as September dawned.

And then, on September 11, 2001, the whole world paused in the wake of the attacks on the Twin Towers and The Pentagon. In the aftermath of that event, we learned one of our classmates, Andy Kates, had been employed in the World Trade Center, and he'd lost his life that day. Andy and I had been in biology class together in high school. I didn't know him well, but he seemed like a nice guy.

How strange that about the same time he'd received a reunion packet—with a survey about how his life was going and an RSVP card to let us know if he'd be joining us— Andy had left home like any other day and never returned to his family.

The events of 9/11 shook the culture of America, and it was sometimes difficult for me to navigate. Like others, I was deeply saddened by the loss of life and the destruction that rained down that day. But I was still uneasy about trusting the government—as I had been since my experience at the CIA in high school—and I was leery of the "mandate for war" the US government assumed after the terrorist attacks. All of this added to my general unease about the future, and my recurring premonitions about a massive, destructive event.

In 2002, during the buildup to the invasion of Iraq, I ran into Alfredo while riding a train from Wyndmoor station to center city.[3] It turned out he lived not far from me in the Chestnut Hill Village apartments on Stenton, between Willow Grove and Ivy Hill Road.[4]

Nov. 2001-CHS'81 20th year reunion (Memorials) at Melrose Country Club, Cheltenham, PA. (David Dornstein image bk. Cornr)

Alfredo and I talked about the impending war and how we thought things were going to get much tougher. It was a tense time. No matter what Saddam Hussein did, President Bush continued to raise the bar of expectations. Clearly, he'd already decided he was going to finish the work his father had started. It didn't matter that Iraq wasn't directly responsible for 9/11. That was a convenient excuse for Bush's war-footing fervor.

Alfredo confided in me that he'd had a vivid dream in which he was riding the PATCO train returning to Philadelphia from New Jersey. In the dream, there was a sudden flash, like an enormous bomb had exploded over Philadelphia. Dream Alfredo had turned to another passenger and said, "Is this really happening?" The answer from the other passenger in the dream was, "Yes, it's happening."

Alfredo's dream intrigued me. It coincided with my experiences in Center City, when I could *feel* parts of the city destroyed around me. I told him about my experiences, and he nodded as if I'd said something obvious. "It sure seems like something bad is going to happen," he said.

We talked more about this over the years. We both had the same feeling: Whatever this perceived future devastation was, it would begin in the 2020s. Sharing these concerns that had haunted me for decades with someone who understood what I was talking about was a relief. At the same time, it was a little scary that someone else—someone I respected and looked up to—had experienced similar forebodings.

Alfredo and I spent more time together. We'd share with each other whenever we had one of those perception experiences. At times, the psychic perceptions would be much stronger, more real. Often, our premonitions would coincide.

"Did it feel especially post-apocalyptic to you today?" I'd say.

"Yes," Alfredo would reply. "Yes, it did."

I even tested him, just to see if he was humoring me. It turned out Alfredo had felt the destruction in many of the same areas that were so strong for me, including the east side of City Hall and the Market Street train station.

Suncoast

I was an avid collector of movies and videos, and a frequent visitor to Suncoast Motion Picture Company, a sister company of the music retail store, Musicland. Most people preferred to rent movies—over time, Blockbuster and Hollywood Video outlets became ubiquitous—but I preferred to own the VHS tapes so I could watch them over and over again. Every Thursday, I made two stops at the Plymouth Meeting Mall: the comic store and Suncoast.

In December 2000, as the gift-buying season was heating up, I was still unemployed, so I told the Suncoast manager I was looking for work. He had a part-time opening, which seemed like a great fit. I could work there—as a movie buff, this seemed like a dream opportunity—and have time to continue working on the graphic novel. I joined the staff for the last push of the holiday season and stayed as a part-time worker.

At a job fair early the next year, I learned of an opening with Amtrak. These days, reservations are taken via an automated phone system "Julie," but in 2001, they still hired a preponderance of real, live people to be reservation agents. Because of my interest in transportation, I really liked the idea of working for Amtrak. And I had experience—the ComPass project, my DVRPC internship, and taking plane reservations—which I figured made me a solid candidate.

During the pre-interview, I asked about being off to observe the Sabbath, and the Amtrak representative was straightforward: "You *will* be working weekends." Like most entry-level jobs, the shifts were subject to a seniority-based bid system. I was excited for the opportunity, and nervous about being discriminated against, so I didn't tell them my religious reasons for asking about the work schedule. I remembered how I'd been plucked from the first orientation at World Marketing Services when I expressed a desire for a religious accommodation. I didn't want that to happen again.

I'd been observant for years at that point, but I debated with myself about possibly working on the Sabbath, at least for a short while. Once I had my foot in the door at Amtrak,

I'd see if I could adjust things in favor of my religious convictions. I went through the drug test, a competency test, and a personal interview, and I was offered a job.

The Amtrak mid-Atlantic call center was located in a warehouse on Roosevelt Boulevard in northeast Philadelphia. My parents and I found an apartment that I planned to lease. They weren't too happy because the route to walk to work included crossing Roosevelt Boulevard, which had a reputation for pedestrian–car accidents. But this was my chance to have a good job, my own place to live, and greater independence.

Until I was sure Amtrak would work out, I didn't officially give up my Suncoast job. I took some time off for the Amtrak orientation.

There were about 40 of us at the orientation, and I sat through the first hour, hardly hearing what was said. My heart was beating fast. There was a lot riding on that day. At the first break, I made a beeline for the personnel office.

"I'm here for the orientation," I said to a clerk there. "I have a big question. How long is the average period of time before a new hire gets weekends off?"

The guy pointed to two very high stacks of folders, each stack with several hundred personnel files. "See that pile on the left? The people who have been here six or seven years? They get weekends off."

The guy at the pre-interview hadn't been kidding. "That's what I needed to know."

That was too long to deny my Sabbath duties. I knew what I had to do, even though I was giving up a good job with a lot of perks. The personnel director was in a meeting, so I told the orientation teacher, "This is a mistake. I shouldn't be here."

"You got the job," she said. "What are you talking about?"

I told her I was quitting, asked if I could keep the Amtrak coffee mug I'd been given, then I went straight to the apartment and canceled the pending lease. Three weeks later, I received a letter from Amtrak telling me I would never be eligible to work for them again.

It wasn't much later that Amtrak introduced Julie, the "virtual assistant" that displaced a lot of call center agents, so I probably wouldn't have worked there long, anyway. But I did feel bad about what had happened. If I had listened to the answer I'd been given initially, I'd have saved Amtrak— and myself—a bit of grief.

I went back to Suncoast and resumed my work there. I was a good employee, even "employee of the month" a few times. I also continued to be one of the store's biggest customers. A lot of my paycheck was turned right back over to Suncoast as I curated my movie collection.

One benefit of the job—compared to telemarketing and phone sales—was I got to know some of the customers, especially those who came in regularly to buy classic movies or reserve upcoming new releases. A lot of our repeat customers came in four or five times a year, but we had a dedicated group of 30 or so who visited weekly. There were some interesting characters in the bunch. (Did I fall into that category, when I'd been "just" a customer?) I got to be friendly with a lot of folks, and even befriended two of the movie buffs: Arthur Tobias and Henry Fairlane.

Arthur Tobias was a gentle giant—tall, nearly bald, and a baby-face—with a voice like a radio announcer. His deep "Hello Ted" resonated through the store. He was a big fan of *Voyage to the Bottom of the Sea* and all manner of science fiction. We had a lot in common.[5]

Arthur was older, and I think he saw me as a son figure. He lived in Ambler and worked for a publishing company that made word-search puzzles. Art wasn't in good health, but he tried to keep active when he could. We met for lunches and other activities. I told him about the progress I was making with the graphic novel, and he was encouraging and supportive.

Arthur could be very spiritual and was often thoughtful and highly ethical. He related to me a personal account of how he'd written to author Harlan Ellison over some activity involving Ellison's work that had concerned Art—and that he felt Ellison should be made aware of. Arthur and his family had originally lived in New York, before he moved to Ambler. As a science fiction aficionado, and denizen of the Big Apple, Arthur, like so many others, had visited Jerry Ohlinger's "Movie Material Store" when it was in Greenwich Village. As a frequent shopper, Art noticed that Ohlinger's was selling mimeographed copies of numerous film and television scripts and other works of Ellison. It seemed clear to Art that Ellison was not being compensated in any way from those sales. Art reported that he had sent a letter to that affect, advising Ellison of the situation and the unfairness of it. In an interesting turn, Ellison apparently never wrote Arthur back, personally, but it seems Ellison remembered him in the acknowledgments section of his definitive compilation: *The City On The Edge of Forever* (1995).[6]

One thing Arthur and I had in common was Arthur's vivid and amazing dream life. He shared one dream I remember particularly well. Art dreamed he was in a modern-day world where everything was different because Hitler had been killed and WWII hadn't happened. In this alternate timeline, millions of Jews hadn't been killed in the Holocaust.

In the dream, Arthur asked, "So what about Israel?"

And the response he got was, "What Israel? There is only Palestine."

In the dream world that had been spared the brutal Nazi crimes against humanity, there had been no push to establish a nation for the Jewish people. I marveled at the amazing details of Art's dreams.

I also became friends with another regular Suncoast customer Henry Fairlane. Henry liked fantasy movies and anime—or anything related to Japan—so we didn't have as much in common, but we did go on a few adventures. One memorable escapade was when he invited me to the preview of the new *Doctor Who* series. We went to the University of Pennsylvania rotunda and got a sneak peak of the first two episodes of the reboot before it was aired on BBC America.

Eventually, I took on more responsibility at Suncoast. I became a floor manager and key holder, and I would often either open or close the store. One of the store managers I encountered was Arliss. I'd been told he was a real hard-ass type, so I was careful around him. It turned out Arliss was a kind guy, and a good manager. There was no question he was in charge, but he was fair and reasonable. After I realized that, I told him what I'd been told about his demeanor.

"You should never believe what people tell you about other people," he said. And that was solid advice.

Crashing

While working at Suncoast—and fifteen years after Barbara and I had parted ways—I had an odd experience. Several women came into the store to look at movies. One of them said, "Aren't you Ted Rickles?"

I had never seen any of the women before, so I was taken aback. "Yes," I said. "Do I know you?"

"No, no. We've heard of you, though."

This was strange. "You've heard of me?"

"You used to go out with Barbara Lewandowski. We were friends with her. She told us all about you."

I was surprised, but I asked whatever happened to Barbara. The women said they'd lost touch with her, but they'd heard she was married and had a couple kids.

Getting to and from work at the mall in Plymouth Meeting was still a hassle, but I managed. One big exception was during a massive snowstorm in late February, 2003. The roads were terrible, with snow plowed to make banks at chest level. The sidewalks were shoveled only to the width of a single person, and you could only access the sidewalks from the intersection.

I was dedicated to my job, and I knew the bi-monthly big reward points weekends always drew large crowds to the store, so I felt duty bound to brave the elements. (Plus, Suncoast was good about accommodating the observation of the Sabbath and other religious events, which I appreciated.) I left home early, knowing the trek to the bus stop would be treacherous and time-consuming.

Everything was going well. There was no one on the sidewalks, and I made slow-but-steady progress until somehow a lone pedestrian appeared at the next crosswalk. He turned into the shovel-width path, with four feet of snow bank on the road side and several feet on the other. There was nowhere to go, and he was slowing me down. Suddenly, I was in jeopardy of not making the bus.

At the next block, I decided to leave the igloo maze of the sidewalk and make a run for it on the street. There was very little traffic, and the plowed street had been salted and wasn't slick. I took huge strides, running faster than I'd ever run before—so fast, I almost couldn't believe it.

As I was running, into my head popped the 10th verse from Psalm 147: *He does not desire the might of the horse, nor does He take pleasure in the legs of man.* At just that moment, I felt a presence to my right, then a sharp pain in my calf. I collapsed, looking back to see who had kicked me, but there was no one there. I thought, *It must just be a charley horse.* I still needed to make the bus, so I struggled to my feet, limped the last 200 feet, and made it just in time.

Deposited at the mall bus stop, I still had to traverse the parking lot. The short rest hadn't helped. My leg was a throbbing mess. I staggered, through the mall entrance, weaving past store fronts, and knocking into trash cans along the way. I took the escalator to the store, limped in, and collapsed into a corner. Arliss was concerned and went to the mall's CVS to get some IcyHot, which didn't really help. He offered to let me go home, but I felt it was my duty to be there, so he assigned me to work the register.

At the end of my shift, my mobility was still compromised, and I dreaded the return trip across the dark, icy lot. I volunteered to stay later, which wasn't a smart move. By the time I left, the pain and weakness in my calf was informing me that the typical 25-minute walk home from the bus stop would easily take an hour or more.

On the bus, I had a brief reprieve as my mind was preoccupied with another matter. There was a woman on the bus I recognized from my tenure at World Marketing Services, and I was trying to remember her name. When I finally recalled it—Kim—I started up a conversation. Another bad move.

Engaged in the act of discourse, I missed my stop at Willow Grove and Stenton Avenues and didn't realize it until I was at the Ivy Hill Road stop. Now, I would have an even longer walk home.

I waved to Kim, thanked the bus driver, and struggled down the steps. Just as I stepped onto the street, there was a loud *bang*, followed by a second impact. It sounded like an explosion, and the bus leapt up a foot off the ground and forward. A car had plowed into the back of the bus, and another slid into the first.[7] Had I been in the stairwell a fraction of a second longer, I would have been ping-ponged in that metal box, and my leg might have been damaged even more!!

Emergency vehicles started to arrive, and at least the bus passengers seemed to be okay, so I started my long, limping journey. Painstakingly, I plodded back up the hill to the intersection I'd missed at Stenton and Willow Grove—where I should have gotten off—then made my way towards home. More snow had fallen, and the sidewalks were treacherous, and I ended up falling again. I was down on the ground, cold, in agony, and I wanted to cry.

Just then, another bus came along, which was odd. Busses don't usually go up Willow Grove after 7pm. Amazingly, the driver who stopped and opened the door for me was one I knew. He told me there was an accident blocking the regular route, so he was driving up Willow Grove. He let me get on the bus and took me to within two blocks of my home.

It's difficult to wrap my mind around the flow of causality in that situation. Even if I had gotten off at the right stop, the pain and poorly walkable sidewalks could still have had me on the ground, crawling and crying in a short period of time. In that scenario, the bus accident might not have happened at all. On the other hand, if I'd exited the bus any slower, I would have been gravely injured in the crash. And if the crash hadn't happened, the other bus wouldn't have been on Willow Grove Avenue to find me, and after another fall I wouldn't have made it home without help. I felt bad that my inattention had been at least partially to blame, but I also felt like G-d was looking out for me.

I was in a lot of pain, and my parents tried to tell me to not go to work the next morning, but I still felt a responsibility to be there. I used the crutches from my California spill, and my parents drove me to the bus stop on Friday morning so I didn't have to walk as far. At the end of my shift, they likewise met me at the Stenton & Willow Grove Avenue stop so I didn't wait in the cold or risk more pain in walking.

It was Friday night and all I wanted to do was have the family Sabbath meal, rest, and recover, but the pain got worse. I knew things weren't right, but my parents counseled me to wait and see how I felt the next day. We had Sabbath dinner together, but even trying to rest in my dad's Barcalounger, the pain continued to ratchet up. I finally insisted I needed to go to the hospital.

Normally, we would have gone to Abington Hospital near Jenkintown, but the roads were still pretty bad and dense fog had joined the wintry mix, so they took me to Chestnut Hill. I was upset this was all happening on the Sabbath, and I felt like I was breaking the rules, even though I was having a health incident beyond my control.

The doctor who saw me wasn't a regular staff member. He was visiting on a rotation from an Air Force hospital, and he was only at the Chestnut Hill hospital every few weeks. He took one look at my calf and knew what to do. He put a long needle in my leg and used a machine to measure the internal pressure.

The other doctors gathered around, and it was like a teaching hospital as this doctor explained the why and how of what he was doing. No one else there had a clue, and if this doctor hadn't been on rotation, I might not have been properly helped. He had experience with this sort of injury, and that was a gift of G-d.

He explained to me—and the medical staff—that I had a compartmental injury. The tear of muscle or ligament I'd felt while running had caused a buildup of blood and fluid, and it was all trapped in my calf area. It was building pressure, and I was close to losing my leg or being paralyzed.[8]

My parents asked if they could move me to Abington.

They didn't want me to be operated on in Chestnut Hill. "You can make that choice," the doctor said, "but you're taking a risk for every minute pressure is building."

Ultimately, the doctor who had diagnosed the problem cut open my calf to drain the fluids, and I was never more grateful for an emergency surgery. Even more, for the near miracle of having a doctor who knew what to do.

I ended up staying in hospital for a month. After the initial surgery, I had to be taken back to the O.R. every few days so that the doctors could determine if any additional drainage would occur.[9] After about two weeks, in order to heal the wound from the surgery, a skin graft was necessary. The cosmetic surgeon came into my room full of swagger, wearing a leather bomber jacket. Dr. Brobyn said, "Listen, we're gonna get you straightened out. We'll shave a thin slice of skin from your upper leg and graft it to your wound."

I'd been through enough and didn't want another surgery, but Dr. Brobyn said to trust him, it was what I needed. When I pressed him for more information, he tried to demur, but I insisted. "Fine. Without the graft, your leg could get infected. It'll go gangrenous and purulent. It'll be oozing and gross, and it might require amputation. Is that what you wanted to hear?"

"Yes," I said. "Thank you. I just needed to know."

He muttered that no one ever made him say it out loud and told me he'd be back the following week.[10] He made sure to let me know it wouldn't be Tuesday or Thursday, because those were the days he took his plane up.

Over the weekend, I developed an allergic rash from elements in my IV, and it was decided we should delay the graft until the rash had cleared. Apparently no one told Dr. Brobyn, because he came bursting into my room before dawn, waking me from what little sleep I was getting in the hospital. I told him the surgery had been postponed, and he said, "We can do it today. No problem."

I was still reluctant, and this went on for a while. Eventually my parents showed up and suggested the surgeon come back on Thursday. (Mom hadn't been given the notice that Thursdays were for flying.) He let her know he'd be in his plane, Thursday, thank-you-very-much. This triggered a disagreement between all parties involved. The doctor wanted to do the graft right away, and my family wanted to delay.

At some point, my mother was trying to be conciliatory. She said, "Doctor, we respect your professionalism. We aren't questioning your expertise. And we certainly aren't concerned about malpractice or anything of the kind."

It was like the doctor had been struck. "You had to say that," he said. "You used the '*M*' word."

Brobyn left the room to talk to his colleagues. When he returned, he informed us (apologizing to me personally) he would not be doing my surgery and that a different surgeon would take care of it. Which is what happened, and everything turned out fine.

I underwent rehab, but I continued to experience ongoing, intermittent incidents of leg spasms in that leg for years. It often flared up after I'd exerted myself physically, but it struck at random intervals. I kept asking if it was related to the compartmental syndrome, but medical personnel insisted it was not. I wasn't convinced.

I went back to Suncoast after that, and life slowly returned to normal. A couple years later, around Christmas, a woman came in to purchase a gift. She paid with credit card, and I saw her last name was Brobyn. "Any relation to the famous plastic surgeon?" I asked.

"Why, yes. He's my husband."

"He's such a marvelous man," I said. "Does he still take his planes for a spin regularly?"

"Oh yes," she said. "Every chance he gets."

In 2006, Suncoast's parent company was downsizing, and our store was on the chopping block. (Musicland and Sam Goody stores were also disappearing at a rapid rate.) I had been a key holder and for the final shift, I was the one to pull the gate down for the close of operations. The Suncoast era had come to a close.

After the store closed, I lost touch with Henry, but Arthur and I remained in contact. He had become a treasured influence in my life.

9

MOVING FORWARD

Cruising with Takei

I signed up for a Royal Caribbean *Star Trek* cruise for December, 2003. Scant days before I had to leave Pennsylvania for the cruise, my friend Steve Hirsh got married! I was joyful that it had worked out that I could attend his simcha, and more, I wound up with a special responsibility of being one of the two witnesses to his Ketubah.[1] The ship was to leave from Puerto Rico, so I flew to Florida, then San Juan. In Florida, I also visited Disney again.

After arriving in San Juan, but Before the cruise, I visited the radio telescope at the Arecibo Observatory, which was pretty amazing! It was fortunate I left a couple days early to sight-see because a big snowstorm hit the eastern seaboard, and a lot of people were unable to catch their flights in time.

Visiting the huge Arecibo radio telescope in San Juan, Puerto Rico
shortly before the launch of "Sea Trek 2003"

There were several actors from *Star Trek: Voyager* on board—including Garrett Wang and Tim Russ—as well as George Takei, Sulu from the original series.

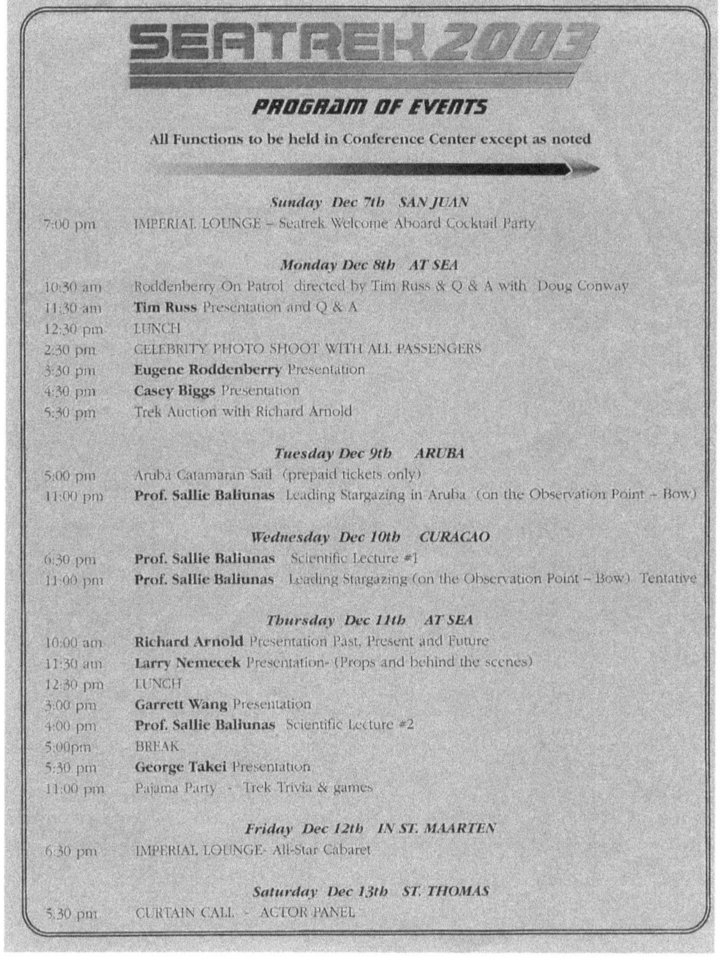

The general schedule of activities aboard ship and ports of travel for Royal Caribbean's "SeaTrek 2003"

I had attempted to meet Gene Roddenberry's widow, Majel Barrett, at a couple conventions, but things hadn't worked out. I thought she might support my *Genesis II* idea. Gene's son—Eugene „Rod" Roddenberry, Jr—was going to be on the cruise. I figured on a cruise ship, I'd have better odds at getting input from someone from the Roddenberry family. I had a five page story treatment printed to show him.

Rod and I actually sat down and went over my idea. He was interested, but he had some bad news: "To tell you the truth, I don't think we have the rights to *Genesis II*. I can ask my mom, but I don't know how much I can help you with this."

This was the first hint of a devastating reality I hadn't considered. The *Star Trek* franchise hadn't been a big hit early on. And there wasn't a lot of money to be made off a TV show cancelled after three years and a few made-for-TV movies. Gene Roddenberry had sold the rights to most of his creations to Warner Brothers to offset various financial needs.

I was too invested in the project to give up, so I decided to push forward, believing if I developed a good product, solicited the verbal support of the Roddenberry family, and found the right publisher, things would fall into place.

"Rod" Roddenberry w/me & holding a page w/photo of the "Genesis II" subshuttle.

Original studio shot w/Gene.

The cruise stopped in various ports, including Curacao and St. Maarten. When we disembarked in St. Maarten, we were told there was a private nudist resort on the other side of the island. The beach was public, but we should be careful to not trespass on the private property. Of course, this piqued everyone's curiosity. I went over there in my swim trunks, and sure enough, there were nude people lounging on beach chairs and frolicking in the waves.

I removed my glasses and trunks and waded into the crystal clear water. The day was so beautiful. I plunged under the water, and when I surfaced, there was a totally beautiful, totally naked woman standing not 10 feet from me. There I was on a tropical island, enjoying the ocean and near a completely nude brunette in her early thirties. Could things get any better?

Pushing my luck, I started to chat her up. It was a normal conversation—Where are you from? Are you staying in the resort? I came on a cruise ship, etc.—except we were both naked. Ratcheting my boldness another level, I asked her if she was at the resort alone.

"I'm here with my husband," she said, nodding in the direction behind me. When I made a full turn to my left, I saw him, not fifteen feet away in the water behind me. "And our son," she continued, as a teenaged boy suddenly turned up at the woman's right side. I was literally in the middle of a family circle where we were all nude in the water!

I wanted to panic! Aside from the absurdity of the

situation, I didn't quite know what to say. I thought for a moment and recalled the popular advice commonly given when you have to give a speech and you're nervous: "Try to imagine the audience in their underwear to make them not so intimidating." Once I knew she had a husband and son, this situation required me to do the opposite. I focused on making a thoughtful excuse—I wished her family well, but said I had to leave—all the while imagining that all of us were fully clothed and that nothing out of the ordinary was happening.

Apparently, I wasn't the only cruise member who had ventured to the forbidden resort. Back on the ship, Garett Wang made a comment as we left port: "A lot of people on that beach didn't have any business being nude." We all laughed at that.

I was on a shoestring budget, so I'd signed up for a quad cabin, sharing living space with three strangers. In the middle of the night—before I was scheduled to go on an excursion to explore some caves at our next port—my leg spasmed. I screamed and fell off the bed and onto the floor. The other guys in the cabin all chimed in, "What happened? Are you OK?" I felt really bad. It certainly wasn't my intent to wake those guys up at 2 a.m.

Later that morning, I went to the ship's sick bay. The doctor there had an accent from one of the islands. He said, "I can give you a couple pills."

"Anything," I said, "to stop the pain!"

I took the pills and headed to board the bus for the excursion. George Takei was on the bus, which was exciting, but I started to feel like someone had slipped me a Mickey. By the time we entered the caves, I was loopy, pirouetting around and walking into stalactites. I'll never forget George Takei's response, delivered in his unique, dramatic voice: "Oh, my!"

Obviously, the ship's doctor hadn't warned me to take it easy or that the pills would have side effects. I went back to confront him. "What kind of moron are you? What kind of medicine are you practicing?"

Klebs Junior

Nearly a decade had passed since I'd started my *Genesis II* project. Despite the news that the rights were owned by Warner Bros., I decided to push forward. I had the basics of the story, and I needed an artist to help sell the idea.

I worked through an artist's agency, Glass House Graphics. The owner, David Campiti, connected me with Klebs Junior, a talented illustrator and art teacher from Sao Paulo, Brazil. We communicated mostly by email and phone, but we also met in person, both at San Diego Comic-Con and when Klebs was briefly in Philadelphia.[2]

We developed artwork for about 10 pages of the book, and it looked really good.[3] Additionally, we managed to commission another major comic book artist, Luke Ross to do an exciting full-color cover! I'd spent several thousand dollars on the concept, and I was convinced the project would find an interested publisher.

After we'd produced sample pages, I took the binder of illustrations to show my father. I wanted him to see I had something to show for the years of planning and research. Just like the dream I'd had in California, I descended the staircase. Dad was reclined in his chair. His sideburns had grayed considerably. That was a nice moment, and it felt good to have something tangible for all the hard work.

"Genesis II" proposed graphic novel-promotional Inked layout artwork courtesy Klebs Junior, editing: Chuck Tooley.-p.3

"Genesis II" Proposed Graphic Novel Promotional inked layouts. Artwork courtesy Klebs Junior; editing: Chuck Tooley; p. 4

Finished Pencil - Genesis II Frontier Project - Feb. 05 ⑤

"Genesis II" proposed graphic novel-promotional Inked layout artwork courtesy Klebs Junior, editing: Chuck Tooley.-p.5

"Genesis II" proposed graphic novel-promotional Inked layout artwork courtesy Klebs Junior, editing: Chuck Tooley. -p.6

"Genesis II" proposed graphic novel-promotional Inked layout artwork courtesy Klebs Junior, editing: Chuck Tooley.-p.7

"Genesis II" proposed graphic novel. Cover design, Ted Rickles,
Artwork and coloring, courtesy: Luke Ross (2004)

My belief in accomplishing a Genesis II graphic novel was buoyed by the work being done by Herbert "Father of the Ferengi" Wright, who I met at a *Star Trek* convention. Herb Wright had worked with Roddenberry on *The Questor Tapes*, another post-*Star Trek* idea I liked.[4]

Wright was working with his friend and associate, Cash Edwards to revive *Questor* and it was in pre-production for a television series. Seeing Herb make progress toward revitalizing one of Roddenberry's other nearly-forgotten works gave me hope I could do the same with the graphic novel version of *Genesis*. (Sadly, Herb died before his project officially started shooting, and without his leadership, the *Questor* reboot never happened.)

I was nervous and excited, but I felt like momentum was growing. Over the next months, I met with several comic book companies. My hopes were high. The artwork looked great, and I thought the story was solid. I knew there were hurdles to overcome, but I also knew the Roddenberry family had some interest in seeing *Genesis II* take on a new life.

I met with the president of Dark Horse Comics, Mike Richardson, at a Comic-Con in San Diego, but they took a pass immediately. I also presented the idea to Moonstone Publishing, Arcana, and Top Cow Comics in association with their media partner, Spacedog Entertainment. There was some idea that with Top Cow and Spacedog, a comic and movie project could be developed, but they ultimately passed.

Spacedog wanted to take over the whole project, rewrite the story, and completely change everything about it. They didn't want me to be involved, creatively, though they offered to give me credit as "concept creator." After all the time, effort, and money I'd put into the project, the only company I could find with any interest in the idea didn't even want me involved.

This was a major blow. I was hurt and upset by the way things turned out.

I was disappointed, not just for me, but for the story of *Genesis II* and the legacy of Gene Roddenberry. I knew Majel and Rod were interested in the project, and I was especially sad I couldn't facilitate the resurrection of a story she had worked on with Gene all those years ago. (I even heard from a family friend that when Majel died, she still had the story treatment for my graphic novel in her bedroom.)

Over time, I began to shift my writing focus. Instead of trying to recover a long-lost fictional property already copyrighted, I decided to write a non-fiction academic book about the cultural impact of science fiction television shows.

A lot of science fiction shows were post-apocalyptic stories, and I had my own interests in that sub-genre. I began writing about science fiction television with that bias, but I eventually figured out I wanted to write about a wider range of topics.

With Majel Barrett Roddenberry at Creation Entertainment, NV

Destabilized

A couple years passed, and I lost track of Laura. She and Richard had moved, and I didn't know how to get ahold of her, even if I tried. Our contact had dwindled over the years, but it was rare to go so long with absolutely no news from her. She had a history of bad decisions that left her vulnerable, and I worried something bad had happened to her. I had no desire to contact her sister—who had been involved in some shady business, including running afoul of the FBI—and I considered hiring a private detective to locate Laura to see if she was okay.[5]

One day, I had Laura on my mind as I was walking near the Elkins Park train station. I recalled that day on Ambler campus when I had looked up to the sky and called out to G-d to send me a companion to make that difficult year more tolerable. As I stood in the station's parking lot—right across from the apartment Laura and I had shared—I was practically in tears. I said, "Please, G-d. I'd like to know, at least, if she is alive or dead."

The very next day, out of the blue, Laura called me. Since then, we've stayed in touch. She lives in Florida, and we still have difficulties navigating a friendship, but I believe it is important to overlook certain eccentricities and differences in order to maintain the connection with someone who played such a large role in my life.

Around this time, I was feeling low on many levels. After

Suncoast had closed, I'd been unemployed again, then worked part-time in sales for Business 21 Publishing. My health was on the decline. The *Genesis* project had hit a roadblock. Things weren't going well.

I saw an advertisement on the bus that said, "Are you depressed?" and I thought, *As a matter of fact, I am.* The ad was for a research study at the University of Pennsylvania, and I wrote down the number and called.

I met Dr. Jay Amsterdam, head of the psychology department. He was studying dopamine levels as a measure of depression. The study randomized a group of individuals: One group would receive 13 weeks of psychotherapy, the other would receive an antidepressant pharmaceutical.

At the start of the study, we were injected with a radioactive tracer that bonded to dopamine receptor sites in the brain and would be measurable in a CT scan. Dr. Amsterdam's associate, Dr. Andrew Newberg, was injecting me, and he said, "You're not going anywhere for a few days, right?"

"No," I said. "Why?"

"You'll be radioactive," he said. "You might set off some alarms if you had to go through security." Hmm, I thought comedically, if it could be that much of an issue, maybe next-time I should get the radiation dose from a spider bite rather than the needle. They didn't get the Spider-Man reference right away, but it still felt appropriate.

I had hoped to be included in the psychotherapy group but was given Lexapro instead. I started on a low dose, which ramped up over the time frame of the study. They paid for transportation to report weekly to a nurse and make sure things were going OK. At one of the checkups, the nurse asked if I had any unusual feelings or strange experiences. I said I was feeling a bit less depression, but there was also an odd side effect. "I've been feeling an increased need for affection. And I've found comfort in skunks."

The nurse made a note. "You said, 'skunks, 'right?"

I explained I'd obtained a stuffed-animal skunk, and I felt better when I cuddled it. The longer I was on the medicine, the more pronounced the skunk magnetism became. I bought more of them and carried one with me for comfort.

After 13 weeks, both study groups were given the radioactive treatment and scanned again to assess whether there was a dopamine difference between the therapy and the medication. Their work was reported in a series of scientific papers published between 2007 and 2012. (I still have my surfeit of skunks and love them dearly. Sadly, they are all plush toys, not real pets.)

The Lexapro seemed to have a positive impact on my depression, so I asked my doctor for a prescription. I remained on that medication for about a decade. Even with the medication, my depression grew gravely dangerous at one point, around 2006. It was the only time in my life I actually contemplated on how easy it would be to step onto a busy street into oncoming traffic. I even made my mind up to do it, but something inside spoke to me, and said, "You don't have to do it today. Just do it tomorrow."

Within a couple days, I met with a psychiatrist who had some advice that convinced me to rethink my decision. Between that inner prompting and the doctor's advice, I had enough time to change my mind before I did something I couldn't undo.

The decline in my health continued to accelerate. If my homeostasis was destabilized, I would have trouble walking. One time, I went to work at Business 21, even though I wasn't well. I wasn't making much money there, but I couldn't afford to lose out on hours.[6]

Their offices were in East Norriton, so after I took the bus to the Plymouth Meeting Mall, I had to catch another bus to get to work. On the way, I stopped in at an ATM to withdraw money, and I couldn't walk straight. It looked like I was going to fall. Someone called the police, and I had to explain I was fine, just having some balance issues.

At work, I was still having trouble. When I got up from my station to take a break, I had to cling to the cubicle walls. My supervisor saw it and asked what was wrong, then told me I couldn't work in my condition. It was the first time I'd ever been sent home because of my instability.

I started to wonder what was wrong with me.

Business 21 closed that office and offered for me to move to the South Philly office, but the pay wasn't worth the distance.

Convention Conversations

I continued to have some great experiences at conventions. I attended the 40th Anniversary *Star Trek* convention in Las Vegas. I'd met Mariette Hartley a couple times, including after she'd performed in the play, *Copenhagen* in Philadelphia, but I finally got a photo op with her at the convention.

I'd always loved Robert Culp, as an actor, and I was gushing with praise when I met him. "Everything would be right with the universe if they just made one more movie with you in it."

"That's very flattering," he said, with a beaming smile. "I appreciate it."

Instead of being glad I'd left a good impression with a favorite actor, I pressed on: "Why not? Look at Adam West. He's from your era, and he's out there making movies. You could do that, too!"[7]

Culp's smile flipped upside down. "I wish you hadn't brought up Adam West."

My knack for saying the wrong thing had bit me again. Apparently, Culp and West had some long-standing Hollywood feud left over from the 1960s. I'd have never mentioned Adam West, had I known.

A few years later, I ran into Adam West at a Wizard World convention in Philadelphia. I asked West and one of his aides, "What happened between you and Robert Culp?"

Meeting Robert Culp at the 40th Anniversary Creation Star Trek Convention in Las Vegas, NV (2006)

At first, West and the other guy were laughing about it, but I said I thought it was shameful. Culp was dead by then, and he'd apparently been really upset by whatever had happened all those years earlier.

Adam West got a bit more reflective and said, "Look, Robert was a nice guy. I respected him. I don't really know why he was upset with me."

In the end, I walked away with less respect for West. I still was a fan, but my deeper allegiance was with Robert Culp.

In 2006, I attended my last Comic-Con in San Diego. The event had grown so popular, it was impossible to find a reasonably priced place to stay.

As with all conventions, there was a lot of time spent standing in long lines. When you stand in line, you overhear a lot of conversations around you. Typically, at a convention like Comic-Con, the conversations are about an upcoming movie or a favorite fandom, but in this instance, I overheard several interesting conversations about the looming economic recession. It was an odd topic for a bunch of comic nerds, but I took note of the uneasiness many people felt.

Comic-Con attendees in the Sails Pavilion, San Diego Convention Center.
Unlikely venue for talk of an economic downturn.

Not long after, I was at a wedding with my parents and my sister Sara. We were seated with a couple who I didn't know, but we all chatted amicably. The conversation turned to the worsening economy. I'd been looking closer at the situation and was convinced the coming recession would be more than just a dip in the market.

"The whole country is gonna be hit hard by this housing thing," I said. "Everything's going belly up. It's going to be bad."

"You know this how, exactly?" the husband said.

I told him I'd been reading and listening to people around me.

He laughed it off, like I was being an alarmist. At that point his wife got involved in the conversation, and the topic of her work became a way to diffuse the difference of opinion. I found out she was a sales rep for Cepacol throat lozenges.

"I think Cepacol are more effective than other cough or sore throat lozenges on the market.," I said, trying to be conciliatory. We had a fine time talking around the table after that.

The Great Recession was in full swing between 2007 and 2009. A lot of people faced tough times. At some point, in the middle of the recession, we received a package at my parent's house: A whole case of Cepacol lozenges. I knew who had sent the gift. I supposed the wife had remembered my prediction and was offering a token of acknowledgement.

CIA, Reconsidered

Sometime around 2008, I attended a lecture at the National Constitution Center in Philadelphia. The speaker was a retired, high-ranking member of the US security apparatus. During the question portion, I recounted my experience as a high school student asking a question at the CIA headquarters. The speaker listened to what I said, but his response didn't ease the dismay I'd been feeling for nearly 30 years.

After the lecture concluded, I approached him to better understand his neutrality and he said, "I understand your distress. I had a high-level security clearance. Every day when I went to work, I still had to be patted down. I was still under intense scrutiny. I couldn't just waltz into the Capitol or bypass the screening at the White House. The consequences for one mistake were too high."

I realized, then, that the concepts of security and safety were not black and white, and while I still found the idea of using marginalized people as guinea pigs to be reprehensible, I also came to realize there were both good and bad people involved in the government, and some of those good people were just trying to do their best in very complex and dirty circumstances.

Abomination

When J. J. Abrams' version of *Star Trek* was released in 2009, I was excited to see the franchise get a fresh start. Until I saw the movie.

Despite the critical and public acclaim, I hated the movie from the beginning. I thought it was an insult to the legacy of *Star Trek* and to the memory of Gene Roddenberry. The other big sci-fi movie of 2009 was *Avatar*, and I thought James Cameron had made a more Roddenberry-esque movie than Abrams.

I despised the 2009 incarnation of *Star Trek* on so many levels. Everyone was so in love with the high-action space battles, and great character enactments, they didn't notice when Abrams re-wrote the canon of the story and destroyed the two planets of Vulcan and Romulus. And then, a colony of Vulcans were saved to ameliorate the disappointment and loss.

I immediately inferred the movie was making a sideways reference to the loss of the Twin Towers in 9/11. It was, to me, like *Star Trek* was being used subtly as a propaganda tool to tell the American people to, "Get over it." What!? I thought, *How smarmy it is to use Star Trek's history and moral high-ground to suggest it was time for the American people to "get over the nearly 3,000 deaths in those two towers!* I was practically fuming when I left the theater.

Beyond that quasi-political interpretation, the whole re-imagining of *Star Trek* as presented by Abrams departed from the original intent of Roddenberry's creation. Abrams was more of a *Star Wars* fan, and his *Trek* movies are filled with homages to *Star Wars*.

He distorted the *Star Trek* canon to promote his own fantasies. In the first movie, Captain Pike says to a young Kirk, "Join Starfleet. It's a peacekeeping armada." But an armada is a fleet of warships, not a force for exploration, advancement, and promotion of peace. It was as if Abrams painted an abstract painting using *Star Trek* colors.

My disdain for the movie was in the distinct minority. (I even asked Walter Koenig, the original Chekov, if he'd ever heard anyone complain about the Abrams film. "No," he replied. "You're the first.")

To me, the film was analogous to a Joseph Goebbels propaganda film. Abrams had snuck a lot of bad values and distorted thinking into the film and made it flashy so everyone would love it.

When the next film in the Abrams series came out in 2013—*Star Trek: Into Darkness*— they admitted they had previously, intentionally written that first 2009 film as allegorical commentary about 9/11.[8]

I've always been a big fan of time-travel stories, and there are a lot of stories about what people would do if they could go back in time. Who would they want to meet? What would they want to see? Could they affect the past in a way to shape the future for the better? In my opinion, if I could go back in time, I can think of no nobler cause than to destroy the 2009 J. J. Abrams *Star Trek* movie before it ever saw the light of day.

Friends Help Friends

My friend Art helped me get a job with the magazine company he worked for. It was just a few hours a day, transcribing and data management for the puzzles they created. It wasn't much, but it was something.

Art continued to be a strong supporter. As I shifted my focus to writing the non-fiction commentary of science fiction television's impact on the culture, he maintained his encouragement and enthusiasm.

The US Census was organizing its decennial count for 2010. I had applied for a field surveying job and was being trained. Kristl and I met for her birthday in June, and she told me she had applied to the Census as well, but they hadn't hired her.

Kristl was a great leader and organizer. After she'd left Temple, she worked at the private school her son attended. She helped grow the school. Whether it was at her son's school, or as a participant in the local planning commission, Kristl had a profound impact wherever she worked. I thought it was strange the Census Bureau hadn't hired her.

A month or two later, she'd finally been contacted, and she

was working in the field office. I was happy she was doing that, and it stoked a sort of kinship that we were working for the same organization.

Since I didn't drive, it was difficult for me to find a good opportunity for me with the Census. Finally, in August, I found an assignment I thought I could do, but I got a call that changed that course of action.

My long-time friend, Peter, had moved from Glenside to an apartment complex in Melrose Park a couple years earlier. He'd had some health problems and couldn't get around much any longer. Peter had a caregiver, but she needed time off each week, and Peter required daily assistance.

Peter asked if I could be his caregiver on the off days. I certainly hadn't done any work like that before, and the pay wasn't very much, but Peter had been such an important friend, I wanted to help. He had treated me with dignity and generosity—almost like a son—and his kindness was a major reason I'd established an enduring connection to the Jewish community.

It seemed like a slight to the Census, but my loyalty to Peter was paramount. I turned down the Census work and served as a part-time caregiver for Peter for about a year.[9]

During that time, I met another person through the synagogue, Ephraim Isaacson. He had come from New York to be near his brother, who lived in Elkins Park. We became friends and started spending time together. I introduced him to Alfredo and some of my other friends—Lou, Joe, and Kyra—who would get together regularly. Ephraim drove, so that was a nice perk to our friendship; plus, he had a bit more money and sometimes he'd say, "Dinner's on me!" which was very generous.

I told Ephriam about my background in sales and sociology, and he shared he was starting a business setting up basic websites for companies. At that time, professional websites were becoming more popular, but they were also expensive. Fortune 500 companies could afford to spend thousands of dollars to have a website, but small companies and family-owned businesses couldn't.

Ephraim had basic templates we could customize to individual businesses; that way they could have an internet presence without spending tons of money. I helped make sales calls, and Ephraim taught me the basics of coding and search engine optimization. He paid a decent wage, but the company didn't really take off the way he'd hoped.

Unfortunately, Ephraim had some psychological problems, and a series of breakdowns followed. I found out later his mental health had been part of the reason he'd left New York. There were two sides to Ephraim. One was extremely kind and friendly. The other was obsessive.

He eventually ended up in the psych ward of the Abington hospital. I went with his mother and stepfather to visit for a few minutes. The ward was small, tight, and congested, and I was sad to see him in that environment.

After he was released, Ephraim told me horrible stories

about being in a locked psych ward. "They were always watching. They even listened in on my phone calls." I felt bad for him, but I wasn't sure how much of what he was telling me was true. It seemed unconscionable.

10

DIFFICULT PERIOD OF LOSS

Slowing Down

In 2010, Alfredo accompanied me to DC to visit the Air and Space museum. There was a massive Earth Day celebration on the National Mall, including an Avatar-themed display. I got a photograph with an actor made up to look like a Na'vi inhabitant of Pandora.

In the museum, I was disappointed to see they'd moved the USS *Enterprise* from its prime location in the main hall to a more ignominious spot: a plexiglass case in the basement gift shop. The new location allowed a more thorough viewing of the model, but I thought it deserved better placement. (Eventually—after some restoration work and adding new lights—the *Enterprise* was moved to a more central and noble spot, even more auspiciously located and once again in the main hall.)

The day went well, and Alfredo and I headed back toward

the Metro station. Alfredo was having trouble walking and didn't want to get on the subway, so we hailed a cab and went to dinner in nearby Arlington. The twilight cab-ride from the mall to Arlington was breathtaking and memorable even to this day!

After dinner, we made our way back to Union Station and took the Amtrak train back to Philly. It was past midnight when we exited the local train near home in Wyndmoor. Alfredo borrowed a stray shopping cart from a nearby supermarket to help him get home. By the time we got him settled, I was feeling fatigued as well. It was very late, my parents were asleep, and there were no cabs at that time of night. I had a 30-minute walk home, and my dizziness and swerving kicked in.

After repeated stability incidents, I'd figured out that, for whatever reason, I could walk *backwards* with more stability.[1] So, I traded one behavior that causes people to stare and report me to the authorities—staggering and running into things—for another behavior that also raises eyebrows.

I walked backwards, in the dark, down Willow Grove, almost two miles. I stopped to rest at Fatty's Bar & Grill because they were still open, but I was so disoriented, I could barely sit on the stool. A waitress asked if she should call someone for me, and I told her I was fine, I just needed a minute. She was really kind. When I left, she asked if I would please call back once I got home and was safe. Otherwise she'd be worried sick. Once I finally got home, I called from the phone in my room to let her know I'd made it.

That night was a turning point for both Alfredo and me.

Within months, Alfredo's doctor diagnosed an advanced form of degenerative arthritis. Alfredo started using a cane and eventually needed a hip replacement, but he kept putting off the surgery until he was confined to a wheelchair. I've tried to help him over the years in whatever way I could.

For me, it was a slower decline, but that night certainly made me think. If a day trip to DC could have that effect on me, maybe it wasn't safe for me to be out and about as much.

Arthur's Passing

July 29th, 2010—the 18th of Av on the Hebrew calendar—my friend Arthur died of a heart attack. I was incredibly sad. Art had been such an encouragement over the years. I knew I would miss his presence in my life.

Arthur's mother and I were commiserating about the loss, and I asked for three things.

First, because Art had been so supportive of my writing, I asked if she would allow me to select a few science fiction books from his collection to further my research and have a sense of Art's continued presence in the project.

Second, Art had a collection of Hebrew texts he studied from, and I wanted to use those books to improve my own study, in Arthur's honor.

Finally, Art had a friend, Richard—a cancer researcher

in New York—with whom he studied Torah weekly, via telephone. I wanted to reach out to Richard, and Arthur's mother gave me his phone number.

"We lost a good friend," I said, when Richard and I spoke. "I'd like to study Torah, the way you did with Arthur. We can continue in his memory."

Richard agreed. We started shortly after Art's funeral and have been studying together regularly ever since. Richard is a decade older than me and someone I can count on for good advice. Each week, we go verse-by-verse through Torah and the commentaries, discussing religious topics that come up in our reading. Each week, I'm reminded of my friend of blessed memory, Arthur, who is still with us in many ways. I am honored to use his Hebrew books and continue the weekly study with Richard.

I'd held a grudge against the town of Ambler for decades. Other than Arthur—and my barber—I thought there was nothing good about the place. In the wake of Art's death, I softened my perception. My bad choice all those years earlier wasn't the town's fault. Ambler hadn't offered me the specific relief from school-induced misery I craved, but it wasn't a bad place: it had been home to my friend, Arthur. And, perhaps without Ambler, I'd have never benefitted by knowing him.

Sometimes I'm slow to release a grudge, but I think it's important to continue to grow and evolve as a person. Imperfect as I am, it's one way I try to improve myself.

Another Loss

On the one-year anniversary (on the Hebrew calendar) of Arthur's passing, I experienced another loss.

For many years, my mother and my maternal grandmother had suffered from a strained relationship. There was a family conflict sometime around 1996, after which my mother had stopped speaking to my grandmother and my aunt. This estrangement lasted almost 15 years.

My mother was so angry, she made me swear to have no contact with her mother. The situation was sad, and although I certainly agreed that my mother had been mistreated, her demands disturbed me. I'd been forbidden to have any contact with my grandmother. So, I had to go behind my mother's back. I didn't want to deceive my mother, but it was equally upsetting to not see my grandmother. I felt trapped.

I made a point to visit her, though. She also enjoyed a good laugh. At one point, I'd been downtown with Alfredo, and we passed a confectionary shop. I went in and got a special treat for my grandmother's birthday.

"It's time someone puts you in your place," I told her when I handed her the boxed treat. "There's an alligator in there, and whichever one of you moves first is gonna eat the other one."

She looked nervous, slowly undid the ribbon of the box, and carefully opened the lid to peek inside. Her eyes went wide: There really was an alligator in the box! She shut the box and said, "Is it chocolate?"

"That's right," I told her. "And since you moved first, you better eat it quick!"

By 2011, my grandmother was in her nineties and growing more feeble. She had what presented as dementia and said odd things. During one visit, she said—apropos of nothing—"Ted, you're going to live to be 64 years old, and you're going to have a good life." At one time, 64 might have seemed old, but that didn't sound nearly long enough to nearly 50 me!

Since my grandmother's health was declining, I thought it important for my mother and her to have a chance at making peace. My aunt agreed, and we had a cousin mention to my mother that my grandmother really missed her and wanted to see her.[2] (That was a slight exaggeration because, by that point, my grandmother didn't have the wherewithal to make such a request.) My mother went to visit, and when she came home, she was really glad she went.

Soon after, we visited my grandmother as a family unit for the first time in years. My grandmother sat on the seat of her walker, my mother beside her, with my father seated across the room. Out of nowhere, my grandmother rose from her seat, walked to my father, and gave him a big hug. It was a strong, lingering hug, the way you hug someone to comfort them. She then returned to her spot as if nothing had happened. My grandmother had always treated my father well, but she'd never shown physical affection in that way. A few minutes later, she repeated the same thing. She stood, walked to Dad, and hugged him. We all thought it was very strange.

The next week, my parents returned for another visit, but I decided to go with Alfredo and his friend Kyra to an air show in Atlantic City. It turned out not to be a great day, and when I got back, things were even worse. I found out the next day that my grandmother had passed away on the same date on the Hebrew calendar as Arthur—18th of Av.

My Mother's Illness

Mom had smoked since she was 15, and she'd had an occasional cough for years. After my grandmother's death, my brother gave my mother an ultimatum, insisting she go to the doctor for a checkup.

She acquiesced but remained tight-lipped about the results of her doctor visit. My father also remained mum, but Mom's demeanor changed, and there was a look in her eyes that was disquieting. We all started to suspect something was amiss. My brother and I had spoken, and he sensed something was wrong, too, but everything was hush-hush. Tension built as the Thanksgiving holiday approached.

I'd been involved in planning my 30th high school reunion, scheduled for November. Since I'd been tasked with commissioning a plaque with the names of our classmates who had passed away, I felt an obligation to be there, but I was also anxious about the growing sense of secrecy hanging over our family. I was preoccupied with the premonition that something terrible was just around the corner. I went to the reunion, even though I didn‘t want to be there. I deliberately got drunk and had a bad night.

My anxiety fed my depression, and I was in a bad state. I sat at the family Thanksgiving table thinking what a charade it was. There was a giant elephant in the room no one was discussing. We were pretending everything was OK when clearly it was not. Everything was a lie.

I was so frustrated, I took a knife and stabbed my hand a couple times, and I didn‘t care what happened to me. The pain of the cut was less than the pain of what was happening around me.

That act of self-harm scared my family, but nobody really reacted. No one called the police or tried to get me help. My wounds weren‘t life-threatening, so it was ignored, just like the poisonous secrecy hanging over us.

A while later, I finally learned what was going on. During her doctor‘s visit in October, my mother had been given an order for an X-ray of her lungs. Looking at the results, the doctor told her she functionally had one lung left due to her cancer's progression. My mother had fainted at the news. She‘d kept the diagnosis secret, but she was dying.

In the middle of all of this, my nerves were frayed for an additional reason. I‘d borrowed and over-extended my credit paying expenses for the *Genesis II* project and other questionable spending. I had tens of thousands of dollars in debt. I'd worked briefly at Corporate Call Center, helping people with open enrollment for Medicare, but between my health issues and my mother's situation, I needed to be home, so I left that job.

Bankruptcy was the only way out. My parents paid the legal fees, and the process took about a year. It was finalized early in 2012. This financial reckoning added to the ongoing anxiety of my mother's illness.

Mom celebrated her 70th birthday on December 19th, and my parents celebrated their 50th wedding anniversary on January 14th of 2012. She received chemotherapy at the Cancer Center at Abington Hospital, but I knew things were getting worse. On March 1st, she got very upset over an incident at home and suffered a heart attack.

She was in the hospital for two weeks on a ventilator. The cancer had spread, and she was unable to breathe on her own. Mom was given a choice: She could be put on a permanent breathing machine with a tracheotomy, or she could accept placement through hospice. She made the choice for hospice, and she passed away on Friday morning, at 8:20.

It was March 16th, 2012, or the 22nd of Adar, 5772.

Much like when Lou's father passed, I encountered the presence of my mother lingering around us after her death. She stayed with us a while before going on.

Reconnecting With Henry

Not long after my mother's death, Henry, who I'd lost touch with after Suncoast closed, called me. "I'll bet you wondered what happened to me!" he said.

I had other things on my mind, and we hadn't been as close as Arthur and I had been, but I told him it was good to reconnect. Henry had been through some rough times—throat cancer, losing all his teeth, living with his daughter, and struggling financially—and he thought it would be nice to get together sometime and catch up.

Henry and I began to meet occasionally, and he joined in on the activities of my friend group from time to time. In the year after my mother's death, I entered a quieter phase of life, but we still met to celebrate birthdays.

Troubles at Home

A couple years after my mother's passing, Sara was diagnosed with colon cancer. She was 48 years old at the time, and she responded well to radiation, at first.[3] However, one of the palliative care nurses told me the life expectancy of someone with stage four cancer was a year and a half.

My own health issues continued. At a wedding in 2014, I was dancing with the men of the synagogue when my back started to bother me. I went to see a doctor and got some X-rays. The disc between my L5 and Sacrum was extended and bulging 40 percent beyond normal, creating intense sciatic pain.

I investigated surgery, but it was high risk, with the reward mostly just forestalling the pain a few years and pushing the problem further up the spine. I've avoided back surgery so far. Instead, I get quarterly epidural injections that keep me going for a while, and when I could, I also did exercises designed to help strengthen the back muscles and help ease the pain.

After my mother's death, our home dynamic changed. Sara and I lived with my father, and my other siblings were living far away. I felt the firstborn's duty to try to run the household as best I could, which caused conflict between Sara and me.[4] I was worried about her health and felt she was taking needless risk. She would disappear for long periods, and I didn't know where she was. Plus, we didn't see eye to eye on how we handled our widowed father.

At some point, as the arguments escalated, a precedent was set for calling the police and having them intervene in our rows. Sadly, things were so bad, the police intervened several times.

During this time, we vetted nursing facilities to select a place for my father to live. We'd found a good spot and were waiting for his time to move. In the meantime, I struggled to keep things going. I was trying to coordinate a communication system with the three of us in the household

My sister Lori and her husband bought my father a new

iPhone smartphone. I was annoyed because I'd actually been trying to teach Dad how to use a simpler, less complicated android phone for the previous month or so, and this was an odd complication to that. The complexity of the iPhone confused him. So, while it was a steep learning curve for me, I thought I had a better chance of utilizing the iPhone for our combined benefit. I suggested we switch phones. Initially, Dad agreed and ceded the phone to me. However, when Lori called to ask how he was enjoying his new iPhone, things went wonky, to say the least!

This issue caused a family spat. My father and Sara were in the kitchen talking to Lori, who was at home in New Jersey. Lori convinced my father the iPhone had been purchased for him and he should ask for it back. I tried to explain I felt a lot of pressure to coordinate the household and medical appointments, and it made more sense for me to have the phone. I'd already set up several applications to help us all navigate household obligations and stay in touch.

"Dad," I said, "if you love me, you'll trust me on this."

My father, though, agreed with Lori and insisted on having the phone back. I felt abandoned. My father didn't trust my judgement, and that stirred a hopelessness inside me that resulted in me taking a steak knife and stabbing my hands and feet.

This was the second time I had done this, and as it was happening, I realized it was a mistake. I wasn't suicidal. I didn‘t want to kill myself. I just wanted to demonstrate how upset I was.[5]

Sara called the police, who knew where to come. I went in the ambulance to the Abington hospital, where they treated my cut hands and feet. I was completely silent. I let them treat me and position my limbs to take photographs of my injuries, but I ignored the questions they asked.

I was put into an emergency room cubicle, under close observation. Obviously, they thought I was traumatized—since I refused to speak—and possibly suicidal. They didn‘t have access to my inner thoughts, and I refused to talk to anyone. When the social worker came to interview me, I talked a little more, but I didn‘t really explain what had happened. I was still processing it, myself. ”Family conflict” was an inadequate description, but how could I convey the whirlwind of pain, loss, abandonment, grief, and frustration that erupted when I felt like I‘d lost my father‘s trust?

Even though I wasn‘t suicidal, the hospital staff recommended me for the psych ward. I was told I could voluntarily commit myself or they would file for an involuntary committal. If I committed myself, I could stay in Abington. If I didn‘t, they would have me committed at Norristown State Hospital, which had a very bad reputation and was far from home.

I chose the Abington option. The psych ward was in a different location than it had been when I‘d visited my friend Ephraim. It was a nicer place than the crowded ward he'd been in. I was closely monitored because they thought I was suicidal. I had a lot of time on my hands, so I was using the hospital phone pretty freely.

Talking to Ellie one day, she asked about the facility. "It's much nicer than when it was in the Rohrer building," I told her. While I was there, my siblings moved my father into his new home. I felt bad I wasn't there to help.

I met with the floor psychiatrist, Dr. Custer. She asked if I'd been institutionalized before, and I told her "no." She had, however, deduced that over time the Lexapro may have begun to act differently in my body. It was a potentially useful conclusion. Dr. Custer came across as a highly experienced and knowledgeable psychiatrist. But she may also have misdiagnosed me. However, She replaced my Lexapro with an antipsychotic medication that was the worst drug I'd ever taken.[6]

After the initial 72 hours, Dr. Custer tried to get a court-ordered extension to keep me institutionalized, and I had to go in front of a judge on a closed-circuit video link to plead my case.

I was told the judge sides with the doctor 90 percent of the time, so I didn't have high hopes. I told the judge calmly I wasn't suicidal. I held out my hands in front of the camera so that he could see that they were fully healed. I was respectful and pointed out that since the initial incident, I hadn't harmed myself in any additional ways.

I further stated my father was in an assisted living facility and needed me to be available. "I don't know why I'm still here," I said, in a humble, level voice.

The judge admitted he was slightly stymied and said he'd have to consider the case. A few days later, he ruled in my favor and I was allowed to leave after an 11-day stay.

Months later, I gained access to the discharge notes. Apparently, someone had been listening to my call with Ellie because Dr. Custer had documented in her notes that while I denied being previously institutionalized, I had admitted on the phone that I was familiar with the old facility. They had taken my comment out of context, thinking I'd been a previous patient rather than a visitor. Ephriam had been right all along... and I should have respected his words.

Sara's Death

After my father had entered the assisted living facility, tensions with Sara diminished. As her illness progressed, I tried to be more supportive and sympathetic. Neither of us drove, so we would hire a car once a week to go grocery shopping and visit Dad.

The medication I'd become acclimated to in the hospital had dramatic side effects. I became obsessed with potential disasters and became perpetually afraid to the point of staying in bed, covers pulled over my head, afraid to face the world. I ruminated over the household, sure the roof was about to start leaking or the water heater was ready to explode.

I felt much less stable on that medication than I'd felt before I took it. I begged the new outpatient psychiatrist to help me get off the drug, but she refused. Thankfully, one of the members of the synagogue was also a psychiatrist. At the 3-year yarzheit of my mother's passing, I approached him, practically crying because I was desperate to not feel the way that drug made me feel. He helped wean me off it.

I had canceled several events during that time because I was just too anxious. I'd planned to go see Harvey in California, but until the last minute, I didn't think I could go. With my meds adjusted, I was feeling a little better, so I made up my mind to try. Three days before my flight, I told Harvey I was going to attempt it, but I was still unsure.

I ended up talking myself into the trip, one step at a time. *You can pack, but it doesn't mean you're going. You can go to the airport, but it doesn't mean you have to get on the plane.* Once the door to the flight closed, I had no choice. Off to San Francisco, then on to the 50th Anniversary *Star Trek* convention in Vegas.

In the weeks after I returned from California, Sara's illness progressed. We made a lot of trips to the cancer wing of the hospital, the same place where my mother had been treated. As she got sicker, my brother came down from Connecticut to stay with me for a few days. He was starting a new job and had family obligations, but he made time to come down. We visited Sara in the hospice center

Sara's last public appearance – Mar. 2017 – standing side-by-side w/brother, Nathan Rickles. This was a Roaring 1920's Gala.

at Warminster and had our meals together. It was somber, but it was nice to have him in the house. I'd been living alone for several weeks, and it was lonely.

My brother asked where I wanted to live, since it would be impractical to maintain the family home with just me living there. I knew right when the time came, my first choice was to move to Elkins Park. The synagogue was there, and I felt at home there.

My sister remained positive, believing the treatments would heal her. She was courageous and strong, but she succumbed to cancer in April of 2017, during Passover. She died on the last day of Chol HaMoed, the intermediate days of the holiday week, so her burial had to wait until Wednesday. As they lowered her casket into the ground, I sensed her soul leaving the coffin.

Both of these deaths were especially hard on my father. He'd lost both his wife and a daughter to cancer.

I was reminded of that scene, just before my grandmother's death, when she had uncharacteristically given my father two mournful, comforting hugs; one for each loss he would soon endure. It seemed clear that she had somehow sensed he would need that comfort and knew she would not be there to offer it.

Realizing this also reminded me she'd told me I would live to age 64. I've often wondered if her prophetic vision for my lifespan will prove to be equally accurate.

Trying to Regain My Footing

I coordinated the emptying and cleaning of the Laverock house. There was a lot of furniture and other items to dispose of. I remember the moment they came and took the kitchen table. It had been a centerpiece where a lot of our family's interactions—good and bad—had happened. What a bittersweet moment.

My balance and dizziness issues continued. I was reluctant to apply for work because my health was so inconsistent. My aunt and uncle were worried about me, and they talked me into going to a neurologist in Flourtown. I was skeptical that the MRI the doctor suggested would show anything.

"Let's say the MRI comes back normal," I said. "Then what?"

"Then you could maybe see a psychiatric neurologist," the doctor suggested.

I had the brain scan and called to make an appointment to get the results. The nurse said, "The doctor doesn't need to see you. The results were normal." I asked about the referral to a psychiatric neurologist, and the nurse excused herself, then came back and said, "We don't make those referrals. You'll have to see your primary care physician."

My primary care physician didn't know anything about it, so I tried searching the internet. There were a handful of psychiatric neurologists in the area, and they treated children under the age of 15.

The whole episode turned me off on neurology. That doctor had done a bait and switch, just to get me to have an MRI. And, it seemed, no one could diagnose what was wrong with me.

I remember having lunch with Kristl during this time and telling her about all I was going through. She listened thoughtfully, as she always did, and said, "Maybe you have some sort of syndrome. Maybe it's not just one thing."

After looking at a few places to live in Elkins Park, I made a selection of a nice, ground-floor apartment. Unfortunately, it was leased before I could finalize things, and they only had a second-floor apartment available. I liked the area, and I took it.

When I went to sign the papers, I noticed I was permitted to have pets. I figured it wouldn't hurt to ask if this included exotic pets. "It depends on the pet," the leasing agent said.

"Skunks?" I asked.

"No skunks. No raccoons. No snakes. Will that be a problem?"

I had gotten by with stuffed animal skunks up until then, so I told her, "Nope. Not a problem."

One new apartment, furnished in the style of "Contemporary American Skunk".

11

ADJUSTING TO NEW REALITY

Overindulgence

After the period of loss and change, I needed something restorative. I planned several trips for 2018.

It started with a promotional phone call that I received. For years, I'd roomed at the Crowne Plaza in New Jersey for PhilCon, ultimately facilitating a minyan group who met during the convention on Friday night and Saturday morning for Jewish prayers. The promoter explained over the phone that I'd been a good customer, so I was eligible for a special program exploring a "new concept in leisure." How did three free days of resort accommodations sound?

My spidey sense should have been tingling, but I figured I could use the free days in conjunction with a planned trip to the *Star Trek* convention that summer in Vegas. So I took a whirlwind trip to see Harvey in Napa and then flew to Vegas. It turned out to be one of the worst trips of my life.

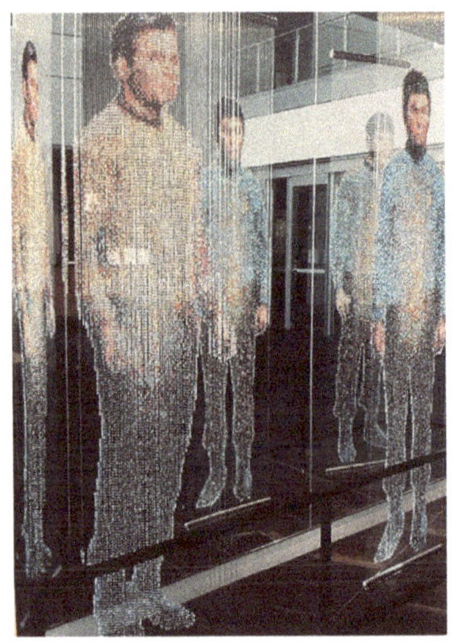

Skirball Cultural Ctr, CA.

W/Michael & Denise Okuda & Doug Drexler; NY.

W/Shatner; NY[1]

W/Keir Dullea & Gary Lockwood; Pasadena, CA.

"Escape Velocity" con in DC.

Air & Space²

On a previous trip, Harvey had introduced me to a friend of his. On this trip, I found out Harvey's marriage had disintegrated, and the "friend" was his new romantic companion. I could tell this woman was better for Harvey, but she and I didn't click. Some of it was my fault. I brought elements of my life back home on the trip, and it caused conflict. Harvey and I ended up having a falling out. I didn't think something like that would ever happen between us. We've talked a few times since, but our relationship has become strained.

I had just gotten my medical-use authorization for marijuana to help manage pain, and I was going hog wild. I was supposed to take three or four inhalations, but I was doing five times that amount. The more often I did this, the less effective the marijuana became for treating my illnesses. On my trip, I bought edibles and oils, reasoning that recreational marijuana use was legal in California and Nevada, so I could indulge. It turned into over-indulgence.

The resort in Vegas was really nice. So nice that, even though I had no money, I almost fell for the time-share scheme this "new concept" turned out to be.

I'd booked a second hotel to overlap with the "free" resort stay, and I needed to transfer my luggage. I left the convention feeling dizzy, and returning to the resort to pack, I stopped at their cafe to eat, but it didn't help. The combination of my health condition, lack of sleep, and overuse of pot had me reeling. Resort security was called, and I ended up going to the ER.

This was a big mistake. The hospital was nothing like I was used to. Apparently, it was a hospital familiar with treating drug overdoses and violent patients. There were armed security guards everywhere. When I changed into a hospital gown, the ER staff took my clothes and removed them to some other part of the facility.

They offered me food, but it was clearly not kosher, so I refused. I kept getting up, but they wanted me to stay in bed. When I needed to go to the bathroom, I was followed. When I opened the door to exit after I'd finished, there was a nurse standing right there. Startled, I quickly stepped back in and shut the door. I felt safer in there.

Eventually, I composed myself and came out. The nurse said my behavior was paranoid. I went back to waiting on the bed, and a security guard came with a wheelchair that had restraints. I was told the doctor would see me and to sit in the chair. I felt like something was wrong, but I complied. I knew if I resisted, I would be labeled the "problem" in the situation.

As they wheeled me along, we passed the sign reading "Psychiatric Ward," and I knew I was in trouble. They kept me there overnight, even though they had no reason to. I later realized that even though marijuana use was legal, if you overdose or abuse it, you can still get into trouble. Thankfully, they let me go the next morning.

I quickly cleared my things out of the resort and settled into the convention hotel. The hotel was huge with three towers, and my room was a long way from the convention. I rented a scooter for the rest of the week. I didn't have much fun at that convention, though I did get a photograph with Nichelle Nichols, Uhura from the original series.

One small blessing came the last day: I found some plush tropical birds on sale in the gift shop. I brought them home and used them as inspiration for a tropical rainforest theme in the bathroom of my apartment.

Even in the middle of a bad experience, you can sometimes salvage something good.

Please Let Me Walk Straight

The other trip I'd planned was a long trip to Israel, with a stop in Paris on the way. I was afraid to take marijuana into France and Israel, so I had to rely on oxycodone for pain management.

I returned to the Palace of Versailles. After walking the gardens and circling the lake, I walked back and stopped to have lunch, after which I planned to walk around inside.[3] My sciatica was acting up, and I took a little extra oxycodone, which really started to kick in as I was walking through the Hall of Mirrors. I was zigging and zagging and visibly unstable.

Hall of Mirrors. (2018)
Just before my dizzy spell.

Hall of Mirrors. (1871)
War Hospital.

Hall of Mirrors. (~1789)
Palace Life[4]

The Versailles EMTs were called. "We want you to be OK. We're taking you to the hospital." They put me in a wheelchair and took me out a side entrance to a waiting ambulance. "Don't worry, Monsieur. It is not like the States. We do not charge for the ambulance here."

The hospital in Versailles was amazing—the architecture, the light from the windows, the bright white surfaces. It was modern and impressive. I was attended to by a pretty, young resident who treated me with kindness. I told her about my back and that I'd taken an extra half dose of the pain medicine.

"Next time," she said, "start with one, then only take the other if it doesn't work."

My experience in France was so much more pleasant in 2018. People were more friendly, and they didn't display vitriolic resentment that I couldn't speak French. All of the shopkeepers and people I interacted with were much more accommodating. It was almost like visiting a different place than I'd been in 1995.

I flew to Israel and spent Rosh Hashanah and Yom Kippur with friends, then went up to Tzfat and spent time at Ascent.[5] I had some near misses in Israel with the local medical personnel. My swerving and instability was an ongoing problem.

For Rosh Hashanah, I was in Jerusalem. I had a vivid dream that night. I was on an airplane, flying somewhere. My old sociology professor, Bob Kleiner, appeared. He had passed away several years earlier, and I'd never really had a chance to say goodbye to him.

In the dream I said, "Bob, what are you doing here?"

"I'm just flying," he said. "Traveling just like you."

The dream was so real. It gave me a peaceful feeling. It was like I had a chance to say my goodbye.

On Yom Kippur, I received a message from G-d, which I've struggled to integrate more deeply into my life. Much like the nearly audible message I'd heard in 1980, this message caused me to re-evaluate my mindset and my way of acting in the world.

Even when you are right about something—when you have the moral high ground—do not overreact. Treat the situation with respect. Handle yourself with care. Don't let your certainty turn into entitlement and self-righteousness.

When I considered conflicts I'd had with Sara, instances where I'd harmed myself, and many other events where being "in the right" justified my impulsivity, I realized how important this new insight was. It was something I needed to ponder and figure out how to correct. I was pretty sure it wouldn't be an easy fix.

I realized as I was packing to leave how sad I always got when I left Israel. I wondered if there was some way I might move there permanently. I wouldn't leave Philadelphia as long as my father was alive, but I began to dream of relocating to Tzfat.

On my way back to the States, I missed a connecting

flight in Amsterdam. The airline compensated by rebooking me a flight to Boston instead of Chicago. By the time I made it to Boston, I'd been on the go for 25 hours, and my body lodged a protest.

Transferring from the international terminal to the domestic side, I dragged my carry-on and myself toward the security checkpoint. I took off my shoes and belt, like a proper traveler, and felt the sensation of my brain unplugging. I couldn't walk straight. I stumbled through the security arch and into the scrutiny of the TSA.

I was told to sit down and interrogated by security. "What's your name?" People had been calling me by my Hebrew name, Eliezer, for the past month, so it took me a minute. "You don't know your name?"

"Which one?" I responded.

They summoned an EMT who took my blood pressure, oxygen saturation, and glucose level. As usual, the numbers weren't significantly out of the healthy range to necessarily justify hospitalization. Nonetheless, based on my behavior, they wanted to transport me to Boston Hospital, but I insisted I would be OK and that I had to catch my flight. "You're already on the no-fly list. You're not flying anywhere."[6]

They tried to pull me from my chair and put me on a gurney, but I resisted. "Give me a minute. I'll be fine."

I was told they wouldn't force me to go to the hospital if I could walk straight. I prayed to G-d in heaven, *Please let me walk straight.*

I walked a few feet, and then came back and sat down. "OK," they said, "do it again."

I managed to walk straight again, and they said they couldn't hold me against my will but I wasn't going to be flying. I'd have to find another way home.

I didn't know what to do. A sheriff's deputy assigned to watch me after everyone else had left was getting impatient. "Come on, man. I've got better things to do than sit here and babysit you."

His attitude made me angry, but I tried to employ the more calm response G-d had impressed upon me in Israel.

"Officer, I appreciate what you do, and maybe you don't realize it, but you're talking down to me."

The officer softened. He asked where I was going, and I showed him my boarding pass. He said to follow him, and at the gate he told me to sit in one place and not move. "If you're not here when I get back, there's going to be big trouble."

I was happy to sit and wait. He returned in a few minutes. "This is what's going to happen. Your flight leaves in one hour. The gate attendant is watching you. If you can keep it together and board the plane without incident, they'll let you get home."

Thankfully, I made it past the intense scrutiny and acted "normal" enough to make it home.

Grounds For Sculpture

The physical effects of my extended return flight lasted several days, expressed in both serious jet lag and attendant episodes of zig-zagging and staggering. Desiring to stay in Israel as long as possible, I had delayed my return until just a few days before my Dad's ninetieth birthday. I knew I wanted to celebrate with the family, and not being there was unconscionable to me. Lori had organized a major family get-together that early October at the "Grounds For Sculpture" in Hamilton, New Jersey. „Grounds For Sculpture" is a phenomenal place filled with 3-D sculptures of many classic as well as contemporary artists, over 700 exhibits, spanning some 42 acres of land! Dad being ninety now, we all plowed into the park's tram and took a 90 minute tour to view the main attractions from the comfortable confines of our open air seats.

After the tram tour, Lori had arranged for the birthday lunch celebration in the park's very famous restaurant, "Rats." I was still highly fatigued, and barely over the jet-lag from my recent return from Israel. Moreover, the sciatica from my back pain and emerging knee pain was making me want to excuse myself from the table and find some place—any place—to lay down flat on my back, and take the pressure off the pinched nerves in my spine.

I looked across the table at my nephew, Axel. At all of eight years old, he had the dull look so common to children who have passed from the pleasant parts of a tasty meal into the monotony of adult conversation. We hadn't seen each other in a while, and I figured he would appreciate accompanying me away from the other adults. Also, if I wound up resting longer than expected, Axel could go back and relate my location to anyone who may have been concerned in our party. I approached Axel and whispered quietly, "Axel, do you want to help me find a horizontal place where I can lay down?" As Axel would later write it up in a narrative for a sixth-grade school assignment, this is what happened next:

"…We left the room and walked to a big round soft bench. A man was cleaning it and my uncle asked, 'Can I lay down there?' … 'No', the man replied, 'a party is coming.' We walked outside and there was a ledge of rocks, and a tiny alleyway and a little bridge. My Uncle whispered, 'Axel, Never do what I'm about to do.' I was scared because I didn't really know what was going to happen. I was also laughing, nervously. My face was getting as red as a tomato and I felt like I couldn't breathe. I didn't know what to do when he started to hobble across the (narrow) bridge. So he starts walking over the ledge and across the little bridge and lays down. I was laughing because I could only see his stomach. I went inside and told my dad…"

Axel saw me bracing myself, above the water side of the bridge (dark area)
slowly approaching a stone wall to lay down.

Sex Dolls and Bedbugs

Having never married, I occasionally sought solace at gentleman's clubs, like Delilah's in Philadelphia. In addition to watching the girls perform their pole dances, I engaged them in lap dances in the private backrooms, often paying two women at a time to dance for me. In addition to the sexplay, I harbored hope that conversation and shared interest would lead to a companion open to transitioning to social interaction outside the club.

Two women—Stella, a psychology student at University of Pennsylvania, and Alice, a single mom with an infant daughter—were open to such an arrangement. They'd gotten to know me over time and accepted an invitation to dinner. They chose The Capitol Grille, one of the premier dining spots in the city. The bill for our meal (and drinks) totaled over $500, which was a bit of a shock.[7]

I waited in the lobby to say goodbye to the ladies, who had excused themselves to the restroom while I settled the check. I lingered a while, but they never reappeared. Eventually, I got a text saying they'd left because Alice's babysitter needed her to come home. Between the enormity of the bill and their bailing on me, I felt more used in that situation than I had as a client at the club.

I realized my loneliness was making me vulnerable, and it was a liability. One possible solution to my problem was the sex-doll market springing up online. I researched several websites, but one in particular promised "lifelike" dolls manufactured in the USA and sold by a Georgia-based company. With a huge selection of models, I couldn't make up my mind, so I ordered three.

They took months to arrive in their long, wooden crates. To my surprise, the dolls had clearly been built and shipped from China. They were beautiful to look at and easy to pose, but not nearly as "functional" as the descriptions had promised. Additionally, the instructions indicated the dolls should be "stored horizontally," which wasn't possible in the limited space of my apartment.

Thwarted in my original intent, I decided to utilize the dolls in a more artistic way. I purchased actual body bags on Amazon, one for each doll, and positioned them as part of a "morgue" display in my living room, where they've stayed, mostly, to themselves.

I ended up settling for a different kind of companionship. My friend Henry was 76 and living with his eldest daughter in a dilapidated section of North Philadelphia. They lived off of Henry's meager social security income until a gas leak drew the attention of the authorities and their apartment building was deemed unsafe. His daughter moved back with her mother and sister in Dauphin county.

Henry loved Philadelphia, and he did his best to stay nearby, bouncing from tiny apartment to tiny apartment. Not long after I'd returned from Israel, Henry got approved for government-subsidized housing, but he needed a place to stay for a few days until his new apartment was ready. I invited him to stay as a guest with me.

I knew Henry had some odd hoarding tendencies. He kept the foil lids of yogurt containers for various purposes (including drink coasters) and washed out ice cream cartons to store and organize his various vitamin supplements. I insisted he not bring those items to my apartment during his short stay.

What I didn't know was that Henry had a long history with a great scourge of apartment dwellers: bedbugs.

By the time I discovered the collection of tiny black dots on the wall behind the guest bed in which he'd been sleeping, it was already a major infestation. I asked Henry to vacate while I figured out what to do. (I later learned that bedbug problems had followed Henry for many years.)

Ironically, this happened the same week as the Sabbath Torah reading, *Tazria*, which details G-d's instructions for dealing with leprosy and infectious impurity in the Jewish community. The connection to my situation wasn't lost on me, and I was reminded how often the mundane things of our daily lives are reflected in the universality of the Torah.

I was scared to report the issue to my apartment management, but I also didn't want the bedbugs to spread to my neighbors. Hope Alloitious—a mutual friend whom Henry had introduced me to—told me she'd suffered through no less than three such infestations during the early years of her friendship with Henry, so she knew the exterminator I should call.

Any anticipation I had for a quick fumigation solution were soon quashed. The exterminator warned the chemicals could be carried through the building's ventilation system, putting plants and small animals at risk. Not only would I never endanger my neighbors 'pets, I was *trying* to keep the infestation hush-hush. I was afraid I would be evicted if the bedbug problem was discovered.

So, we treated the problem the slow and painful way. For weeks I boxed up all of my possessions. I sealed chemical kill strips inside the boxes, and moved the boxes into two storage units. The exterminator and his son helped, including moving the three sex dolls that weighed around 100 pounds each! They applied several rounds of treatment to my apartment, but the bugs seemed to get ahead of the effort to control them. They spread throughout my apartment and, apparently, they considered me a tasty treat upon which to feast.

Hope had advised me I could be a carrier and that I should notify people I was in contact with. At first, I thought I could skirt the issue by being extra careful. I even went to a dental cleaning without informing the hygienist of my problem. Halfway through the procedure, I began to worry that, despite my precautions, I might cause harm to this woman's home and family, and I confessed my apartment had bedbug problems. She tried to appear unfazed, but the second half of my cleaning was not as thorough as the first half.

I decided I didn't want to be responsible for bringing that grief to anyone else. So, the summer before the rest of the world would isolate due to Covid-19 fears, I was practicing for pandemic lockdowns. I avoided visiting Dad at the assisted living facility, and I recused myself from my brother's 50th birthday party.

I researched, and consulted my exterminator, to learn precautions I could take when I needed to go out, but it was a laborious process. I had to arrange pest-free sets of clothing and shoes outside my apartment to change into. Once I'd figured out the logistics of being safe, I contacted the dentist's office and asked for an appointment for another cleaning, since the last one hadn't been thorough. I was told I was welcome back only if I had a note from my physician.

I made my case that bedbugs were not a disease and a note from my doctor wasn't appropriate. I told them I had researched and learned how to take proper precautions to keep others safe. The receptionist explained the owner and main dentist had made the decision. I was a long-time patient, and I asked that the dentist call me so I could speak to him directly. He phoned a few days later, but the conversation was pretty much the same. He'd made up his mind. As a last-ditch effort, I gave him my exterminator's number and asked that he confirm all of what I'd told him.

Three months passed. My bedbug situation was resolved,

but the dentist's office still refused to see me. The dentist had never contacted the exterminator. Clearly, I was not a valued patient, so I found a new dentist.

As the problem with bedbugs began to subside, I returned to Delilah's to visit Stella and Alice. The ladies showed they'd missed me by encouraging me to part with my money. Alice texted saying they wanted to see me again. Rather than saying no, or confronting them with suspicions they weren't actually interested in a real friendship, I tried a delaying tactic. I told them I might have an infestation of bedbugs, and I didn't want to put them in jeopardy.

I did still have some residual effects from the bedbug bites I'd suffered, so I told Alice I couldn't get together with them in good conscience. Alice tried to insist it would be OK, but I declined her offer. Alice was a mother; I was shocked she would risk such a thing.

An hour later, I got an angry call from Stella, who was upset that she'd cleared her schedule at Penn for the possible meet-up. She seemed more upset over the inconvenience than she was about the implied health threat from bedbugs. I finally intuited I was getting nowhere with them and admitted to myself my method of seeking companionship wasn't healthy for me either.

Convinced of their true intentions, I sent them a group text stating that true "friends" would have been concerned for my well-being—which neither woman had expressed—and would have appreciated my caution in protecting them.

It was clear they were only concerned about the money they could make, not about me, and I ended things. In the end, I'd conveniently used one set of bed bugs to get rid of another set of "bed bugs."

Disordered Conversion

My stability issues were an ongoing nightmare. I'd gotten used to the sensation and I knew how to navigate the situation, but to an outsider, I looked inebriated: staggering, zigging and zagging, clutching solid objects, and clinging to phone poles. Walking backward sometimes helped, but it invited a different reaction. I've had multiple run-ins with police and EMTs because they think I'm either drunk (if I'm dizzy and walking forward) or crazy (if I'm walking backward).

Before Philcon one year, I was really struggling with a whole host of health issues. I'd been utilizing medical marijuana to mitigate pain, but it was less and less effective over time.

I planned to leave for New Jersey on Thursday morning, early enough to visit with Ellie prior to the convention. But that morning, I got so dizzy I fell down outside my apartment. My pulse was extremely high, and I was scared something was really wrong with me.

I went to the hospital Thursday night, and they put a heart monitor on me. Laying there, I talked myself down from my fear. *I'm feeling better,* I reasoned, *and this test isn't going to show anything anyway.* I really wanted to get back to my apartment, gather my things, and get on the bus to New Jersey, so I skipped out of the hospital the next morning with the EKG leads still stuck to my chest.

The bus took me to New Jersey, and the weekend proceeded mostly as planned, except I continued to smoke the marijuana to manage my physical symptoms, and by Sunday morning I was a total mess again. I was dizzy and falling down. Dennis, a liaison for the convention, approached me to ask what was happening. "Do we need to call an ambulance?"

I told him what had happened before I left home, and the man looked at me and said, "Who the hell leaves the hospital when they might have serious heart issues, just to attend a science fiction convention?" They called for medical help, and I eventually figured out I was taking too much marijuana, which triggered additional symptoms rather than just helping manage my other illnesses.

After I realized my problems were increasing to the point of making travel almost impossible, I decided to try one last time to make sense of my condition.

When Sara was sick, she'd had a rare adverse reaction to one of the drugs she'd been prescribed and had a seizure. She went to the same neurology practice where I had my bad experience. Thankfully, she'd seen another doctor, who was empathetic and professional.

I made an appointment with the doctor who had seen Sara. He was patient and sympathetic. The doctor thought I might have conversion disorder, where neurological symptoms defy medical evaluation. My stability symptoms were much more dependent on my mental health than I'd realized. Physiological stress was part of the triggering mechanism, but in conversion disorder, there is a strong bond between a person's symptoms and mental and emotional distress as well.

This was a lightbulb moment, and this doctor was the first to point me in the right direction. (Ironically enough, Kristl had been the second closest in her layman's opinion that I suffered from some sort of multi-faceted syndrome.)

I began outpatient physical therapy and balance therapy at Chestnut Hill hospital.

Unfortunately, it's still been a rough road. I've had numerous run-ins with police or paramedics who think I pose some kind of threat to myself or others. My knee has gotten progressively worse. As I was waiting to lose weight to get a partial knee replacement, it deteriorated to the point of needing a full replacement. I've also been diagnosed with vertigo and diabetes. Sadly, as my body declines, I'm left to wonder if my grandmother's prediction of my lifespan wasn't accurate.

A New Path

Even with a diagnosis of conversion disorder, I was still searching for ways to keep active and be able to travel. In the days prior to the Covid-19 outbreak, I accidentally overdosed on a powerful marijuana-based oil I'd obtained through the medical marijuana dispensary for my increasing knee and back pain. It was very potent, and I found myself dizzy and unable to move. I was practically paralyzed and couldn't even open my eyes. Just as I felt I was losing all movement, I dialed 911. I could barely crawl out of my apartment and onto the landing as I waited for help to arrive.

The police came and saw how out of it I was. They wanted to get me into the ambulance but needed my ID and insurance card, which I'd left in the apartment. I gave one of the officers my keys and instructions to look for my ID beside my bed. He was gone for what seemed like a long time. From inside the apartment, I heard odd banging and the sound of something heavy dragged across the carpet.

Finally, the officer came out and admitted he couldn't find the ID and insurance card. He took hold of me and asked in a gruff voice, "What's with the dolls in the body bags?"

In my incapacitated state, all I could muster was, "Just dolls. That's it."

Later, my friend Hope pointed out I'd missed an opportunity for some humor. "You should have said, 'They're just dolls, but you're welcome to borrow one.'"

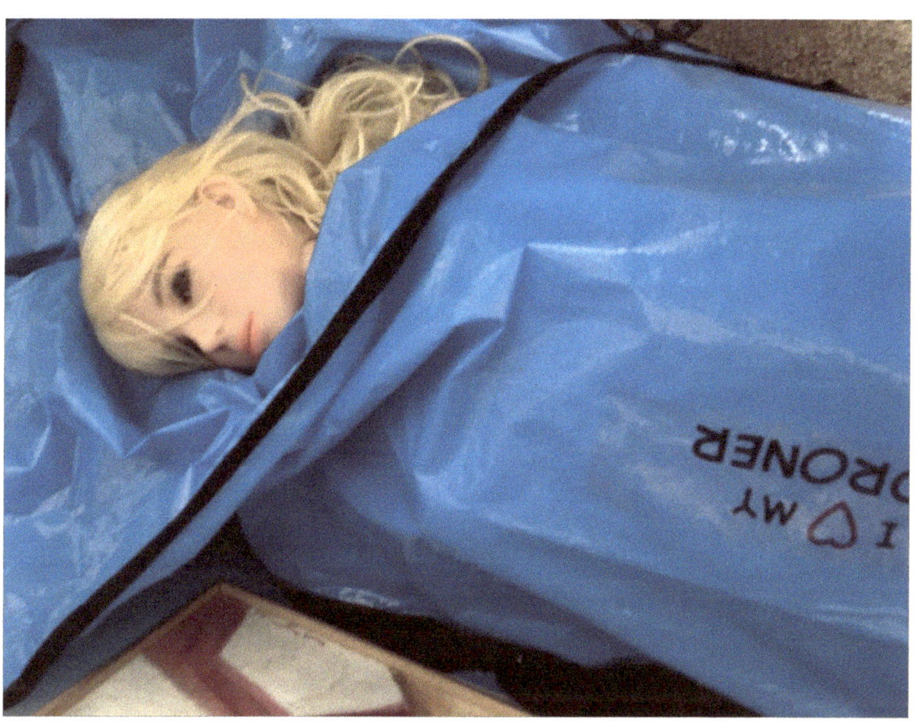

"Bethany" in her body bag, probably surprised to be "awoken" by the police!
But, what charge would they be investigating?

In 2020, the last part of my prophetic dream from California came true. I had a powerful marijuana experience, and I got up from the table more quickly than I should have. As I pushed up from the table, I had the sensation of being propelled upward, without restraint. It felt like I was flying out of my body.

I didn't die, obviously, which was a relief. I had worried about that scene of the dream being a premonition of my death.

But it did feel like the death of an era of my life. It was the end of one period and the beginning of another. All of the parts of that dream had now been fulfilled. I had a new path to follow.

Kristl's Illness

Kristl was diagnosed with a devastating and aggressive cancer. Like she had been throughout her life, she was very sensible and level-headed about this new challenge.

In the last months before she died, we weren't able to get together for our semi-annual meet-up, but we did have a chance to talk. We last spoke in February of 2021. It was a devastatingly sad conversation. She said, "Ted, if there were an airplane to fly me away from this pain, I would take it."

I was so sad, and I was crying on the phone. Kristl asked why I was crying, and I said, "I'm crying for you. I'm not ready to not have you in my life anymore."

"You're crying for me?"

"Yes."

"Thank you," she said. And then she added words I will never forget. Kristl said, "I love you, Ted."

As painful as that moment was, it also seemed to close a loop that had been open since I'd told her I loved her back in 1987.

In the last days, Kristl was in the same hospice in Warminster where my sister had been. But, thankfully, when she succumbed to the cancer on March 3rd, 2021, it was in the comfort of her home, and surrounded by her family.

The family scheduled a memorial service on a Saturday in June, after Kristl's birthday. I made sure I was there. It was Shabbat, and I observed the religious rules as best I could. I walked from my hotel to the church where her memorial was held. I made an exception to my rule of not going inside Christian churches. Despite a vast difference in our theology, Kristl had been a servant of G-d. She did a lot of good in her life. My life, and the lives of many others, had been blessed by her presence in it. She served the Creator well.

Dr. Walker came to Temple w/many academic degrees. She became head of Student Affairs, 7 years into Kristl's 20-year tenure[8]

Entitlement vs. Enlightenment

My two remaining siblings live hundreds of miles away with their families. Being the only child left nearby, it falls on me to assist my father on a regular basis.

Dad has an uncommon blood-platelet condition that requires a hard-to-find medication. Most pharmacies don't stock it, including hospital pharmacies. So, if my father is taken to the hospital—as happens periodically, due to complications of COPD—someone has to take this special medicine to him.

My father had been hospitalized several times, and the assisted living facility couriered the medicine to him. The staff decided they wouldn't do that any longer, so they asked the family to devise a solution.

We developed a "go bag" with items my father needed, including enough medicine to hold him over until more could be brought. I asked a nurse for three of the pills, which I put in the bag. This arrangement worked just fine. Dad was hospitalized in June of 2021, and the medicine was there when he needed it.

Dad bounced between the hospital and a rehab facility for several months. Meanwhile, I hatched an idea to leave shortly after Thanksgiving and surprise my sister in Miami, then go to the Florida Keys for a few days. When my father returned to the nursing facility in October, I wanted to be proactive about resetting his go bag, so things would be ready for me to be away.

I went to the nursing station to ask for three of his pills and was promptly told the policy had changed. Patients were no longer allowed access to their medications. I explained why it was necessary—not least because the facility didn't want to take the medicine to the hospital for my father—and how we'd recently been through a scenario where the go-bag precaution had worked exactly as intended. "Plus," I said, "my father was a pharmacist. He knows what to do with medications."

It didn't matter. Rules were rules.

I had several weeks before my trip, so I took a deep breath and decided to address the issue with the director of nursing. On my next visit, I asked the receptionist to tell the nursing director I'd like to speak to her, but apparently she "got busy," and we didn't speak that day. She also didn't phone me during the week, as I'd asked.

The next visit, I again asked to see her and waited for two hours before I felt fatigued. My conversion disorder was kicking in. I didn't want to be a spectacle and give her reason to not take me seriously, so I left before she came to Dad's room (if she ever came).

I was getting anxious. I couldn't travel with a clear conscience if this medicine wasn't available to my father. I didn't want to ruin the surprise visit, so when I told my siblings what was happening, my sense of urgency wasn't reciprocated. Lori had a good rapport with the staff—she's the kind to bring cookies or cakes to the workers—and she said she'd email and see what answers she could get.

Around November 20th, she received a reply from the director saying it wouldn't be a problem to have the medicine in the go bag, and she'd delegated the task to one of the staff. I had a rush of relief. We had it in writing. It was going to happen.

On Thanksgiving Day, I went to visit my father. As I was preparing to leave, I saw the red bag. *I'm probably being over-cautious*, I reasoned, *but let's make sure*. I unzipped the bag. The promised medicine was not there.

The flash of anger was immediate. We'd been promised this would be taken care of, and here it was, three days before I was set to leave. I told my father I'd be right back and marched to the front desk, resentment building with every step.

"I don't care whose holiday dinner you have to interrupt," I told the receptionist, "but someone is going to make sure three pills are pulled from the dispensary and put in my father's bag." I slammed my fist hard on the counter.

"Ted," she said. "You'll not speak to me that way."

"This isn't personal," I replied, "but I'll speak however I need to, to get some action. If someone doesn't take care of this, right now, I'll have the entire police force here."

She left the reception area. While she was gone, I considered how precarious my threat was. If the police did come, I was the one who had slammed my fist and made a threat. I realized I needed to be very careful with my next move.

Apparently, the receptionist had called my sister to report what was going on, because my cell phone rang and I could see it was Lori on the ID. I declined the call. I didn't want to get into the whole thing, and I also didn't want to reveal my surprise visit.

The receptionist was visibly frightened. "Ted, you have to leave."

I sat in a chair and refused to leave until someone fixed the situation. I knew I wasn't thinking clearly, so I texted my brother: "I know it's not a good time, but I'm in trouble here."

Nate called, and I went to the public men's room and sat in the stall, trying to have privacy while I explained things. Nate said I needed to let it go and leave. I argued that the right thing was for them to fix the problem.

"Listen," he said. "If you leave, I'll get it taken care of tomorrow. But if you stay, I'm not going to help."

"You would do that," I said, "to Dad?"

"I don't want to, but you aren't making any sense. If you aren't going to be sensible, neither am I."

Nate always has a way of getting through to me, and I left the bathroom stall resigned to doing things his way, though I didn't let on I agreed. "I guess we'll see what happens."

Just then, one of the male staff came into the bathroom. He said, "I've been asked to escort you from the premises."

I told him I wasn't leaving until I said goodbye to my father, but he insisted. "You were violent, and you're going out of here, right now."

I was still on the line with Nate, and I put him on speaker phone. The man said, "I'm going to have to call the police on your brother here, if he won't leave."

Nate didn't know I'd actually decided to not make things any worse, so he responded, "I guess you'd better call the police, then."

"Really…You're telling me, it's okay? You're okay with me calling the police on your brother?" he repeated. Then he said, to me: "You heard what your brother just said."

"Do what you've got to do," I replied. "But I'm going to go see my father before I go."

"You're not going anywhere." I was braced against the bathroom sink, and he approached me, fists up. I repeated that I wanted to leave the bathroom and see my father, and he said, "Are you gonna fight me to get out of here?"

"I just want out of here." I was inching toward the door. "If you want a fight, you're gonna have to hit me first."

He braced his arm against the doorway to block me; I tried to slip beneath it. He locked arms with me, and I pushed him as hard as I could. As he stumbled backward, I started out the door, but he rushed me from behind and tackled me through the opposite door, into the women's restroom. My head was bruised. When I tried to stand, he pinned me with a full nelson hold to immobilize me.

Witnesses started to gather, and I was released but told to not get up. The police and EMTs showed up. I was injured and on the ground, and they thought I was the victim. They tried to help me stand, but my instability had kicked in after the rush of adrenaline had faded. I collapsed again, and they asked if I needed an ambulance.

I thought it might look better for me if I went in the ambulance, so I agreed. I was wheeled out of the facility on a gurney. It was little satisfaction that the threat I'd made had come true. At least five Upper Dublin emergency and police vehicles were lined up at the curb as my gurney was placed into the ambulance. It looked, in fact, that just as people would have been sitting down to their Thanksgiving dinners, I had seemingly brought the entire local police department onto the premises.

In the aftermath, the facility director visited my father and told him all of the staff was scared of me and I was banned from visiting. Mysteriously, someone brought the three pills to my father and made sure they were in his bag, which was a good thing: While I was traveling, my father ended up in the hospital, and he needed the medicine.

I visited Lori in Florida, but after all the fuss I'd caused, I decided to tell her I was coming, not just show up on her doorstep. After my visit to Florida, I took a diversion to California to visit Vasquez Rocks, which was a bucket-list item for me.

While I was gone, I had a decision to make. The police

thought I should press charges because the nursing home employee had physically injured me. I contemplated using the threat of a charge as leverage to have my ban rescinded, but the more I considered it, the more my stance softened.

I was reminded of the lesson G-d had tried to teach me during my last trip to Israel. Just because I was right didn't excuse my actions. I'd approached the situation with righteous indignation and acted irresponsibly, which had triggered a whole chain of unfortunate events. The employee had also overstepped his place out of his own sense of entitlement and "rightness." I decided I would not press charges.

It was an important lesson, learned the hard way.

12

LESSONS LEARNED

Struggle is a Part of Progress

My ongoing health issues continue to frustrate me. The balance and coordination problems associated with conversion disorder intermingle with my diabetes and are exacerbated by knee and back problems. It's difficult to discern exactly how and where these conditions overlap, and it confuses the issue of treatment.

When I'm experiencing a particularly severe spell of dizziness, the public safety personnel or medical staff who approach me do so with an intent to "fix" me. They'll too often try to collate their observations with bystander accounts, looking for "catch-all" categories such as low-blood-sugar diabetes, simple dehydration, or Ataxia. They aren't often interested in hearing the full story. I understand their position: They want to quickly identify and address the problem, and they assume their medical training and knowledge must make them right. If they can quickly put my situation into a neat little box, they can move on to the next crisis.

But my lived experience is more complex than, "You have condition X, so we have to do Y right away." Even when I try to explain I'm actually OK, I just need a minute to rest, they assume they know more than I do about my condition.

It is frustrating to be pigeonholed and my condition is unusual enough that I fear a note I carry won't always be given credence by just-arriving EMTs. My instinct is to clam up. This hinders communication and makes things worse. I know it is counter-productive, but it is soul-sucking to speak and not be heard.

A recent experience is indicative of what I've learned from dealing with my various medical conditions. I was in the hospital after an appointment and was trying to regain enough stability to safely navigate to the exit. I was dizzy, so I was walking through the hospital halls backwards. One woman passed by and suggested, "It might help if you turned around so you can see where you're going." A few feet further down the hall, a different individual commented, "I'm sure there's a reason why you're walking backward. Just be safe, OK?" Those two attitudes captured both ends of the spectrum when it comes to reaction to my medical condition. I just wish more people were like that second person.

After a long history of dissatisfaction with medical care, I still struggle to find answers to my problems. I'm thankful to have made some progress in understanding what's going on, but there has been no "one cure" to help me improve. There are no magic pills, only continued behavioral therapy with some lifestyle adaptations. It seems for now that my health continues to deteriorate, which makes daily life more difficult and curbs my ability to travel and plan for the future.

The US is an imperfect society, guided by an imperfect government, and I see parallels to the fall of the Roman Empire in our present culture and governance. This perspective leads me to doubt the long-term viability of the US. I hope I'm wrong, but even if I'm not, those things are beyond my control.

As apocalyptic visions and declining health propel me toward my grandmother's prediction of death before my 65th year, it's sometimes hard to maintain hope. While I certainly think people make individual choices and inroads into self-improvement, I've come to accept that there is an equal—or greater—force at play: Destiny. Many of the prophetic dreams and impressions I've had have convinced me that while our human perception of time is linear, in reality all time is happening at once. And, while time is real, our perception of it is an illusion. There are too many variables beyond my control. While some things may be fated or unavoidable, I also recall the wizened words from my brief encounter with that Rabbi in Palo Alto, so many years ago.

Back then, when I was fretting about the negative aspects of my decade-spanning dream, he'd counseled: "You've been shown one path, but there is still time to change it."

The Jewish concept of competing inclinations—yetzer hora and yetzer tov (the bad and good)—describes my internal struggle. Most philosophies and religions recognize the human desire to do right is often counter-balanced by the proclivity to do wrong. Judaism teaches an additional lesson: Even when doing wrong, something good can come from it—through repentance—Teshuvah. So many times, my mistakes were the fertile soil of deeper learning.

My path has been inconsistent and unsteady, but the underlying truths G-d has attempted to teach me remain applicable, even when denied or ignored. Thankfully, G-d has a way of dragging me back to truth until I take heed and submit to it.

After my "psychic surgery" with Cindy, I periodically visited spiritualists and psychics until I accepted the only entity that I should allow influence over my soul is G-d. I learned to not tiptoe around "gray areas." The work of transformation should come from the inside, uninfluenced by outside forces of questionable origin.

I've often felt guided and protected by G-d, beyond what I deserve. Sometimes that protection didn't reveal itself until years later. After my first Israeli trip, I was nudged away from my teenage "bomb buddies" and was protected again when I had the terrible idea to solicit Lee's help in "waking up" my college campus. The full import of G-d's guidance was made clear in 2017 when Lee Kaplan was sentenced to life in prison for 17 hideous crimes. There, but for the grace of G-d, go I.

Sometimes, the lessons were multi-faceted. The bomb plot that ended my stint at Ambler helped me navigate a situation decades later.

A few years ago, my brother's in-laws hosted a wedding celebration. My sister, and brother were invited, but I was not. I was upset by this perceived slight, and I considered plans for retaliation.

I intended to crash the wedding. I wouldn't make a big scene, just slip into the wedding and prove the point: I should have been invited.

Planning my subtle protest, I was reminded of the Ambler incident. My attendance at the wedding might cause collateral damage I couldn't control. If someone recognized me and knew I wasn't invited, my brother would bear the brunt of complaints and criticism. Just like I couldn't be sure no one would be hurt by a pipe bomb in 1982, I couldn't guarantee my brother would be spared the social shrapnel of my actions. A social bomb could be as unpredictable as a pipe bomb, so I stayed home.

I'm also thankful for the mentors, teachers, and friends who have been servants of G-d and impacted my life. I've tried to mention many of them in these pages, to honor their influence on me.

The community of Young Israel of Elkins Park has given me the impetus to grow and evolve as a person, but also the freedom to be more authentically myself. The eclectic gathering of people in our religious community gives me confidence to share my thoughts, even with people I know have a different perspective and probably disagree with me.

It often takes a long time to internalize and act on the things I've been taught. The unfortunate incident at my father's nursing home last year demonstrates I don't always get it right, but I continue to apply the things I've learned, and that is progress.

Despite the hurdles, I hope to move to Tzfat, Israel. I can't change the world, but I can change myself. I may only have a handful of years left, but in that time I can live a life that is a little better today than it was yesterday. I can improve the ways I treat others and take care of myself, one imperfect step at a time.

If Life Lands you with Lemons . . . Lift off with "Lamed-Aid"

I have learned that there are really two sides to the issue of transcending boundaries. On the one hand, the desire (especially when young) is to push through boundaries or extend them. It is often how we learn. We may find success while moving forward on some dimensions, and learn limitations and how to course correct when encountering resistance or turbulence in other areas.

In appreciating and accepting others, we learn to approach others' personal spaces with humility and compassion. In her profound work, *Passages (1984),* psychologist Gail Sheehy wrote of our "seeker selves" and our "merger selves." For me, "the seeker self" resonates with the famous introductory words to the original *Star Trek* series. As we look to colonize our own lives and futures, we're encouraged like the U.S.S. *Enterprise*, to "Boldly Go…" and take on new tasks and adventures in life! At the same time, we adapt to the urges of our "merger selves," endeavoring to slow the pace of accomplishment so that we can share with others, build solid relationships, create families and nurture the young while supporting our communities.

At times, both our "seeker selves" and our "merger selves" have to learn to let go of things. I wrote early on of the influence author Michael Crichton had on my thinking and development. The most profound impact came from his own autobiography, *Travels* (1988). *Travels* was, in large part, the inspiration for the very book you hold in your hands. Many of Michael Crichton's reflections on his own change and growth came about through a learned process of "letting go." As we move through life's lessons, it's often those work-around concepts and wool-gathering artifacts that need to be swept away, clearing the decks for new phases of life and learning.

Long before we became familiar with Mr. Spock's famous

hand salute and farewell phrase—"Live Long and Prosper"—the Jewish people had the tradition of encouraging friends and relatives to, "Go from strength to strength!"

I've been fortunate that my own journeys in life have brought me into the company of many thoughtful and caring friends. They've been there to celebrate my insights and help me "course-correct" where needed. They've never pushed or prodded, only offered different ways of seeing things!

As 2023 and the 50th anniversary of Gene Roddenberry's *Genesis II* approaches, it is cautionary to look back on the genre of post-apocalyptic film and television series. Yet, at the same time, signs persist that the coming years and decades may present new hardships and challenges.

We may not always comprehend it, but a Greater Force guides our destinies—G-d! And although we cannot always see it, *Everything* is connected! In that vein, there is nothing to fear! There is still time for all of us to step out of the shadows, find illumination, and be the change that we wish to see in the world around us!

Now it's your turn! Whatever your Path…
May You Go from Strength to Strength!

CHAPTER ENDNOTES

CHAPTER ONE: Beginnings

1. Mom and sister Joyce's parents were Theodore Schuster and Charlotte (née Gerson) Schuster (later, Adler). They were both German immigrants to the United States, unaware of each other until they arrived and met in New York City sometime around 1936. Ted Schuster and his family had been residents of Bebra, Germany. Charlotte, or Lottie, as she was affectionately known, had resided with her family in Oberwessel, Germany near Frankfurt Am Main. Their two cities of origin, Bebra and Oberwessel, were roughly 261 kilometers apart and they might not have met had it not been for their status as immigrants, and the opportunity to meet at a singles social dance in New York subsequent to settling into jobs and homes in New York. Ted and Lottie married in January of 1938.

2. Gallaudet Pharmacy served the neighborhoods of Gallaudet University, a special college for the deaf and hearing impaired in Washington, DC. For the several

summer months of 1952 that Haskell Rickles worked as an assistant pharmacist at the pharmacy, many of the customers he served were likewise deaf or hearing impaired.

3. Shoemaker and Busch was a premier wholesale supplier to druggists and pharmacies beginning on April 3, 1892 (succeeding the prior management of Roller & Shoemaker). It was headquartered in Philadelphia at 602 Arch Street. *(See- The City of Philadelphia As It Appeared in 1893: A Compilation of Facts for the Information of Businessmen, Travellers, and the World at Large;* Philadelphia Chamber of Commerce and Frank Hamilton Taylor; published by Geo. S. Harris & Sons; 1893. Shoemaker and Busch prided themselves on supplying "any and every article required by the retail druggist".

4. To the 1970's and 1980's generation of television viewers, Mariette Hartley was most readily identified from her commercials with co-actor James Garner in promoting Polaroid instant cameras. She could also be seen cohosting CBS's "The Morning Program". Hartley also performed in a number of science fiction programs. In addition to *Star Trek* and *Genesis II* (1973), she costarred with Robert Lansing in *The Twilight Zone* episode, "The Long Morrow" (1964); guest-starred in *The Incredible*

Hulk (1978) episode, "Married"; and in an episode of *Logan's Run* (1978) "FuturePast".

5. Poul Anderson's "The Fatal Fulfillment" (1970) was also published in *The Magazine of Fantasy and Science Fiction* Vol.33, No.3 (March, 1970); p. 4-45. The story was nominated for a Nebula Award for best novella of 1970. A few years later, the discipline of sociology itself would make its own foray into an academic connection with science fiction. *Sociology Through Science Fiction* was published in 1974, released through St.Maarten's Press and edited by John W. Millstead, Martin Henry Greenberg, Joseph D. Olander and Patrick Warrick.

6. Crichton's *Five Patients: The Hospital Explained* 1970) provides a non-fiction introduction to the experience of hospital work as well as several fiction works he penned under the pseudonyms of either John Lange, or Jeffrey Hudson, which often involved medical conditions as part of the plot. *Five Patients* remains a great read for prospective medical students. TV viewers from the 1980s may also remember the long-running television series, "ER" that Michael Crichton created. In addition, Crichton was an accomplished film director in his own right, He directed a number of now classic science-fiction film gems including: *Westworld* (1973); *Terminal Man* (1974); *The Great Train Robbery* (1978); *Coma* (1978)

and *Looker* (1981) (recognized as the first film reference to real-world full-body computer assisted tomography). Numerous successful science fiction films as well as the *Jurassic Park* franchise of films are based in his work.

7. Robert Lansing had a wonderful capacity for portraying sensible, principled, competent and charismatic military or police officers. Lansing had himself served two years in the US Army. One of his most entertaining roles was as Lt. Jack Curtis in the campy sci-fi television series, *Automan* (1983-1984). In addition to his role alongside Mariette Hartley in the earlier mentioned classic *Twilight Zone* episode "The Long Morrow", older viewers may remember him as the obsessed scientist in the classic SF film, *4-D Man* (1959).

8. The page with photos from my attendance at the 1975 Star Trek Convention includes four columns of a logo at top and bottom of the page. The logo appears as an image of the Earth being intersected by a paper airplane (that may be being ridden by an ant?). This was the graphic logo of "The Committee" which organized and managed the original *Star Trek* Conventions in the 1970s. (YES! There were original *Star Trek* conventions before Creation Entertainment came on the scene). "The Committee" shepherded five *Star Trek* Conventions (1972, 1973, 1974, 1975 and 1976). I placed the four

columns (Top & Bottom) across the page to indicate that this was their forth convention (as well as to draw attention to the fact that it was a pretty cool logo for the time.

9. A useful book from the 1970s that presented an academic survey of the field of parapsychology – from describing psychic phenomena to discussing research techniques in the field is: *Handbook of Parapsychology*, edited by Benjamin B. Wolman, 1977; by Von Nostrand-Rheinhold Company, NY, Litton Educational Publishing, Inc. 967 pgs.

CHAPTER TWO: Teen Years

1. I was also present at the Atomic Energy Forum hearings on the events at Three Mile Island (TMI) occurring on March 28, 1979. Those hearings were held either in the summer of 1979 or 1980 (?)?They reviewed the events and handling of the partial meltdown of the number two reactor which led to what may have been the worst nuclear disaster in United States history. I was there as the personal guest of my uncle, Lester Schuster (1925-2014). Uncle Lester was there in his capacity as an atomic health physicist on staff with the New York Department of Labor.

2. The United News Company of Philadelphia had been the city's fully independent book and magazine distributor, delivering to pharmacies, supermarkets, and newsstands throughout the Philadelphia region. It was acquired in 1991 by the Chas. Levy Company, LLC of Chicago, IL and operated for a time as "Levy United News". See: the internet article, "Chas. Levy Company, LLC."on the World Wide Web in www.encyclopedia.com.

3. In those days Lee and his mother lived at 1507 Juniper Avenue in Elkins Park, with the house titled in the name of Lee's father Herbert Kaplan.

4. Susan Judith Rickles (Mom) had a wonderful sense of humor-such that sometimes it was difficult to tell whether she was being facetious or serious. This remark that she had made regarding not sharing our address with the police was in fact one of those uncertain times.

5. In those days the university's main repository of books, magazines and research materials was in the Samuel Paley Library adjacent to the campus bell tower and occupying the block on 13th Street, with a strip of lunch trucks separating it from the next block on which the Student Activities Center (SAC) then stood. In the late 1980's the strip of lunch trucks was moved to its current location adjacent to the Humanities Building, and in the early 2000's the Student Activities Center underwent a massive refurbishment and was renamed the Howard Gittis Student Union Center (1755 N. 13th Street)

6. Many wonderful people attended that August 1980 tour of Israel from Adath Jeshuran Synagogue. They included: Cantor Charles Davidson, his wife Frances and two daughters; Philanthropist Milton Dauber and his wife; Kalman and wife Suzan Fine as well as many others.

7. Hollingshead, Michael. "B.F. Skinner" in *Omni*, September, 1979; Vol. 1, No.12. pp.76-80.

My conclusion is that on the simplest level, Ben Bova, as editor was correct in his short response to my query. In addition to Skinner's own seminal works such as *Walden Two*, others have written extensively about his ideas. However, the four page interview, should you read it, is noteworthy for the range of topics it spans, as well as the retrospective voice with which Skinner reflects back on the ideas of his life's work.

CHAPTER THREE: Israel And Beyond

1. This list of past-presidents of Y.I.E.P. includes, but may not be limited to: Marvin Berman, Sidney Bernstein, Steve Bernstein (unrelated to Sidney), Michael Feinberg, David Lazowick, Avroham McConnell, Daniel Robbins, Bart Scheinfeldt, Daniel Scheinfield, Dr. Frank Schwartz, Zvi Schwartz (Unrelated to Frank), Dov Simons, Stanley Sved, and Tom Wolpert (several of these people served multiple terms).

2. Larry Caroline was that administrator, working at the Beth Jacob Day School, but also supportive of the fledgeling Orthodox Minyan of Elkins Park. He recalled in a telephone conversation with me having left a bottle of scotch with a note for "best wishes" to the new congregation just prior to their first convening of Sabbath services, which is understood to be Parsha Breishis (*Genesis*), just following the holiday of Sukkot, October 1980/5742. (Source: Telephone conversation between the author and Larry Caroline, July 14, 2022; 1:00pm)

3. As founder and first president of O.M.E.P./Y.I.E.P., Sidney Bernstein emanated a definite charm, warmth and charisma. I recall one wonderful experience at a Sabbath day meal that he and his wife hosted at their

home for those who had gathered for worship services that day (Spring, 1981). It's necessary to presage the account by first explaining that it is customary during the meal to sing songs (Zemirot) to celebrate the joy that accompanies the Sabbath Day. On one occasion, Sid led us in a rousing rendition of *Yom Zeh Mechubad* ("Crown of Days, Above All Blest"). Impressed as I was, I asked Sid from my place at the table, what was the origin of the song? He gently explained that it was the invention of a 19th century little old Rabbi in Poland. The winters were harsh, Sid explained. So, to comfort his Talmidim (students), the Rabbi would take them out on the frozen lake and they would skate in circles, singing *Yom Zeh Mechubad* to keep warm together. Incredulous as I was to such a romantic origin for the song, I asked Sid, "Really?" – At which point Sid smiled and responded: "No, not really- I made that up."- and everyone laughed, but I was still amazed that he could make it sound so true! (See: www.Zemirotdatabase.org)

4. The year before I had first gone to Israel, those "bomb buddies" were not the only group I hung out with. —This other group, however, was a bit more constructive. I had conversations and some activities with "The Philadelphia Anti-Missionary Institute". Essentially, these were two Jewish guys, Scott Gould and Mickey Miller who had reacted to the cult concerns of the times and the fact

that Christian missionary groups were "preying" on wandering Jews to convert them to Christianity. Oddly enough, one example that stood out at the time was a "Jews for Jesus" Assembly led by Martin Chernoff, a Jew who had converted to Christianity and wanted to lead other Jews on that path. Around that time, as I've written here in this book, I had started investigating other religions between my high school sophomore and Junior year. I, like many Americans, had taken an interest in the debate as to whether religious cults were an example of freedom of religion, or whether they represented an unhealthy form of mind control over their members? Some groups like the Hare Krishnas and the "Moonies" (Members of the Unification Church and followers of Rev. Sun Myung Moon) were suspected of relying on their status as religions to retain a tax shelter- and to retain privacy as to their inner workings. The mid 70's saw a plethora of psychologists come out and warn that such groups drew wandering and shiftless youth into their fold with their theologies, but then used brainwashing techniques including isolation, "groupthink" and poor nutrition to meld them into adherents to their religious and sometimes quasi-political agendas. The questions raged back and forth in the media with religious advocates stating that people had the right to worship as they chose and psychologists and behaviorists questioning the sudden personality conversions that parents, friends and others attributed to these new religions. CBS television in fact ran a couple of "60 Minutes" news segments on young men and women who had undergone such sudden conversion to new religions. A few books came out as well, one of which I had read: *Snapping: America's Epidemic of Sudden Personality Change* by Flo Conway and Jim Siegelman (1978). In addition to my occasional meet-ups (and some-under-cover infiltration I did for Scott and Mickey), I was also on the lookout for other sources of information. One of these turned out to be Michael Masch (1950-2021) who in later life would serve positions as a senior vice-president and chief financial officer of Howard University as well as holding Pennsylvania state and Philadelphia local budget oversight positions. Back then, though, in the late 1970's, he was just Mike Masch, but a dedicated and involved member of Germantown Jewish Centre (where my parents and my family were members). Mike was also an avid reader of comic books and I would run into him on more than one occasion down at Fat Jack's Comic Crypt at 20th and Sansom Streets where we both went to buy our comic books. Anyway, the Germantown Jewish Centre Men's Club would arrange, once-a-month, to have a speaker talk for an hour on a contemporary topic of importance to the country as well as the Jewish Community. The lectures were promoted in the synagogue newsletter and I convinced my Dad that we should attend. Mike

Masch spoke at length about the issues regarding cults and missionaries. It was a phenomenal lecture delivered by an erudite speaker! Masch's lecture, combined with my book readings and discussions with Scott Gould and Mickey Miller formed the basis of the multi-part series I would write for the KIFTY Bulletin after my return from my first trip to Israel. The Guyana Tragedy, in which 909 members of "The People's Temple" later in 1978 essentially committed suicide under the direction of cult leader, Jim Jones, put the question to rest for many Americans who reasoned that any religion or religious leader who would lead his people to death did not constitute the "life-affirming" values with which most traditional and commonly accepted religious groups practice.

5. Unlike many other languages (including English), Hebrew has more levels of meaning then simply phonetic, graphic, and ordinal. For example, in English the letter "L" has the "El" phonetic pronunciation and sound, the graphic "L" visual identification, and ordinally it is the 12th letter in the English alphabet. Hebrew, however is more multi-dimensional. The Lamed (ל) even though it is also the 12th of 22 letters in the Hebrew alphabet has a separate mathematical value beyond it's ordinal position. Mathematically, it has a value of "30" as an individual component in combination with the mathematical

values of other Hebrew letters in any particular word. (The mathematical equivalents of Hebrew words is also termed the study of "Gematria".) Beyond this 4th level of mathematical value, each letter in the Hebrew alphabet also has a conceptual value. Lamed (ל), for example has the conceptual or spiritual meaning of "learning" and it's upswept head reaching up is a visual cue to reach up and acquire learning and spirituality. When Lamed is combined with the letter "bet" (ב), the word לב ("lev") is formed, meaning "heart". The heart is also an organ of teaching and learning through commitment and love. The bet (ב) has a mathematical value of two (in this case identical to it's ordinal value). The heart (לב) is also an organ that has duality in that it can serve either the person's good inclination (their Yetzer Tov) or their evil inclination (Yetzer Hora)- because all humanity have both! The gematria of Lev (לב) is 32 (30 +2). The Torah teaches that 32 is also the gematria of the word כבוד (Cavod) meaning, glory. Among the spiritual connections here may be the fact that it is through our heart, and connection to the inner (versus the outer world) that we may glorify G-d.

The spiritual component and mathematical values of each of the 22 Hebrew letters in combining to make words (with their gematria equivalents) are almost "chemical" or "physics-based". For example, the first verse of Genesis in the Hebrew of the Bible (as given over 2,000 years ago) tells us that G-d created the Heaven and the Earth. The Hebrew word for heaven is "Shamayim", written שמים. However,if we remove the letter, shin (ש) from the beginning of the word, we're left with the word "mayim", (מים), which translates as water. This expression is interesting because it relates to what we know of the chemical nature of water, that when it breaks down, it evaporates and returns it's elements to the atmosphere. Moreover, the Hebrew word for water, מים is structurally equivalent to it's modern day exposition of 2 hydrogen atoms and one oxygen atom. In other words, we might read the two mems (מ)'s as representing the heavier hydrogen elements, and the single yud (י) as representing the single oxygen atom). Again, these words are from the original Bible and have been written this way for thousands of years! Moreover, Jewish tradition teaches us that before the creation of the world, G-d looked into the eternal Torah and he used the primordial letters of the Hebrew alphabet, in various combinations to create our world through a composition of "black fire upon white fire" (Source: *Breishis Tanchuma*). While this sounds purely alliterative, we've learned over the last century, or so, that wavelengths and energy signatures can be related to form and function in a multiplicity of relationships that constitute the physics of our universe. Math and music have relatable sequences. So, Kabbalistically or in physics, it strikes a believable tone, that while it is beyond our comprehension, that our Creator did literally speak us into existence and through His utterances, recreates our world and each of us moment by moment! Related to this is G-d's commandment to the Jewish people to blow the ram's horn (termed a "Shofar") on Rosh Hashanah, which also celebrates the Birthday of our World on the sixth day of creation. The "Tekiah", "Shevarim", "Teruah" blasts as we hear them, are meant to awaken our souls to seek positive change in bringing ourselves closer to G-d. It may be a gift from G-d, allowing us as we hear the Shofar blasts to resonate with the opportunity to "recreate" ourselves and create new worlds of positive influence and abidance with G-d's laws on a physical plane. In this it may be spiritual, as a metaphor for the powerful utterances with which He himself created us.

6. My recollection is that my actual tour of Syracuse University took place sometime after the "open-house" visit to Temple Ambler's campus in Spring, 1981. In fact, my Syracuse visit may have been July 7, 1981. This makes sense because I recall the chatter on Syracuse's campus generated that day by President Ronald Reagan's appointment of Justice Sandra Day O'Connor as the first woman Justice to sit upon the Supreme Court.

CHAPTER FOUR: Lows And Highs

1. Temple University operated a small shuttle bus on a circulator route (nearly hourly) connecting the Ambler campus to the SEPTA Ambler regional rail station. It was a great benefit for Temple Ambler attendees who did not have cars or other means of personal transportation. On Thursday evenings, I would board the University's shuttle bus to the SEPTA rail station. SEPTA's own Lansdale/Doylestown train then made stops at Ambler station as well as stopping at Elkins Park on it's route inbound to center city Philadelphia. Temple also operated a larger bus that made direct connections between Ambler campus, the Tyler Art Campus (then situated in Elkins Park), the university's medical school campus, Main Campus and the Temple University Center City Campus (TUCC).

2. I would search the cafeteria offerings because I was trying to be "that Kosher" at the time. Almost everything that was presented looked like it could have been cooked on an open grill with any combination of meat and milk and would have been non-Kosher. Egg salad and tuna fish seemed my "safest" options.

CHAPTER FIVE: Temple Undergraduate Years

1. What was then the Benson Apartments is today the "100 York" Apartments. In the 1980's however, there was a popular restaurant on the ground floor that served residents of the building as well as walk-in customers.

2. Temple's Mitten Hall, located on the University's Main Campus, has a rich and "storied" past. In 1936, President Franklin Delano Roosevelt spoke there. Other historical figures whose presence has graced the venue include Charles Sandburg, Amelia Earhart and Charles Barclay (source: Temple University).

3. Peter Goldstone had an office in Ritter-Annex. I would occasionally spend time with him there, but also attended a few of his graduate classes in Ritter Hall as his guest.

4. Laura taught me some key principles of advertising and marketing. She introduced me to the mnemonic "AIDA", which was created in the late 19th century by businessman Elias St. Elmo. The mnemonic summarizes the stages by which an advertiser can evoke the purchasing urge of his or her targeted consumer. "A.I.D.A." means that the advertiser should catch the Attention of the prospective customer; arouse their Interest, create a Desire for the

item or service and instigate the Action to buy it. Laura also had a well honed approach to marketing-research in terms of revealing a consumer's conscious as well as unconscious influences for purchasing something. I had a rudimentary understanding of some of this even years before having met Laura from my reading during high school of Vance Packard's *The Hidden Persuaders* (1957). There are of course certain basic draws for a consumer, such as brandname and familiarity, ease of use, and economical pricing- but Laura was keen on the principles of "probing" and "qualifying", so that in any interview or survey, the marketing researcher captured all possible reasons and impulses that the consumer might be influenced by in the purchase.

5. Elkins Park has had a lot of history to it for the Jewish people. The past Prime Minister of Israel, Benjamin Netanyahu and his brother, Yonatan Netanyahu (who died in the raid on Entebbe in 1976), both lived in Elkins Park for a few years while briefly attending Cheltenham High School. My mother's family also resided in the Lynwood Gardens Apartments of Elkins Park for the first few years after her family moved from New York to Pennsylvania around 1952. Today the area is much more diverse with a rich mixture of nationalities. However, the three synagogues in Elkins Park (Keneseth Israel, Beth Shalom and Adath Jeshuran) located on Old York

Road between Township Line Road (to the North) and Ashbourne Road (to the South) constitute a Kehillah (Assembly) of synagogues along the Old York Road corridor. This year will also see the re-locating of several Yeshivot (academies for Torah learning) into Elkins Park.

6. During the 1980s, Sandra Kessler had the reputation of being one of the premier dealers on the east coast of the US for buying and selling antique toy robots and collectibles.

7. Rabbi Zelig Pliskin is the author of several books on self-improvement, notably *Love Your Neighbor* (1977); *Guard Your Tongue* (1979); *Gateway to Happiness* (1986); *Gateway to Self-Knowledge* (1986); and many more recent successive works. Because of his background and experience in psychology, I went to meet with Rabbi Pliskin. I do not recall whether that meeting was here in the states, or during my summer social work course in Israel in 1987. It was, though, sometime between 1986 and 1991. I took the opportunity to briefly discuss with him the extent of my obsession with the Dean. He demonstrated for me a series of hand movements in combination with thoughtful affirmations which were aimed at distracting me and breaking the cycle of obsessive thinking. I did try them, but with limited success.

8. There was - and remains- a consistency to these experiences. I'm reminded of a miraculous story of my father's youth that he related to me on at least two occasions. My father, as a young boy, was riding his bicycle out on the street near his home on North 8th Street in Logan. He was probably no older than five years old, so this was perhaps around 1933-'34. Anyway, a car ran over him and although he needed to go to the hospital and may have required stitches, he was relatively unscathed (ב"ה). In my own life, I've had the frequent experience that some form of inexplicable help or aid would suddenly materialize out of seeming nothingness in time to shield, protect, or move me away from some threatening, difficult, or potentially risk-laden circumstance- enabling me to escape danger, or just a bad situation (ב"ה).

9. Dr. Merton also autographed a text-book for me at the time that this photo was taken. He signed his name along with the words, " To Ted Rickles of Temple University my own Alma Mater, Robert Merton 870502, Boston". Merton's contribution as a father of sociology's structuralist-functionalist's approach is incalculable. His book, *Social Theory and Social Structure* (1949) is considered a seminal work. Merton put forth a theory of deviant behavior, respective to different types of social adaptation. He also defined the terms "latent

function"vs. "manifest function". Merton's early use of focused interviews led to the mainstream use of "focus groups" in marketing research campaigns.

CHAPTER SIX: Temple Graduate Years

1. One of the major initiatives during those years at the DVRPC was the support and advancement of TMA's (Transportation Management Associations). The DVRPC provided analyses of trip data and recommendations for a number of TMA's including the North Penn TMA, the Eastgate TMA in New Jersey and several others. The origin and development of TMA's came about historically as a response by "campus"business leaders to deal with the congested ride-to-work experiences of their employees. So, TMA's, often led by the President or representative of a major company, also represented the collective interests and concerns communicated by the other companies within the campus of such major industrial office parks. I would analyze trip "ride-to-work" and "work-departure" times as well as the volume of trips by time-point, and write up the reports with recommendations, which were then sent to the respective TMA chairperson. The recommendations were often in terms of suggesting additional car-pooling, consideration of lobbying local government for inclusion of high-occupancy vehicle lanes on the expressways leading to the industrial park, company institution of "flex-time" to alter high traffic arrival or departure times, and alternative staggered shifts. It was interesting

work, which at one point, even brought me to the World Trade Center (1991) to accompany other DVRPC staff to a regional transportation conference.

CHAPTER SEVEN: Post-College World

1. Other dedicated inbound phone lines to WMS handled calls for Topper's Spas, purchases of study software for the MCAT and LSAT entrance exams, as well as Dutch Gardens. Additionally, I recall one particularly odd job where Vice-President Mark Morris pulled me off plane reservations with Travel Bargains in order to "cold-call" wholesale manufacturers of industrial freezers- using the yellow pages. (I never really found out what that was about- but I did it!)

2. I think that the appreciation of Sequoia's as a dining venue is something that Lori and I continued to share throughout the years. In 1998, when she married her husband, Cuong, their wedding was held in Embassy Row and the families of both bride and groom shared an enjoyable pre-wedding dinner at Sequoia under a late summer's night sky.

3. This reference is based on a telephone conversation between the author and Stanley Sved on July 21, 2022 between 6pm and 7pm.

4. Up to a point, Gene Roddenberry's journey with *Genesis II* (1973) paralleled his experience in getting the

network "nod" to get *Star Trek* on the air in 1966. The first "pilot" that Gene produced for *Star Trek* was "The Cage", which the network execs deemed "too cerebral". Fortunately, for the many Trek fans throughout the world, Gene didn't give up there and went on to make a second pilot, "Where No Man Has Gone Before". Likewise, when *Genesis II* was turned down for a series, despite garnering significant Nielsen ratings in its March 23, 1973 airing, Gene rebounded with a second made-for-television pilot, *Planet Earth* (1974). It too was rejected and a later third attempt, significantly altered and without Roddenberry's involvement- Strange New World - was aired by ABC in 1975. Gene had seen the writing on the wall back in the Spring of 1974 because CBS had already scrapped their interest in *Genesis II*. The network purportedly had only one opening for a sci-fi television series for the Fall, 1974 programming season - and they chose the *Planet of the Apes* TV series instead. The Apes franchise had taken the public eye, and CBS likely believed it had greater staying power. However, the *Planet of The Apes* TV series was also beset by a number of plot problems and was cancelled after only one season.

5. One of the things I had hoped to accomplish when I returned to Paris in 2018 was to solve the mystery of that photo of the two Nazi SS officers smiling while posing

in front of the Eiffel Tower. After a twenty-three year absence from the monument, it did seem a bit farcical when I rode the tower's pillar elevator along with a crowd of noisy enthusiastic tourists. For those tourists, the elevator, or "lift", we were in was only a means to get to the tower's mid-level restaurants, or to the top for a breathtaking city view of Paris. However, though I did partake in these activities as well, my main interest was in the elevators themselves. I rode a couple of times up and a couple times down, asking each of the elevator attendants if they knew anything about the photo which I described as posted in 1995 on the outside of the elevator shaft wall at the tower's mid-level. Most of the attendants were too young - only one was past seventy and his memory had dimmed in ability to recall events of over two decades earlier. The answer to the mystery did not come until I got to Israel the following week. I had planned to spend the Rosh Hashanah holiday with friends who lived in Ramat Bet Shemesh Aleph, a suburb of Jerusalem. In addition to myself, there were two elderly guests, a married couple. They were clearly of mixed nationality. The wife, I believe was Israeli, but the husband spoke with an apparent French accent. It turned out that he was a French national and had had a career working in the Louvre. After hearing my question, he explained that 1995 marked the 50th anniversary of the end of World War II, and as such, the photo I saw was likely one of a variety that could have been posted throughout Paris as a reminder of the pain that the war had cost France. It could have been part of a national effort to remember, but also a reminder to never let such things ever happen again.

6. Between 1999 and 2001 the San Diego Convention Center underwent a major expansion, doubling its size. Simultaneously, the composition of Comic-con was changing and growing to include much more of a media presence in the booths that took over the exposition areas and panel programming which filled conference rooms to promote new upcoming film and television releases. Likewise, the attending public swelled to 160,000 people. The experience for return attendees such as myself was as if Comic-Con had doubled in size to fill an additional football field! Comic-Con filled the expanding convention space to capacity, even as the extensions were completed! It was both phenomenal and exhilarating! By the time of my last attendance, despite the completion of this expansion, Comic-Con planners had to institute "crossing-guards" at the aisle intersections on the convention floor, regulating crowded pedestrian traffic to permit short flows of foot traffic at perpendicular aisles.

7. Unfortunately, there is little on the internet regarding World Marketing Services having existed throughout the 1990s. However, it is referenced in the obituary of its president, Bahir Browsh, who sadly passed away in September, 2021. See: www.Olearyfuneral.com.

CHAPTER EIGHT: New Millennium

1. Blue Sky Tours is currently listed as operating out of Albuquerque, NM. As of this writing, there is no confirmation as to whether the Blue Sky tour bus company that I utilized in the Santa Barbara-Ojai region of a southern California in 2000 is, or ever was, an affiliate of the current company.

2. Aside from her role as Lois Lane in the first four *Superman* films (1978,'81,'83 & '87), Margot Kidder had many other outstanding performances. Two of my favorites were as Zazel Pierce, opposite Gene Wilder, in the 1970 film, *Quackser Fortune Has a Cousin* in the Bronx; and as Marcia Curtis in *The Reincarnation of Peter Proud* (1975).

3. The SEPTA Wyndmoor rail station was rebuilt in its current location in 1930. But that location, at 256 E. Willow Grove Avenue and Wyndmoor Street was previously a portion of an old civil-war hospital. Mower General Hospital had additionally spanned the current area of the Chestnut Hill Village apartments and occupied a full 27 acres of land situated between Stenton, Germantown, Springfield and Abington Avenues including areas that now contain town houses. Mower Hospital had been one of the largest federal military hospitals during America's

Civil War. It had operated from January, 1863 through May, 1865 and 20,000 soldiers were treated there over the course of those years (source: Wikipedia).

4. Whether intentional or incidental, the Chestnut Hill Village Apartments complex, which now occupies a portion of the space upon which the old Mower Civil War hospital (1863-1865) resided, has in recent years (2018 or later) had its buildings repainted from red to a shade of grey-blue So, oddly enough on what would have been the 160th anniversary of the opening of the hospital (January, 2023), an odd shade that mixes both union & confederate colors adorns the buildings for area residents, as well as the traffic coursing along that section of Stenton Avenue.

5. Originally, before the television series of the same name (1964-1968) by Irwin Allen, there was a film starring Walter Pidgeon and Robert Sterling also titled, *Voyage to the Bottom of the Sea* (1961). It was, in fact, the basis for television series of which Arthur was a very devoted fan!

6. See: Ellison, Harlan. *The City on the Edge of Forever.* Limited Edition. Borderlands Press. Baltimore.1995. p.8

7. I was in significant pain and did not question other bus passengers, arriving officers or paramedics in the moments after the crash's impact. I did however observe from a distance that the second car that had plowed into the first appeared badly "accordioned" and I believe I witnessed the arrival of "jaws-of-life" equipment to safely extricate any passengers that may have been in the vehicle at the time of impact. The event was also related on the late night news that evening.

8. To understand Compartmental Syndrome and it's seriousness, one has to know that there are parts of the human body that are "chambered" other than the heart. So, for example, your biceps as well as your calves are chambered. In my case, somehow in running as I had never run before, I accidentally tore a tendon, ligament or other connective element associated with the compartment of my right calf. The result was that internal fluids were seeping into that chambered area, building up Internal Compartmental Pressure (ICP) that, over time and in my acute case, would eventually crush the existing nerves and muscle inside the calf. Had the condition not been properly diagnosed on the spot, and a fasciotomy performed immediately to drain the fluid, I could have been either paralyzed from the waist down, or even required amputation!

9. I am grateful that during the month I spent at Chestnut Hill Hospital throughout March of 2003, that good friends, Frank and Joye Schwartz as well as Ben Silver and David Toplin came to visit me.

10. Whether or not apparent from the account I've written, I was both annoyed and put-off at the time by what I perceived as Dr. Brobyn's very dramatic and emotional resistance to describing what would happen to my leg if I did not have the skin graft.I was really very ignorant. I didn't understand why a skin graft was needed and assumed beforehand, that the cut created by the faciotomy would heal over time on it's own and at worst only required stitches? Without Dr. Brobyn's forthcoming explanation, I could only assume that the skin-graft was cosmetic in nature. Dr. Brobyn's emotional, almost tearful reticence to explain the process of purulence, gangrene, etc. that would otherwise set in without the skin graft, seemed to me to be simple enough that he should have been able to explain it in an objective detached clinical manner. But instead, he put his head in his hand and went very sad, telling me that he could not believe I was putting him through the verbal detail of the consequences. Dr. Thomas Brobyn passed away in 2019. Until reading his obituary, it was unknown to me that he'd been a veteran, serving his country in the Vietnam War and seen his share of medical trauma, while posted to the 229th Medical Detachment and 3rd Field Hospital.

CHAPTER NINE: Moving Forward

1. A "Ketubah" is a Jewish marriage contract. It contains the names of the Bride and Groom, the date of the wedding and agreements of what the couple commit to each other in the face of G-d during their marriage. It requires the signature of two witnesses that they were present at the occasion as well.

2. Sadly, Klebs Moura Junior passed away of cancer on November 21, 2021. During the time I knew him he was a great friend and encouragement to me. His dedication to the graphic arts and comic books, in particular, is an inspiration to all of us! First and foremost, he was a teacher willing to work with anyone who wanted to use the visual arts to tell a story. He was one of the founders of Studio Impacto Quadrinos in his native São Paulo. It didn't matter if his students were financially challenged, or where they came from in São Paulo. If they had an interest in art, it was his joy and life's pursuit to encourage it! This was endemic to his personality and I experienced it first hand in the interest he took in me and the encouragement he gave me, not only on our project, but in his suggestions that I should try to seek employment with DC Comics, Dynamite, or other companies (I did not feel at that time, though that that was the career direction I wanted my life to take- But Klebs made it clear that he

believed in me and supported me.) We were together in San Diego on one of the last Comic-Cons I attended in the early 2000's. Some years later he had cause to come to the publishing offices of Marvel or DC in New York and made a side trip to Philadelphia so that we could see each other. Sure enough, when I met him at the Amtrak 30th Street station on his arrival from New York, he was not alone. He proudly introduced me to one of his students who, he said had great talent and whom he had brought along from São Paulo. Impacto Quadrinos was likely the predecessor to Kleb's later IHQ Studios. As a graphic artist, Klebs was sought after by both Marvel and DC and others and had many successful comic book contributions to his credit. He worked for several years on his own major work, a graphic novel titled, *Patra Armada* ("Armed Homeland"). In 2016, it received the HQMIX award for best Brazilian miniseries. Although the work that Klebs did on our proposed *Genesis II: Alone Against Tomorrow* graphic novel never went much further than the sample art shown here, I am proud to have at last presented it within the pages of this book. R.I.P., Good friend!

3. Charles ("Chuck") Tooley (1957-2021) had an editorial role in shaping portions of the story as well as the look and feel of the work we did on Genesis II: Alone Against Tomorrow. First and foremost, Chuck was the capable manager of two of the three incarnations of the comic

book store on the second floor of the Plymouth Meeting Mall between the early1990's until about 2005. Initially operated as *The Comic Stop*, the store moved one space over and became *Legends*, retaining Chuck as its manager. However, whenever he had a free moment that didn't involve helping a customer, or conversing with fans, he would opportunely convert the exchange into a teaching moment. Chuck was incredibly well read. He'd also worked as an editor prior to coming to be manager. Because he was a an effective manager, the owners of the comic book store acquiesced to Chuck's near ultimatum that they incorporate sales of classic paperbacks from as much as a half century earlier. It was Chuck's strong belief that comic books were in fact a jumping off point for readers to move to books and even the classics. While he managed those stores, it was a great experience to walk in and peruse the countless paperbacks that filled the walls, sharing space with the latest new releases of comic books!

4. The *Questor Tapes* (1974) was the third of four made-for-television movies that Gene Roddenberry produced between 1972 and 1977. Retrospectives on the making of *Star Trek: The Next Generation* (1987-1994), often point out that the android character of Questor (portrayed by actor Robert Foxworth) was the basis for Roddenberry's character of "Data" on The Next Generation. However, had Questor been developed as a television series,

his android character would have had an historical background far different from Data's. Data was explained as the unique creation of a reclusive scientist, Dr. Noonien Soong. Questor, on the other hand, was the last in a line of "Lazarus"-like-androids who had originally been placed on Earth thousands of years ago to help shepherd humanity through its development- helping to avoid wars, famine and other traumas to mankind. In the pilot film, the activation of Questor and upload of his trans-generational programming was incomplete. The pilot film paired Dr.Jerry Robinson (actor Mike Farrell) as Questor's human companion, to assist the android with human perspectives on the crises they would face and to integrate emerging pieces of programming he retained from his predecessor. Had the series materialized, the stories would have likely proceeded on Earth with contemporary problems, as opposed to those faced by Data in his role as crew member aboard a galaxy spanning starship.

5. Laura's sister, Sandra Lee (Kessler) Tamler was investigated by the F.B.I. in 2010, along with her business partner, Richard Cohen as part of a raid on the businesses they managed, Prime-Tel Communications and "National-A1 Advertising", (also the parent company of Hotmovies.com). On October 27, 2010, the F.B.I. descended on the company's Philadelphia offices then

at 106 S. 7th Street (the Washington Square Building) and 1912 Rittenhouse Square. The F.B.I. raid also investigated associated charges that the company may have been involved in an illegal escort service. Subsequent to the bureau's probe, Sandra left Pennsylvania and for a time relocated to Carmel, California where she lived with husband, Dr. Bradley Tamler. (Sources: "Federal Investigators Continue Philly Porn Raid"; 6ABC.com.); and "Prime-tel Communications"; Wikipedia; and Instant Checkmate.com "Sandra Lee Kessler")

6. If you've read this book all the way through- there's got to be one question you're asking yourself. If this guy (me) got his driver's license back in 1984, and he's been renewing it all this time- how come he never drove after getting it?? It's a very fair question. Periodically I also did take refresher courses, thinking I would get a car, even a rental, and drive. Obviously, not having a car was one factor that restricted my access to jobs (along with my refusal to work on Saturdays- the Sabbath for Jews- and despite my thoughts of breaking my religious observance for the Amtrak job, I never did!- and have maintained a continuous record of refraining from work on the Sabbath since I was twenty!) Anyway, back to the car issue. Oddly every time I would start to take refresher courses and consider a move to get a car, some incident would very soon occur to dissuade me from it. At one point, I

had made arrangements for driving lessons, again, and was going to start research to buy a car. However, that weekend I was in a car with friends headed for the Jersey shore and we wound up in a fender-bender on the PA-NJ turnpike. The friend who was driving had failed to observe a nearly hidden on-ramp for merging traffic. That was enough to put the kibosh on my driving plans at that point. However, after my neurological condition was diagnosed in 2018, and I began to recognize that a loss of focus accompanied my dizziness, I began to suspect that it probably wasn't safe for me to drive with that kind of medical problem. My episodes of dizziness had been less frequent when I'd been younger, but I was already beginning to realize that stress was a trigger- also not a good thing if you're a regular driver. So, again, I think G-d knew long before I realized it that driving was not a safe gambit for me. Today, I get around with a reduced disabled transit pass or Uber.

7. Robert Culp starred alongside actresses Gig Young and Majel Barrett Roddenberry in Gene Roddenberry's fourth and final made-for-Television pilot, *Spectre* (1977). Culp portrayed William Sebastian, a former criminologist and occult expert who is called upon to combat demonic forces at an estate in England. In previous years, Robert Culp had become well known through his time on the popular "I-Spy" TV series (1965-1968). The series had

won a Golden Globe award in 1967 for best TV show. In 1964, Culp starred in one of the only two original *Outer Limits* episodes penned by SF writer Harlan Ellison. This was *Demon with a Glass Hand*, one of my all time favorite television works. In later years Culp entertained TV viewers as FBI agent Bill Maxwell in *The Greatest American Hero* (1981-1983). He even portrayed the President of the United States in the 1993 film adaptation of John Grisham's novel, *The Pelican Brief.*

8. Before supporting the opinion I put forth in this book's central body, I give credit to Mr.Abrams as an excellent television series creator and producer. Abram's work on his numerous television series: *Alias* (2001-2006); *Lost* (2004-2010); *Fringe* (2008-2013); and *Person of Interest* (2011-2016) are some of the best and most compelling television series ever aired. Unfortunately, when it comes to his big screen ventures, I cannot be nearly as generous, as they often come across in my mind as "formulaic" to say the least. In the case of *Star Trek* (2009), Abrams did admit in a pre-release statement that, "the film was not made for fans of the original series", but, "made for future fans of the franchise and for people who just want to go on a thrill ride" (Source: Shuker, Lauren A.E. And Peter Sanders, "Hollywood Starts Over: From 'Star Trek' to 'X-Men', Studios are Betting on Prequels for the Summer Blockbuster Season," *The Wall Street Journal*, April 24, 2009, pp. W1, W4).

I also reprint here the text I supplied on Ms. Bjo Trimble's Facebook page in retrospective discussion of the film, May 27-28, 2013

"… In the immediate wake of 9/11 so many (scheduled) release films, like Shwartzenegger's "Collateral Damage" or "The Bourne Identity" were pulled or delayed from distribution in theaters, out of the studios' concerns that the public was sensitive to terrorism. Abrams comes out with a film, before the decade is out, twisting an alternate timeline into a way that we can understand that "mass loss" in peacetime is part of life and that the common man, "Nero" as captain of a mining ship, can be a terrorist. This is a statement, an exposition of our (current) reality, but it lacks a visionary hope for reducing its occurrence or giving us real hope for change. Star Trek used to be in the business of Hope."

My having intuited that the film was in fact making a direct reference to 9/11 was corroborated shortly before the release of its sequel, *Star Trek: Into Darkness* (2013) by an uncredited writer on the 2009 film, Damian Lindeloff. The following is excerpted from an article appearing in the *New York Times* and written by Dave Itzkowitz, printed May 3, 2013 and titled, "Hopping From One Galaxy to Another: J.J. Abrams on his New 'Star Trek' and 'Star Wars' films:

"Narratively, Mr. Abrams 'Star Trek' used a sly time travel subplot to establish its young Starfleet officers without annihilating the 40 years of storylines that preceded the film. But it also destroyed Spock's home planet of Vulcan –

an occurrence that Mr. Lindeloff called 'our 9/11 moment in the Trek-verse"

The fact that I addressed a number of friends and fellow movie-goers at the time, back in 2009 (who'd also seen the film) —and no one else had this realization is disturbing to me. People seemed to be willing to be hypnotically led through the 127 minute film, happy to be thrilled with the characterizations of Kirk, Spock and McCoy, Engineer Scott, and the various others along with thrilling space battles. Movie goers do this (and the studios know it), because viewers already enter the theater with the intention to be entertained, and nothing more. Given that premise alone, any highly experienced and intelligent film creator, who has been"knighted" by the film industry can write a political subtext into his/her film knowing full-well that it will go under the radar of the viewers- because the viewer him/herself is biased to consciously ignore any such messages. This however was not always true, and a number of overtly political films were released in the 1970's because the cultural verve of that decade looked specifically to use main-stream film as a way to explore political issues. *Three Days of the Condor* (1975) explicitly interrogated the possibility that a hidden intelligence agency could arise within the C.I.A. to influence its policies and operations. Another film, *Black Sunday* (1977). was a well-made, fictitious dramatic film about a terrorist plot to use a dirigible to bomb the Super Bowl!

Prior to 9/11 Black Sunday would frequently be aired from year-to-year around the time of the actual Super Bowl. However, the anxiety that networks had in regard to anything that involved themes of terrorism resulted in it being generally pulled from television broadcast after 9/11. Additionally, the original *Star Trek* series has often been praised for many episodes that did explore political themes such as racism, war and labor relations. The episodes, "A Private Little War" and "Errand of Mercy" are two episodes credited with the exploration of political and humanitarian issues associated with colonialism and war. However, in the original series, the tone and consideration were quite different. Those original series episodes, while representing the issues, usually ended with an acknowledgement of their complexity and a sub-narrative invitation to the viewer to ponder alternatives-they were stories told with moral inquiry.

As far as my comparison to Abrams' 2009 Trek movie and the films of Hitler's Minister of Propaganda, Joseph Goebbels, Goebbels was skilled and artistic in using the casual and day-today elements of society to obscure hidden truths of his subjects' conditions. I am not speaking here of the more numerous films he made to glorify the Reich, but rather the several films he made concerning the treatment of Jews in the ghettos and concentration camps that were produced for dissemination throughout the world. The Red Cross and other international agencies had received reports of atrocities committed on Jews and other groups under German occupation. To counter these reports, two such films were made of the Terezin Ghetto (1942, 1943) in which Jews were posed (upon pain of punishment or death) as listening intently to concerts, or playing recreational activities to suggest that the ghetto was really a place of liesure and enjoyment. Clever soundtracks and focus on the activities obscured the horror that could only be exposed much later in the post-war years. Similarly, Abrams' 2009 Trek film, in addition to its messaging on 9/11 also encoded negative treatments of officer ascension (characters in the film often advance in rank through death of a higher officer and with little to no time for preparation). Also, the respect and proper address of officers is caricatured in the ways in which Captain Nero responds to and treats the Starfleet commanders and officers he engages with.

9. Dr. Peter Goldstone passed away on January 27, 2020 at the age of eighty and was buried in Chicago, IL. He was a great personal friend to me and a constant support to our synagogue. Just as I incorporated change into my life following the passing of Arthur Tobias to honor his memory, likewise, I began wearing Tefillin more regularly both as G-d's commandment in the Bible specifies, as well as to honor the memory of Peter who was in all ways committed to G-d and his fellow man.

CHAPTER 10: Difficult Period of Loss

1. Walking backward utilizes a different set of motor-neuron connections (different pathways in the brain)), than walking forwards.

2. This was my cousin, Ellen (Simmens) Barbash.

3. Sadly, it was not until recently (May, 2021) that the US Preventative Service Task Force did lower the recommended age for colorectal screenings to age 45. My sister Sara was a victim of the previous shortsightedness. All the indications were there, even before she had turned 48. She'd had inexplicable weight loss, a small abdominal lump and perhaps other signs. But the insurance companies refused to cover the screening for someone under fifty, making it a very expensive out-of-pocket gamble. As our concern mounted, Sara's doctor had to write a letter to the insurance company justifying from his perspective why the screening was necessary at that point, and that they needed to cover it! Unfortunately, as we would discover from a biopsy taken during that screening, it was already too late. The polyps were malignant and the cancer had already spread throughout her body.

4. The strife that Sara and I endured has an all-too-common basis in social-psychological behavior. Quite often in families and relationships, when one (or more) members of a primary group passes away or is unable to function- the surviving, or remaining members tend to assume the role, and or characteristics of the person who has been lost or otherwise compromised. This can have positive or negative effects, but is often unconscious and arises out of a desire to maintain the group's stability and function. In our case, Sara and I were essentially vying for the same role as the primary care-giver to our widowed Dad.

5. On all levels, I was much more aware of what and why I needed to inflict these stabbing cuts in 2015 than I had been when committing a similar act in 2011. The 2015 cuttings were virtually pre-meditated, as, I thought just before performing them that I really did not want to fatally injure myself. I deliberately looked at my hands and feet, looking to avoid major arteries and looking primarily for non-vessel area. It was a calculated effort to let loose my pain, but not compromise my life. In actuality, it was the two earlier efforts at suicide which were much more dangerous from an involuntary perspective. My 2011 impulsive and emotionally traumatic cutting as well as my 2006 considered walk into traffic were much closer to real threats to my life. As a general note, "Cutting" and

any form of self-inflicted wound is contraindicated in the Torah. While my behavior in these acts of self harm do not favor me as an "observant" Jew - they do place me squarely in the 5% of the humanity who respond to crises of emotional pain, or inability to express one's self, by acting out through cutting or self mutilation. Again, each of us, regardless of our religion or faith, have a *Yetzer Tov* (a good inclination) as well as a *Yetzer Hora* (an evil inclination). It's important for all of us, as we go forward, to recognize that our *Yetzer Hora* is not just capable of doing evil to others, but quite often to ourselves as well. For more understanding on "cutting" and other forms of self-harm, self-mutilation and psychiatric ways to treat it, check out: https://mhanational.org/conditions/self-injury-cutting-self-harm-or-self-mutilation.

6. This was Geodon (also known pharmaceutically as Ziprasidone). For many people it can offer relief from psychosis. However, despite having seen occasional psychiatrists, I have never been diagnosed as schizophrenic (and gratefully so) nor psychotic. So, the drug did not work on me as it may have worked on others who have been diagnosed as such. Being forced to be on Geodon for over 6 months was the worst drug experience of my life!

CHAPTER 11: Adjusting to a New Reality

1. The glass etched transporter beaming vignette from Star Trek's original series with Kirk, Spock and McCoy was photographed by me during a tour of the *Skirball Cultural Center* exhibition: "StarTrek: Exploring New Worlds"; Los Angeles, CA (December 8, 2021).The adjacent photo of myself with Denise and Michael Okuda and Doug Drexler was taken in 2018 during a tour of the ship at *Star Trek – The Original Series Set Tour*, Ticonderoga, NY. The married couple of Denise and Michael Okuda are technical staff, having worked every incarnation of Star Trek as well as authoring several books of their own. Likewise, Doug Drexler is a Special Effects artist, designer, sculptor and illustrator who has worked on several Star Trek series and films as well as the *Battlestar Galactica* reboots and several mainstream films. The picture on the ship's bridge of Bill Shatner in the Command chair, with me standing behind him and the skunk, "Fle'uer" posed on the armrest of the chair was taken on July 24, 2021 on the occasion of Bill's visit to Ticonderoga and celebration of his 90th birthday.

2. "Celebrations of the Anniversary of 2001: A Space Odyssey"- The photo of me, shoulder-to-shoulder with

Keir Dullea and Gary Lockwood was taken some time around 2002 (most likely in Pasadena, California at a Creation *Star Trek* Convention). The other two photos are from 2018 during actual celebrations of the film's 50th anniversary. The photo of me posing between Discovery One's EVA suit and space pod is from a display in 2018 at the *Escape Velocity* Convention held May 25-27th in National Harbor, MD at the Marriott- Gaylord Hotel. "Escape Velocity" is an event organized on behalf of the Museum of Science Fiction (MOSF) founded by Greg Viggiano. The final photo, in "The White Room", was a wonderful immersive recreation of the film's white room maintained as a temporary exhibit on the first floor of the Smithsonian's Air & Space Museum from April 8, 2018 through to the end of summer, 2018.

3. Unfortunately, during December 26-27, 2000, violent winter storms rampaged through southern France, destroying 270 million trees, including 10,000 on the historic site of the majestic gardens of Versailles Palace. The damage to the gardens destroyed what had been essentially the same landscape that had, up until then, survived untouched since the reign of Marie Antoinette. The clean-up crews and landscapers worked for months, day-after-day, to restore some semblance of the gardens as they were. But I could not help but feel, on my return trip to Versailles in 2018, that much had in fact changed.

Only the lake remained for me as a familiar comfort to what I had experienced in 1995.

4. Versailles *Hall of Mirrors* is here related in three different eras. Sometimes, when I walk into buildings or places, I actually feel connected to them through impressions of past (or possibly in the case of central Philadelphia) future conditions. This did not actually happen to me on my visits to the Palace of Versailles. However, as I wrote this biography, I stumbled across historical images that reflected the exact same space in two earlier time periods, relative to the photo I took upon being there in 2018. Putting them together here, simulates for the reader, the experience I have of overlapping time zones often experienced in other locales and places. Learning a place's history makes any of us "time travelers".

5. Ascent of Tzfat is a hostel and institute of learning located in Tzfat since 1983. It's a place of contemplation, reflection and spiritual growth. Rabbi Shaul Leiter, a founder of Ascent, has been a driving force in maintaining Ascent's spiritual mission to provide hospitality and learning to those traveling to and from Israel. When I visit Israel, I always visit Tzfat- and in Tzfat, I try to spend Shabbat and time learning in classes that Ascent provides. If you go, it's

recommended that you email and or call in advance. Check them out at www.Ascentofsafed.com. (By the way, if you are confused in this book about the use of different spellings of this city's name- Don't be! Safed is literally, the only city in the world that has twenty different and all common, legitimate English spellings. If you visit, you'll experience the diversity of spellings, varying in store names and restaurants from one street to the next. I have a t-shirt and mug that list all twenty correct spellings! Of course, in Hebrew, it has the same pronunciation- but only one correct spelling "צפת".

6. The problem here at Boston's Logan Airport was that I myself did not yet know the medical term for my condition, nor was I even certain of its etiology. I had begun to suspect that it was neurological in nature, but without an MD's diagnosis, my conjectures were mere speculation. So, when the TSA questioned me, I truly could not explain to them what was wrong with me with any confidence or basis. They and the paramedics who arrived attempted to use physical force to convey me to the hospital. This I knew was wrong, counter-productive and an unnecessary waste of my time and money and their resources. I knew this because I'd already had multiple trips to the ER and repeated brain scans over the last few years and they had all showed normal brain structure without any physical abnormalities. It would be a few

months after I returned from Israel that I would get a proper diagnosis of "Conversion Disorder" or Functional Neurological Disorder. This is a condition that was first diagnosed by a Parisian, Jean-Martin Charcot (1825-1893). Dr. Sigmund Freud (1856-1939) who diagnosed numerous cases of functional neurological disorder, had also previously spent five months studying under Charcot at the age of twenty-nine. Unfortunately, there is no pill or serum that can minimize or potentiate the effects of the condition, the primary treatment for the condition has historically been behavioral therapy and modification, which I continue to do today! (see: neurosymptoms.org)

7. As I've noted earlier, my efforts to keep fully Kosher became a strain on my relationships with my family. My parents, brother and sisters stayed with Conservative Judaism. Many more successful Baal Teshuvahs (Jews who return to Torah Observance) make a fuller, more complete transition than I have. But I've learned in the struggle, that all of us, whatever our religion, and whatever our connection to G-d are all on a path toward greater connection, from different points on that path. Also, I feel that as long as we're striving toward complete observance of the Bible and G-d's Commandments, that we're on the right side of our relationship with our Creator. It's somewhere written that Hashem, (G-d) does not expect us to always complete something, but

He does expect us to at least Try. At this point, because I do still strive to maintain connections with less religious family and friends, I compromise to the extent that I will not eat meat in a non-Kosher restaurant (and I maintain Kashrut at home). I do however eat salmon, flounder, cod, monkfish, Tilapia and Kosher fish as well as meatless salads in restaurants. Unfortunately, since my diagnosis of diabetes in late 2021, my choices in restaurants have had to exclude bread items as well.

8. In 1990, at the time Dr. Valaida Walker was advanced to become Temple's Vice-President of Student Affairs, she had already achieved a storied administrative career in special education within the university itself, and the City of Philadelphia. Both Dr. Walker and Kristl Lynn (Mehnert) Wiernicki could call Temple University their Alma Mater. In Kristl's case, her experience was wholly within Temple University. She filled a thirty-year straight commitment to Temple as she moved from undergraduate student, receiving her B.A. in Journalism as a Communications major in 1974; acquiring her J.D. from Temple's School of Law in 1981; being hand-picked as Vice-President H. Patrick Swygert's Executive Assistant during 1982; and then being advanced to Dean of Students and serving in Student Affairs until her departure from Temple in 2004. Additionally, while attending as a student herself, she worked in

Temple's Office of Financial Aid, assisting students with the completion and processing of their financial aid applications. Ultimately she was awarded the position of Associate Vice-President of Student Affairs. Kristl's ascension was subtly influenced through sharing a kinship-cohort experience with Peter Liacouras and Pat Swygert, with all three of them having shared time together academically in Temple's School of Law, where Liacouras had previously served as Dean of the School and Swygert had been a law professor. The professional association between Kristl Wiernicki, Vice President H. Patrick Swygert and then President Peter J. Liacouras was a powerful and a significant one. As stated on the University's website (www.Fox.Temple.edu), Liacouras is directly credited with "the evolution of Temple from a commuter school to an Urban learning Hub". To that end, as President, he was shrewd enough to advance those individuals that he had shared experience, values, and skills and whom he knew could achieve his agenda under his leadership. Swygert and Liacouras correctly identified Kristl as that person. While we can appreciate the honor due Dr. Walker, it may be an unfortunate oversight by Temple that Kristl (Mehnert) Wiernicki, who served so capably for students and the University, goes virtually unsung as an envoy of responsible empowerment during Temple's vital transformation.

AFTERWORD

(Reprinted with permission from the author and *The Jewish Press,* and as originally published: *The Jewish Press* Friday, November 4, 2022; Pg 11)

Remembering Rabbi Dov Aaron Brisman
By Baruch Lytle

Philadelphia said farewell to one of its foremost rabbinic authorities, Rabbi Dov Aaron Brisman, who passed peacefully in his sleep on Monday, September 19, at the age of 69. Brisman served as the *Rosh Beis Din* of the Philadelphia Beis Din, head of Keystone-Kashrus Agency, senior rabbi of Young Israel of Elkins Park and *Rosh Beis Din* of Igud HaRabbonim-Rabbinical Alliance of America, an umbrella organization of over 900 Orthodox rabbis.

Born in St. Louis and raised in Los Angeles, he was an extraordinary person from a young age. In Los Angeles, he studied at Ohr Elchonon Yeshiva under Rabbi Simcha Wasserman, son of Rav Elchonon Wasserman. In Baltimore, he studied at Yeshivas Ner Yisrael under Rabbi Moshe

Heineman and Rav Yaakov Moshe Kolefsky. Later, he attended Mir Yeshiva in Jerusalem under Rav Chaim Leib Shmuelevitz and Rav Nochum Partzovitz. He received *semicha* from Rav Schneur Kotler of Bet Medrash Govoha in Lakewood, New Jersey.

"He was from a bygone era. He came from a long line of great *rabbonim* in Europe, many of them authors and great scholars," Rabbi Yitzchok Leizerowski, Rav of Bet Medrosh Harav, he told *The Jewish Press*, "and he was himself an incredible in-depth scholar. In Elkins Park, he took a community that was barely there and built it up into a community of *talmidim chachamim*, which is still flourishing today. He was involved in writing halacha with many of the *gedolim* of Eretz Israel, and questions poured into him from the biggest rabbis internationally, very weighty halachic questions." Leizerowski said one of the biggest *ravs* in Israel once said of him that "his pen is something that you haven't seen in 150 years. Brisman was able to write tens of pages of thought off the top of his head. "Many rabbonim would give him their works to edit," said Leizerowski,"and because of that he did not have the time to work on more of his own works."

"As a member of the (Philadelphia) *beis din,* his knowledge was encyclopedic," rav Mordecai Terebelo, 22-year member of the *beis din* and *rav* of Ahavas Torah in Philadelphia's northeast community, told *The Jewish Press*. He was very well respected among the great rabbis in Eretz Israel and in America. His views carried a lot of weight, and yet he was always inquiring about how our [members of the *beis din*] kids were doing. Nothing and no one was below him. I sincerely believed if a boy came up to him and said, 'Rabbi Brisman, I would like to learn Gemara with you for ten minutes a week' he would do it. He had the patience to teach everyone."

As Rabbi Terebelo predicted, Brisman's love for children shined even outside his home and the families of the *beis din:* it meaningfully affected the families of the community he led in the Philadelphia suburb of Elkins Park. "He had a very special relationship with our son, Rafael Micha," said Dr. Saundra Sterling Epstein, whose family has been members of YIEP since 2000. Epstein recalled the time her son was a young student at Torah Academy, where Brisman was a *rebbe*. Young Rafael Michael ran out of his class line when he saw Brisman head into the library. "Hi, Rabbi Brisman. What are you doing at my school," the boy asked. "I am studying, just like you are, Rafi," Brisman said. Suddenly, at only six years old, the young boy shared with Brisman a word of wisdom. "Keep studying Rabbi Brisman, and when you grow up you will be a great *talmid chacham*!".

"For every kid in the shul he had a different joke, and a nickname and every kid thought he was they were his best friend," Rabbi Reuven Goldstein, member of the Philadelphia *beis din* and successor to Brisman at Young Israel of Elkins Park (YIEP), said. "He was able to relate to everybody."

In reality, everyone, young and old, was a student to Rabbi Brisman."He took me under his wing," Goldstein said. "For me, his brilliance was a sense of security. I always knew if there was a question I did not know, I'd say, OK let's take this to Rabbi Brisman."

"Growing up with my father was very interesting, to say the least,"Brisman's older son, Yaacov Mayer Brisman, said. Yaacov remembered his father, "would stay up into the wee hours of the morning, then get up at 5 a.m. to give a *sheor*. As I grew up, I came to learn how that type of diligence was incredibly rare."

"He was an extraordinarily honest man," Brisman's younger son Gedalia Zev Brisman said. He was honest and diligent. He was extremely hard-working not just in the community but in his own *middos*. There was a major stress on personal honesty when we were kids." And when it came to learning Torah, "he specifically stressed to me the importance of constant review and the power of struggling to understand the ideas behind everything in the Torah."

Rabbi Brisman oversaw the conversion process for aspiring candidates in the Philadelphia area who underwent the rigorous multi-year process. His conversions were accepted readily by the Israeli Rabbinate for converts looking to make *Aliyah*, and his name appeared on the Rabbinate's conversion *beis din* shortlist. "Converting with Rabbi Brisman was a *Bracha,*" Rachel Schwartz, member of YIEP, said. "He set clear expectations and his standing in the community gave me confidence. His passing is a huge loss to conversion candidates in Philadelphia."

Rabbi Eliezer Hirsch, rav of Mekor Habracha, is one of the trailblazing rabbis of the fast-growing downtown Philadelphia (Center City) community. Being separated from the heart of Philly's Jewish communities in the northeast and along the Main Line, the community faced many halachic challenges in meeting the needs of its growing membership. "For the Center City community to thrive, we needed someone with stature to [understand the challenges we faced]," Hirsch shared with his congregation at Mekor Habracha. "Rabbi Brisman helped our community considerably by supporting some crucial decisions we made in [Center City]."

In summary, Yaacov said, "He was somehow able to balance his greatness in learning with being the most down to earth humble unassuming person when it came to dealing with people one on one. And that was something that we took to heart when we became older – to treat everyone with respect."

Rabbi Brisman is survived by his wife, Libby, and their four children – in addition to Yaacov and Gedalia Zev, Matti Stahl and Fayga Laya Taylor. Yaacov requests any stories or memories readers may have about his father to be emailed to rabbi- brismanmemories@gmail.com.

INDEX

<table>
<tr><td>Index</td><td>Pg</td></tr>
</table>

SELECTED IMAGE REFERENCES

Page 11: "Axelrod Pharmacy 1960" – Photo Credit, Harold M. Lambert (book on business practices)

Page 19: *Five Fates*- Photo Credit- Doubleday, 1970.

Page 22: Graphic logo of the Earth intersected with a paper airplane and rider- photo credit, "The Committee", 1972, 1973, 1974, 1975, 1976).

Page 28: *The Poltergeist*- Photo Credit- Signet Books, 1972.

Page 37: "Lee Kaplan" aged 17- Photo Credit, *El Delator* (Year book); Cheltenham High School, 1982, Vol. 72.

Page 53: "Rabbi Yosef Caro"- painting purchased by the author and credit unknown, Tzfat, Israel, 2018.

Page 62: "Cheltenham High School 1953-1959"- photo credit World Wide Web

Page 63: "Peter J. Goldstone"- Photo permission through family members, 2022.

Page 75: "Presidential Daily"-Reproduction of the Itinerary of the Presidential Classroom for Young Americans, Thursday, March 12, 1981;

"Paul Chretien" Central Intelligence Agency; Photo Credit, Brian Yarboraugh

Page 81: "Mr. Joe Gyenes" Photo Credit, *El Delator* (Year book); original uncropped photograph, Cheltenham High School, 1981, Vol. 71, p.26.

Page 87: "Ambler Campus Entrance" circa 1965; photograph by Bob Martin and used with permission from the Temple University Libraries' Special Collections Research Center (SCRC); Reference Identifier: HTUAPZ201906000154; (SCRC CODE 202); Permission filed 9/8/2022.

Page 113-114: "The Compass Program: A Two Year Evaluation of SEPTA's Commuter Pass Program as Administered for Temple University Students"; Temple Student Government; 1990 (Temple University Special Collections Research (SCRC) Catalog ID: 99102691392970381 1; Temple SCRC/Urban Archives

Page118: Collaged Articles:

Carrington, Penelope M. "Wiernicki Claims Students Expect More Activities". Temple News, October 12, 1989. Vol. 80. No. 15, Pg.1 (Photo Credit: Brian David Holloway)

Dixon, Amy Lynn. "Improved Relations for Ambler",

Temple News, April 12, 1991; Vol. 82, o. 31. Pg. 1

Friar, E. B."Wiernicki Optimistic for Fall Alternative Housing", Temple News. March 23, 1989. Vol. 68, No. 75. Pg. 1

Isselmann, Jack. "Dare Seeks Students to Analyze Drinking".Temple News. October 19, 1988. Vol. 68, No. 22. Pg.1 (Uncredited Photo).

Herbert, Keith D. "IFC Bows Under University Pressure to Conrol Parties". Temple News. October 23, 1987. Vol. 67, No. 16. Pg. 1 and 5. (Photo Credit: Aaron J. Walker)

Kee, Rob. "TSG Looks at Tuition Plan". Temple News. March 27, 1987. Vol. 66, No. 52. Pg. 1 and 3. (Uncredited Photo)

Mummert, Hallie. "Wiernicki Practices Preventative Medicine". Temple News. April 3, 1989. Vol. 68, No. 29. Pg. 1

Watson, Jennifer M. "Administrators Says Cancellation of Classes is 'Last Resort'". Temple News. September 19, 1990. Vol. 81, No. 3. Pg. 1 (Photo Credit: Steve Winokur).

Additional Image Elements- photo credits:"Reception for new dean Kristl Mehnert" www.digital.library.Temple.edu and "Support for the Wiernicki Family" www.gofundme.com.

Page 127: "Sandra and Mildred Kessler"-Flea Market Photo (Courtesy, the Kessler Family).

Page 154: "Abbie Hoffman", Licensed from Getty Images.

Page 224: "Arecibo Observatory: The Largest Radio Telescope on Earth" Photo Credit: Angel Ramos Foundation Visitor's Center, cover of trifold guide brochure. National Astronomy and Ionosphere Center. (www.naic.edu).(2003).

Page 227: "Gene Roddenberry with Subshuttle" (circa 1973) sourced: world wide web, various sites.

Page 280: "Glass-etched Transporter tryptch (Kirk, Spock and McCoy)"- Photo Credit,-Skirball Cultural Center, Los Angeles, CA. Exhibition-"Star Trek: Exploring New Worlds" October 7, 2021–February 20, 2022.
"Transporter Beam-in with Michael Okuda, Denise Okuda and Doug Drexler", and "With Bill Shatner on the Bridge"Star Trek: The Original Series Set Tour, Ticonderoga, NY. (2018 and 2021).

Page 285: Versailles Hall of Mirrors 1871, "War Hospital"- Photo Licensed, Getty Images. Versailles Hall of Mirrors ~1789, "Palace Life", unique illustration, credit unknown, purchased on eBay, by the author.

Page 292: "Rats Restaurant" Photo Credit: Grounds for Sculpture, Hamilton, NJ. (www.ratsrestaurant.com)